Paul Adam has written several critically-acclaimed thrillers for adults. His books have sold widely around the world, have been translated into several foreign languages and are now available as e-books. Adam has also written television and film scripts. He lives in Sheffield with his wife and two sons.

PAGANINI'S GHOST

It's the most exciting concert Cremona has seen in years. The headliner is a brilliant young Russian playing a violin once owned by the 19th century master, Nicolo Paganini. But the triumphal performance is immediately overshadowed by the murder of one of its sponsors. Solving the murder will require a journey into musical history — and to make that journey, Cremona's police chief will require the assistance of Gianni Castiglione, elderly charmer and only mildly larcenous expert in violins.

Books by Paul Adam
Published by The House of Ulverscroft:

A NASTY DOSE OF DEATH
UNHOLY TRINITY
FLASH POINT
ENEMY WITHIN

PAUL ADAM

PAGANINI'S GHOST

Complete and Unabridged

CHARNWOOD
Leicester

First published in the United States of America
in 2010 by Felony & Mayhem Press
New York

First Charnwood Edition
published 2014

The moral right of the author has been asserted

All the characters and events portrayed in this work
are fictitious.

A catalogue record for this book is available
from the British Library.

ISBN 978–1–4448–1836–9

Published by
F. A. Thorpe (Publishing)
Anstey, Leicestershire

Set by Words & Graphics Ltd.
Anstey, Leicestershire
Printed and bound in Great Britain by
T. J. International Ltd., Padstow, Cornwall

This book is printed on acid-free paper

1

Over the half a century that I have been working as a violin maker and repairer, I have had instruments brought to me in many different ways. Most were nothing out of the ordinary — a musician simply turning up at my workshop with a violin in a case — but one or two have been more remarkable.

There was the Guadagnini, discovered under a pile of wooden crates in a hayloft near Bergamo, that was delivered to me wrapped in newspaper and an old potato sack. Then there was the famous, but decidedly eccentric, international virtuoso, whom discretion forbids me from naming, who showed up on my doorstep one day with his Stradivari nestling in the bottom of a supermarket carrier bag. Perhaps most extraordinary of all was the Amati belonging to a well-known Italian soloist, which his wife — a neglected, highly strung woman, tired of playing second fiddle to a piece of wood — had smashed over his head during a particularly violent marital argument. The soloist filed an assault charge against his soon to be ex-spouse, and several months later the violin, or, rather, the bits of it, being Exhibit A in the prosecution case, were conveyed to me for repair in eight separate police evidence bags.

But none of these events, bizarre though they were, were quite so memorable as the one that

1

was now unfolding before me.

There were six vehicles in the convoy. I had been telephoned half an hour earlier to be given advance warning of its arrival, so I was waiting outside my house when the procession appeared on the horizon, speeding towards me along the road from Cremona. At the front was a blue-and-white police patrol car with its roof light flashing, but its siren mercifully silent — a show of restraint not normally associated with the Italian police. Behind the patrol car was a shiny dark blue Alfa Romeo with tinted windows, followed by a black armoured van like the ones banks use for delivering cash to their branches. Fourth in the line was a red Fiat Bravo, then a silver Mercedes saloon. Bringing up the rear was a second marked police car.

I had never seen anything like it. My home is relatively isolated, a former farmhouse surrounded by fields of maize and potatoes. The nearest house is a good kilometre away. I usually enjoy the privacy the location affords me, but today, for once, I was sorry that I didn't have any closer neighbours who could share in this curious spectacle. Such an ostentatious convoy seemed wasted on me alone.

The first police car skidded to a halt just past the entrance to the gravel forecourt at the front of my house, the driver indulging a worrying penchant for exhibitionism by braking heavily and slewing his vehicle round so that it blocked the carriageway. Two scruffy uniformed officers climbed out, both sporting the mirror sunglasses, stubble, and institutional truculence that seem to be de rigueur in the Polizia Nazionale.

The two vehicles immediately behind — the Alfa Romeo and the armoured van — turned off the road onto the forecourt and stopped beside me. Two men got out of the Alfa Romeo. They were so similar in appearance that they could have been twins. Their smart black suits, white shirts, and highly polished black shoes were identical. Even their ties, a silvery grey silk with a black diamond pattern, were the same. They were in their late twenties, wearing mirror sunglasses like the police officers, but a class apart in every other respect — sleek, well-fed leopards to the policemen's mangy alley cats. With their discreet but stylish clothes, their alert manner — heads constantly moving, eyes searching for possible threats — and the walkie-talkies clutched in their hands, they looked like the bodyguards you always see accompanying the U.S. president or other heads of state. And I suppose bodyguards is what they were, only the body they were guarding was made of maple and pine, rather than flesh and blood.

'You are Giovanni Battista Castiglione?' one of them asked me curtly.

I nodded.

'Your workshop is where?'

'Round the back, in the garden,' I said.

'Show me.'

I led him down the side of the house to the old farm smithy that I have converted into my workshop. His companion remained at the front, but the two men kept in contact by walkie-talkie.

'One-storey brick building, set apart from the house,' the bodyguard murmured into his radio. 'Garden' — his eyes scanned my lawn and flower beds — 'large, open. Good visibility. No perimeter barrier. Fields beyond.' His gaze came back to me. 'Let's see inside.'

He studied the heavy wooden door and sturdy lock approvingly as I opened up the workshop, relaying his findings to his colleague. Then he inspected the interior of the room, checking the windows first before turning his attention to the workbench and cupboards.

'That's a safe?' he asked, staring at the steel door set into the recess that had once been a hearth.

'Yes.'

'Looks pretty solid.'

'I handle a lot of valuable instruments,' I said.

He prowled round the table in the centre of the room and opened a couple of cupboards warily, as if he were expecting some assailant — presumably a very small one — to leap out and attack him. Then he raised the walkie-talkie to his lips again.

'Okay, it's secure. I'm coming back now.'

We returned to the front of the house, where a small group of people had gathered — the occupants of the Fiat and the Mercedes, which had been obliged to park on the verge at the side of the road because there was no room for them on the forecourt. A diminutive man in a grey suit and rimless spectacles stepped forward and held out his hand.

'Dottore Castiglione, it's a pleasure to meet

you. I am Enrico Golinelli, assistant curator of antiquities for the city of Genoa.'

I took his hand in mine. His fingers felt so slight and fragile that I hardly dared squeeze them.

'I apologise for the short notice,' Golinelli went on. 'It is most kind of you to help us.'

'Not at all,' I replied. 'I'm honoured that you asked me.'

'Nothing like this has ever happened before. I don't know what it can be. The instrument was checked over thoroughly before it left Genoa. But Signor Ivanov is absolutely sure that . . . ' Golinelli paused. 'Forgive me, I'm forgetting my manners.'

He turned away from me and gestured at the man and woman standing next to him.

'Allow me to introduce Yevgeny Ivanov, and his mother, Ludmilla Ivanova.'

Ludmilla Ivanova offered me her hand. I didn't hesitate to clasp it firmly in my own. There was nothing delicate about *her* fingers, or her grip. There was nothing delicate about any of her, in fact. She was a big woman, tall and statuesque, with thick black hair pulled back and fastened with a clasp at the nape of her neck. She was wearing red high heels and a scarlet-and-black knee-length dress that was perhaps a shade too low-cut for her mature years, but she had the figure, and the confidence, to carry it off. Her build, the strong, determined set of her jaw reminded me of a Wagnerian soprano and I wondered whether she had been an opera singer once. When she spoke, her voice, too, had the

5

powerful resonance of a Brünnhilde.

'Dottore, I've heard much about you,' she said in fluent Italian, the words muddied round the edges by her strong Russian accent. 'They say you are good, the best luthier in Cremona.'

I inclined my head modestly, but she was not expecting a reply.

'I hope they are right,' she continued. 'We are in urgent need of your expertise. Whatever is wrong, you must fix it. My son's recital is only hours away.'

She glanced at the young man beside her. He gave me a shy nod, then seemed to shrink away, retreating into his mother's shadow. He was shorter than Ludmilla and much thinner. His face had a gaunt look that was accentuated by his high cheekbones and deep-set dark eyes, and though his shoulders were broad and his bone structure robust, there was so little flesh on him, he appeared painfully emaciated.

'People are expecting to hear this instrument,' Ludmilla said. 'Without it, the recital will not be the same. We shall have to cancel.'

'Let us not be premature, signora,' Golinelli said, breaking in quickly. 'The problem may be easily solved. I suggest we proceed immediately, if our escort from the insurance company will permit it.'

Golinelli turned to the two bodyguards.

'Gentlemen?'

'Everything appears to be in order,' one of the young men said.

'Then let us get on.'

The bodyguards signalled to the driver of the

6

armoured van, who nodded and put on his crash helmet and thick, padded protective vest before climbing out and walking round to the rear of the vehicle. The rest of us gathered round to watch him open the doors. There were twelve of us — me, the two bodyguards from the insurance company, Ludmilla and Yevgeny Ivanov and a nondescript-looking man whom I took to be their driver, Golinelli, a young woman with a severe academic face who had to be the assistant curator's assistant, and the four police officers who had strolled over from their cars to see what all the fuss was about. The insurance company escorts weren't happy about that. This was *their* show. They didn't want the local cops muscling in on it. One of the bodyguards glared at the policemen and said sharply, 'You're supposed to be watching the road.'

The police officers nodded indifferently, their eyes hidden behind their sunglasses, but they didn't move. They weren't going to take orders from a civilian in an Armani suit.

'Okay?' the van driver said. His voice was soft, muffled by the Perspex visor of his crash helmet.

The bodyguards took a last look round, scrutinising the forecourt, the road, the fields.

'Okay, go ahead.'

The van driver inserted a key into the lock, turned it, and swung open the heavy armour-plated doors. The watching group — me included — edged forward, necks craning to see into the interior.

It was something of an anticlimax. At first sight, the van appeared empty — just bare walls and a large vacant cavity. Then the eye was drawn down to the floor, to a web of straps and buckles that were holding something in place. In the centre of the web — looking very small and insignificant — was a rather shabby rectangular violin case.

The driver climbed inside the van, unfastened the straps carefully, and picked up the case by its handle. He passed it to one of the insurance company men, lowered himself back down to the ground, then took the case back.

Quietly, without needing to be given instructions, we somehow organised ourselves into a rough line. The bodyguards were at the front, the van driver sandwiched between them; then came Golinelli and the Ivanovs. I was next, just ahead of Golinelli's assistant and the Ivanovs' driver. The four police officers clustered at the rear and, like mourners at a funeral, we all processed solemnly round to my workshop.

Everything about the occasion — the policemen, the bodyguards, the armoured van — seemed so over the top that I was almost inclined to laugh. But the precautions were understandable, for this was no ordinary violin we were escorting. This was a Guarneri 'del Gesù' — the most valuable, famous Guarneri del Gesù on earth. This was *il Cannone* — the Cannon — the violin that had belonged to Nicolò Paganini.

2

No one can be absolutely certain when and how Paganini came by his Guarneri. The experts, who are notoriously loathe to agree with one another about anything, are divided on the matter. But the generally accepted story is that it was in Livorno in 1802. Paganini was staying in the Tuscan city, but without his violin, which he had probably pawned to pay off one of his many gambling debts. He was nineteen at the time and, since breaking with his tyrannical father and leaving home, had been enjoying his newfound freedom in the manner of all young men throughout the ages — with a surfeit of drink, cards, and women. He had not yet acquired the longhaired, cadaverous appearance and the Mephistophelian notoriety that was to come a few years later, but he was already renowned in northern Italy as a violinist of extraordinary talent. The Livornese asked him to give a concert in their city, overcoming his lack of a violin by lending him a Guarneri del Gesù that belonged to a wealthy local merchant named Livron. The merchant was so overwhelmed by Paganini's playing that he made him a gift of the del Gesù after the recital. It was Paganini who christened the instrument 'the Cannon' — because of its powerful, booming tone — and, though he owned other violins during his lifetime, *il Cannone* was always his favourite, the instrument with a unique place in his heart. When he died, in 1840, Paganini left the del Gesù to his home city of Genoa, where it is kept in a glass display case in the town hall most of the time, emerging only once every two years when the winner of the Premio Paganini international violin competition is permitted to play it as part of the prize.

I have seen the instrument on display in Genoa and once, many years ago, had the privilege of handling it in the workshop of the city's then conservator of violins, an old friend of mine from my apprentice days in Cremona. But I had never had the responsibility of examining and quite possibly carrying out work on the violin, until now.

It was a daunting prospect. This was a very special instrument. I tried not to think about how much *il Cannone* was worth. *Priceless* is how it is usually described, but the insurance company would undoubtedly have quantified that adjective into something a little more tangible. Ten million euros? Twenty million? How do you put a price on a voice, on a sound that can move an audience to tears?

The case was on the bench in front of me. I gazed at it for a long moment without touching it. I was aware of the people round me — the two bodyguards breathing down my neck, the police officers and the others crowding in on all sides, everyone waiting expectantly for a glimpse of the violin. I felt like a physician at a royal birth, about to deliver the heir to the throne with a throng of idle courtiers looking on.

My fingers trembling slightly, I reached out and unfastened the catches on the case. I paused for a second. My workshop suddenly seemed very cramped and stuffy.

'If you could move back just a fraction,' I said. 'I need more room.'

The spectators withdrew, though not very far. In the confines of the small workshop, there was almost nowhere for them to go. I flexed my shoulders, pushing back the young men from the insurance company, who seemed reluctant to be separated from me. Then I lifted the lid of the case. In an instant, everyone was back, pushing and jostling to see the contents. One of the police officers let out a contemptuous snort — as if to say, All that fuss over this? — and turned away. His disappointment was contagious. I sensed the excitement in the room abate, the spectators' curiosity vanish abruptly. I could almost hear the crash of expectations being dashed.

In a way, I could sympathise with them. *Il Cannone* is not an obviously attractive violin. In fact, it has an almost scruffy look to it. It is more than 250 years old, of course, which doesn't help, but it is not just its age that is the problem. We have come to expect our violins to be smooth and perfect, as if their makers had only just finished them. We expect them to have a vivid colour and almost dazzling sheen, but that is not how Guarneri — or Stradivari, for that matter — made them. Eighteenth-century violins did

11

not have a high French polish. To understand an instrument like the Cannon, you must not let your first impressions influence you. You must look below the surface to fully appreciate its qualities; you must study the detail, the craftsmanship, looking for substance as well as style. You must keep your mind open, eliminate preconceptions and prejudices, like an anthropologist travelling to some distant isolated community where the definition of beauty is different from our own.

And the Cannon is a beautiful violin. There is no doubt about that. The colour has faded and the front plate, between the f-holes, is black with impacted rosin, but the back still has a magnificent lustre, a pattern of russet stripes over a glowing gold base that is like gazing at a sunset through a slatted wooden blind.

Was I the only person in the room who could see it, who could truly appreciate the greatness that was manifest in every line and curve of the instrument? I didn't care. I was besotted with it. With her, I should say, for a violin is always female. There were a dozen other people in the room, but I no longer noticed them. I had eyes only for this voluptuous little lady in the box before me — a new love in my life, albeit a fleeting one.

Enrico Golinelli cleared his throat.

'Dottore Castiglione, if I might press you,' he said anxiously. 'Signor Ivanov's recital is at eight o'clock, and it is already nearing five.'

I looked up.

'Yes, yes, of course. We must get on. Let's have

12

a look at her, shall we?'

I reached into the case and grasped the Cannon by the neck. My fingers closed round the wood and I felt a shiver run up my arm, a strange, unsettling tingle. I knew it was ridiculous, but it seemed to me as if I could detect the imprint of Paganini's fingers on the instrument. I released my grip, my pulse suddenly throbbing.

'Dottore Castiglione?' Golinelli said. 'Is everything all right?'

He was peering at me with concern, his eyes very large behind his thick spectacles.

'Yes,' I reassured him. 'Everything is fine. It's just that . . . there are too many people in here. I cannot work with everyone watching.'

'Yes, I should have thought. We must clear the room.'

Golinelli looked round and raised his voice. 'May I ask you all to leave, please . . . '

Ludmilla Ivanova opened her mouth to protest, but Golinelli broke in before she could speak.

'Signora Ivanova and Signor Ivanov excepted, of course. You must stay.'

'We need to stay, too,' one of the insurance company men said. 'We have orders not to let the violin out of our sight.'

I saw Golinelli hesitate, so I stepped in. This was *my* workshop, after all. The last thing I wanted was a couple of intimidating security guards standing over me while I tried to do my job.

'What could possibly happen?' I said. 'The

13

violin is safe with me; I can assure you of that. I have worked on many important instruments — Guarneris, Stradivaris — and I have never yet had anything go wrong. The best protection you can give this violin is to wait outside and give me the space to find out what's the matter with it.'

The insurance men looked at each other. Then they shrugged and turned towards the door. They ushered everyone else out, then followed, closing the door firmly behind them. Looking through the window, I saw them take up positions on the terrace, from where they could prevent anyone approaching the workshop.

Only Golinelli, the Ivanovs, and I now remained round my workbench. I lifted the del Gesù out of its case. There was no shiver this time, I was glad to see, just the warm solidity of the maple. I gave it a perfunctory inspection, plucking the strings to check that they were in tune. Then I looked at Yevgeny Ivanov. He was half-hidden by his mother's formidable bulk.

'Describe to me the problem,' I said. 'What exactly did you hear?'

Yevgeny stepped to one side, giving me a clear view of his slender face, but before he could say anything, Ludmilla answered my question.

'It is a slight vibration,' she said. 'Like a buzzing noise.'

'A buzzing noise?' I repeated.

'Not loud, but Yevgeny can hear it. He can feel it. It disturbs him. He cannot play with that kind of noise in his ear.'

'And you noticed this when?' I asked, looking at Yevgeny.

14

Again, it was Ludmilla who replied.

'This afternoon. During the rehearsal in the cathedral.'

'You didn't hear it before, in Genoa?'

'No, he didn't,' Ludmilla said. 'Just this afternoon.'

Golinelli turned to me, rubbing his hands together nervously.

'As I said earlier, the violin was checked before Signor Ivanov's concert in Genoa, then again before it was put on the van to be brought to Cremona. Perhaps something has been disturbed by the journey. It really is very important that we diagnose the fault and correct it. Very important. The Cannon is a national treasure.'

I reached out and stilled his fidgeting hands.

'Stop worrying,' I said soothingly. 'We will find the fault; have no fear of that. And we will put it right.'

'But time is not on our side, Dottore. We have only a few hours.'

'We have time enough,' I said.

I held out the violin to Yevgeny Ivanov.

'Let me hear it.'

Yevgeny took his shoulder rest from the case and attached it to the instrument. Then he removed his bow and tightened it. He slid the violin under his chin. That one small act seemed to transform him. The quiet, shy young man suddenly changed and became a different, more confident person. I have noticed this before in great soloists. They often have a humility about them, a self-effacing modesty that seems surprising in a person whose job it is to perform

15

— literally to show off on a stage. But you put them with their instrument and it is as if a missing part of their body has been restored to them. They have become a whole person again.

He played a sarabande from one of the Bach unaccompanied partitas. I could see, and hear, at once why this unassuming young man had won first prize in the Premio Paganini competition. There was a quality to his playing that was immediately arresting, that made you sit up and listen. His tone was rich and powerful — and that wasn't solely because of the Cannon — but it also had a haunting sweetness that lingered in the ear. He could draw out a melody, could make his violin sing, perform that magic trick that I always think of as nothing short of miraculous: taking horsehair and gut and a wooden box and making such rapturous music with them.

'Give me the full dynamic range,' I said. 'From pianissimo to fortissimo and back again, on each string in turn.'

'There . . . ' Ludmilla said. 'Did you hear it?'

'Yes, I — '

'You must have. What is it?'

'One moment, signora.'

'But did you hear it?'

'Yes, I heard it.'

It was very faint — like the intermittent buzzing of a drowsy wasp outside a closed window — but I could detect it nonetheless. My heart sank. A faint buzzing noise is a luthier's worst nightmare. The whole raison d'être of a violin depends on vibrations. That is how the

16

sound is produced — from the strings, through the bridge, to the sound post, to the front and back plates and the very air inside the instrument. But a flawed vibration like a buzz could have any number of causes, some minor, some very serious. The problem is identifying which cause, or combination of causes, is responsible for that flaw, and that is never simple. A violin, like the human body, is much more than the sum of its parts. Everything is interconnected; even the tiniest component is important and, when malfunctioning, can have an effect that far outweighs its size.

'Let me see it,' I said, holding out my hand.

Yevgeny passed the violin back to me. I held the instrument up and studied it carefully from all sides. My fingers were trembling slightly, my heart fluttering. *Il Cannone* had been Paganini's violin for nearly forty years. It was with him throughout his entire mature career, through all the triumphs as he set Italy, and then Europe, ablaze with his dazzling virtuosity. There was history in this violin. What tales it could tell, I thought, if it had a human voice, instead of just a musical one.

It must have had its share of knocks during those four decades of relentless travelling, jolting round in the back of innumerable stagecoaches and wagons on rough, unmetalled roads as Paganini moved from city to city. But it was still in remarkably good condition for a violin its age. It had been in a museum for the past 150-plus years, of course, although that kind of stifling inactivity is not necessarily good for a string instrument. Without regular playing, they can dry out and shrivel, just like people who are shut away and forgotten.

Guarneri made it in 1743, during the last two years of his life, when he was at the height of his powers as a luthier. Its dimensions are not excessive, but it feels like a large violin. The ribs and arching are higher than on most of his instruments and the plates are extremely thick — much thicker than Stradivari's, or the plates of violins we make today. This massive construction is undoubtedly one of the reasons for the Cannon's impressive tone, but it cannot be the only reason, or we could all copy the measurements and produce an instrument with a comparable sound. Paganini spent years searching for another del Gesù to match il Cannone, but he never found one. It is unique. Its unforgettable voice is due not just to its dimensions but also to those unquantifiable ingredients a luthier adds to his creations — a mixture of love and craft and, in Guarneri's case, a flamboyant, monstrous genius.

I checked the strings to make sure they weren't beginning to fray, then the nut and pegs. The peg box is astounding — cut out with a gouge rather than a chisel, the rough bare wood left unvarnished. The scroll, too, is asymmetrical and somewhat crude in its carving, as if Guarneri couldn't have been bothered to take much care with it. On the back of the scroll is an ugly red wax seal that was originally on the back plate of the violin — stuck on, in an incredible act of vandalism, by some overzealous Genoan official when the violin was first bequeathed to the city, then moved some years later, equally incredibly, to the scroll, where it has remained like a vivid scab on the face of a beautiful woman.

'What do you think?' I said to Yevgeny Ivanov. 'Can you detect where the buzz is coming from when you play?'

'Of course he can't,' Ludmilla said testily. 'That's why we've come to you.'

'Signora,' I said politely. 'I was asking for your son's view.'

'Yevgeny does not speak much Italian,' Ludmilla said, adding, a little acidly, I thought, 'and I'm sure you don't speak much Russian.'

'Perhaps there is another language we can use, then?' I said. 'Do you speak English, Signor Ivanov?'

'He can speak Russian, and I will translate,' his mother said. 'We are wasting time. Are you going to fix the violin, or not?'

'Yes, I speak English,' Yevgeny said.

He spoke quietly, tentatively. His voice was light, but pleasantly warm.

'What is your feeling?' I said in English. 'You are closer to the violin than anyone.'

'It seems to be low down, when I play on the G string,' Yevgeny replied.

I examined the left-hand side of the violin, tapping the plates and ribs to see if anything was coming unstuck. Then I took a small torch and a dentist's mirror and looked through the f-hole at the underside of the front plate where the bass bar is attached. I prayed that there wasn't a

19

problem with the bass bar, for dealing with it would require the opening up of the violin — not something I had any intention of doing, even if Signor Golinelli were to allow it, and I knew he wouldn't. The Cannon has a team of very distinguished luthiers looking after it in Genoa. Any work of a serious nature would have to be carried out by them.

'You have found something?' Golinelli said, his hands beginning to fidget again. 'Is it bad? Dottore, you must tell me.'

'The bass bar looks fine,' I said. 'It must be something else. I'll check the sound post.'

'Dottore . . . '

I lifted my head. Yevgeny was gazing at me earnestly, pleadingly, as if he were trying to send me a silent message.

'Perhaps if you and I . . . ' His voice petered out and his eyes flickered from Golinelli to his mother.

I sensed instinctively — almost telepathically — what he wanted but was too afraid to articulate.

'Signor Golinelli,' I said. 'Signor Ivanov and I need to put our heads together and really get to the bottom of this. And we need to be alone to do it. Would you be so kind as to take Signora Ivanova into my house for a short while? I have tea and coffee and wine in the kitchen. Make yourselves at home.'

Ludmilla started to protest, but I cut her short.

'It is the only way, signora. Your son and I can sort this out.'

20

'Well, really, this is ridiculous!' Ludmilla exclaimed indignantly. 'This surely isn't necessary.'

'I believe it is,' I said firmly. 'We need peace and quiet, the workshop to ourselves, to resolve this.'

'If you really think so . . . ' Golinelli said uncertainly.

'I do,' I said. 'I will call you back as soon as we have anything concrete to tell you.'

Ludmilla didn't move. Her mouth was set tight and she was glaring at me resentfully.

'Time is running out,' I said, putting the Cannon down on the bench so that it was clear I wouldn't continue work until they had gone.

Ludmilla muttered something in her native tongue that I was glad not to be able to understand, then turned on her heel and stalked out of the workshop. Golinelli went after her, pausing on the threshold to say, 'The minute you have something, I must be informed. At once, you understand? I am responsible for the violin.'

'You will be the first to know,' I said. 'You have my word.'

I waited for the door to close, then turned to Yevgeny.

'Well?' I said in English.

He wandered over to the window, obviously checking that his mother and the assistant curator weren't listening at the keyhole. Then he came back to my bench. He seemed more at ease than before, but I could still detect a tension in his body language. He was fragile, brittle, like a

21

twig that might snap if the slightest pressure were applied.

'That was brave,' he said. 'My mother does not like to be told what to do.'

'So I gathered,' I said dryly.

'I can trust you, no?'

'You can trust me.'

'I have confession to make. But you must not tell my mother, or Signor Golinelli.'

'What kind of a confession?' I asked.

'I believe I may have damaged the violin myself.'

'Go on.'

He hesitated, then began to pace up and down in an agitated manner.

'At the cathedral, in Cremona, they give me a room,' he said. 'A dressing room. To leave my things in, to get changed. I have the violin with me. I take it out of the case. I am careless; I don't look. There is this thing — a tall metal candlestick — next to me. As I turn, I hit the candlestick with the violin.'

'Which bit of the violin?'

'I am not sure. I think maybe the bridge.' A note of panic crept into his voice. 'If I have harmed it . . . it would be very bad. A violin like that. You must help me, Dottore Castiglione. You must put right what I do.'

'Easy now,' I said. 'Whatever it is, we'll deal with it.'

'My mother, she must never know. She would be very angry with me. Signor Golinelli, too. He would take the violin away from me, maybe the Premio prize, as well. My reputation, my career

22

would be finish. Promise me you don't tell. Please.'

I warmed to him. He must have been twenty-two or twenty-three years old, but he seemed like a small boy, terrified that he would be punished severely for this mishap.

'No one can take the Premio away from you,' I said. 'It's yours. You won it on merit. No one will blame you for what you did. It was an accident.'

'But you won't tell?'

'No, your secret is safe with me. Now, pull up a stool and sit down.'

I held the Cannon up to the light and peered closely at the bridge. I could detect nothing with my naked eye, so I took my jeweller's loupe and had a look through that, squeezing the soft wood of the bridge with my fingers to see if it was damaged.

'Ah, here we are,' I said.

Yevgeny leaned forward, squinting at the bridge.

'You find something?'

'A hairline crack. Just here.' I touched the edge of the bridge beneath the G string.

'That would make buzzing noise?' Yevgeny said.

'Yes.'

'But violin itself is all right?'

'As far as I can tell, yes.'

He sat back and exhaled with relief.

'Thank God. It is not original, the bridge?'

'No, it's not Guarneri's. This is a modern one, put on relatively recently.'

'You can fit new one?'

'Easily. But I must consult with Signor Golinelli first.'

The assistant curator was as relieved as Yevgeny had been.

'Just the bridge, nothing more serious?' he said when he and Ludmilla had returned to the workshop and I'd given them my diagnosis. 'It will need a new one, no? You have time to do it?'

'Plenty,' I said.

'You'll have to hurry,' Ludmilla said. 'We have to get back to the cathedral. Yevgeny will need to warm up, to prepare himself for the recital.'

'Let me check with Genoa first,' Golinelli said. 'I can't authorise any work without their say-so.'

He pulled out his mobile and phoned the city's chief violin conservator. He explained what had happened, then passed the phone to me. The conservator and I had a brief discussion before I handed the phone back to Golinelli.

'He says go ahead,' I said.

Golinelli eyed me uneasily.

'A crack? How did a crack suddenly appear?'

I gave a casual shrug, careful not to look at Yevgeny.

'These things happen. Wood is a temperamental substance. It can react in unexpected ways. Temperature changes, a different humidity, the journey in the van — any of them could have caused it. Now, if you'd leave me alone for a while, I'll get the job done.'

I was conscious of the time ticking by as I worked on the violin, but I tried not to let it disturb me. I also tried not to think of the status of the instrument. I had to regard it as an ordinary violin, not the violin that had belonged to the most celebrated virtuoso in history. But it wasn't easy. Every time I touched it, I was aware that Paganini's hands had been there before mine. His fingers had held it; his chin had rested on the front plate; his breath had drifted over the varnish.

Somewhere deep in the soul of the instrument was the indelible memory of that one great man.

Handling the violin gave me a strange feeling of transience. It had been made two centuries before I was born and it would survive long after I was gone. It wasn't passing through my life; I was passing through its life, just as Paganini had passed through it.

I must have fitted hundreds of new bridges in my years as a luthier, but none so carefully as this one. It had to be perfect; it had to become part of the violin, to complement it so that its distinctive voice would remain unchanged. When I finished, I put the strings back on and tuned them, then sat for a few minutes just gazing at the instrument.

The work was good; I knew that. But how would the violin play? I had to get Yevgeny back in immediately to try it out, but I procrastinated. I wanted more time alone with the Cannon — an opportunity like this would never come my way again. But I didn't want simply to look at it, delightful though that was.

I glanced furtively round the workshop, as if I feared someone might be watching me. Why not? I said to myself. Why shouldn't I? Yes, it was presumptuous of me, but was it not also necessary? It wouldn't be much, just a preliminary check before I called Yevgeny in. Any conscientious luthier would do the same.

My arms trembling — with anticipation and no small measure of guilt — I slipped the violin under my chin and picked up the bow. I hesitated. Paganini had played this instrument, and since his death only the Premio winners — gifted musicians in their own right — had been allowed to use it. Now I, Giovanni Battista Castiglione, humble luthier and third-rate amateur violinist, was going to have a bash on it.

I dug the bow into the strings and recoiled at the sound. It echoed round the workshop, the same booming cannon noise that had inspired Paganini's nickname for the instrument. It was loud, reverberant, but rich and warm, too. A dark, sonorous voice that grasped you by the throat, leaving you breathless but gasping for more. Most importantly, the buzzing on the G string had disappeared.

I'd never played a violin like it, and I took full advantage of the moment. I tried some Bach from memory, steering clear of the sarabande Yevgeny had played to spare myself the depressing comparison between our respective performances, then had a go at a Schubert sonatina and the 'Meditation' from Massenet's *Thaïs*. I was tempted to risk something by Paganini himself, one of the caprices, perhaps, but I know my limits. Even *il Cannone* would not enable me to play those. Paganini, if he was watching me from above — though, given his satanic reputation, he was more likely to be down below — would undoubtedly have been laughing at my wretched antics, but I didn't care. I knew I didn't sound very good, but I was certain of one thing: I sounded better than I ever had before, and ever would again.

Finally, my curiosity and vanity satisfied, I left the Cannon on my bench and went into the house to find Yevgeny. He was alone in the back room, standing by the piano, leafing through one of my many piles of chamber music.

'You have much music,' he said.

'Chamber music is a passion of mine,' I said. 'Particularly string quartets.'

'You play in a quartet?'

'Yes . . . well, I *did*. I used to play every week with three friends.'

'But no more?'

'One of them died,' I said.

It was more than a year since Tomaso Rainaldi had been killed, but the memory still brought a lump to my throat.

'You like quartets?' I went on.

'I play very few,' Yevgeny said, a wistful note in his voice. 'I wish I had more chance. My first year at the conservatoire, I get together with other students sometimes. But my mother, she does not like. She want me to concentrate on my solo career.'

'It is one of life's great pleasures,' I said. 'Making music with other people.'

Yevgeny nodded.

'Perhaps in few years I find time to try. At the moment, it is impossible.'

'Ah, you're here. You have finished?'

I turned my head and saw Ludmilla entering the room, a cup of coffee in her hand.

'The violin is ready,' I said.

'Then what are we waiting for? Yevgeny must try it.'

Ludmilla deposited her cup on top of the piano and strode purposefully out through the French windows on to the terrace, where the insurance company men were still standing guard. Enrico Golinelli joined us in the workshop and I handed Yevgeny the Cannon. He played some scales, then the Bach sarabande again. I listened very carefully, but I could detect no flaws in the sound. Nor could Yevgeny.

'Very good,' he said, putting the violin down. 'She sound better than ever.'

'You are satisfied?' Ludmilla said to her son.

'Yes, I am very happy.'

'Then we must get back to the cathedral. Your recital is' — Ludmilla checked the gold watch on her wrist — 'less than ninety minutes away. Signor Golinelli, we have no time to lose.'

The assistant curator sprang into action. The insurance company men were summoned into the workshop; then the driver of the armoured van was called round from his vehicle, the four police officers tagging along behind. *Il Cannone* was put back in its case and we retraced our steps, trooping round to the front of the house in a straggling line.

As the violin was being loaded into the van, Yevgeny held out his hand to me.

'Thank you, Dottore Castiglione.'

'It's Gianni,' I said.

'Thank you, Gianni. For saving my recital' — he lowered his voice to a whisper — 'and for saving me.'

'It was nothing.'

'Please let me give you a ticket to the concert.'

'I have one already,' I said. 'I'm looking forward to it immensely.'

'Then come to the reception after — in the town hall.'

'I will be with friends.'

'Bring them, too. Please, you must.'

'Yevgeny!'

Ludmilla was waiting impatiently by the gate. 'Our driver is waiting. We must go. *Now*.'

Yevgeny gave me an apologetic glance.

'Until later,' he said, and hurried away to join his mother.

Golinelli came to thank me.

'Send your bill to me in Genoa,' he said.

'There is no charge,' I replied. 'It was an honour just to touch the Cannon.'

Golinelli shook my hand, then trotted out to the Fiat on the road. The police cars and the Ivanovs' Mercedes had turned round and were waiting in a line. The armoured van and the insurance company car reversed out of my drive and took up their positions behind the leading police car. Then the convoy moved off. I watched from my front step as the vehicles sped away along the road towards Cremona, getting smaller and smaller, until they vanished over the horizon.

3

The cathedral in Cremona is one of the undiscovered treasures of Italy. It is smaller and less spectacular than the more famous basilicas in Florence or Rome or Venice, but those great churches seem to me to have lost their true purpose, to have lost touch with the common man. There is something overwhelming and intimidating about their size and grandeur. They are places of worship still, but they are not conducive to spirituality on an individual level. Perhaps they never have been. St. Peter's and St. Mark's and Santa Maria del Fiore were built to celebrate the glory of God, but I wonder sometimes whether the glory of man were not the greater imperative in their makers' minds. As architectural wonders, they inspire and impress, but as places for the personal expression of religious faith, they have become hollow shells. They are shrines to little more than the patron saint of tourism, mere points on a holidaymaker's itinerary to be visited and ticked off.

I see faith, of any persuasion, as a private matter, to be followed quietly and without ostentation. The trappings of religion — the churches, the priests, the ceremony — are not a necessary part of that faith. They have their place, and they can be a comfort to many, but faith is not an occasional luxury, to be indulged only on a Sabbath in a consecrated house. It is an integral part of your daily life, a guiding hand that defines your actions and thoughts whether you are conscious of it or not.

Cremona Cathedral is a magnificent building, but it is on a scale more suited to a religion that was founded on simplicity and self-sacrifice. It has its share of tourists, yet they do not detract from the cathedral's purpose. It is still a place where any individual, whether he believes or not, may come to reflect on his life. There is a soothing tranquillity to the high vaulted interior that encourages and supports contemplation, and also, at the right time, celebration — the celebration of life and death, of marriage and birth, and, tonight, of music, that wonderful, uplifting gift that in my own small way I have spent my life helping others to share and enjoy.

The nave was packed with people, every seat occupied. This was a recital that no one wanted to miss. Cremona is many things to many people, but to its residents, and to the world at large, it is, above all else, a city of violins. All the great luthiers lived and worked here. Stradivari, Guarneri, Amati are so fundamental to the city's history, and its sense of identity, that it is impossible to exaggerate their importance, or their unique standing in a world that is so obsessed with wealth and status. These were not noble men. They were not rich or powerful. They were simple craftsmen, woodworkers, but their names are known and venerated round the globe.

It was no surprise, then, that the citizens of Cremona should turn out in force to hear the

31

most famous instrument made by one of its most famous sons. *Il Cannone* left the city more than two centuries ago. It has been appropriated by Genoa, a gift from that city's own most famous son, and is normally heard only there. The Premio Paganini prizewinner's recital on the violin is always held in Genoa. Yevgeny Ivanov had already done one recital there, but this year — in a break from tradition — he had been allowed to perform a second recital in Cremona. No wonder I could detect such a sizzling atmosphere of expectation and excitement in the cathedral. *Il Cannone* was coming home, and everyone wanted to be present to welcome it, to hear it sing.

I was in a seat in the centre of the nave, some distance from the front. The first few rows had been reserved for various civic dignitaries and their guests — the reverence we show our dead luthiers does not, alas, extend to their living successors. I saw the mayor and other local politicians and the usual rent-a-celebrity mob that seems to show up at significant cultural events like this. I recognised a couple of well-known actors, several television personalities, and an A.C. Milan footballer whose on-the-pitch belligerence and inarticulate post-match interviews had hitherto not led me to suppose he had an interest in violin music.

I also saw someone else I knew — the plump, well-fed figure of Vincenzo Serafin, the Milanese violin dealer with whom I have a longstanding, if not always harmonious, business relationship. He was sitting in the second row with his mistress,

32

Maddalena, beside him. Trust him to get one of the best seats in the house. He turned his head, stroking his silky black beard with smug satisfaction, and surveyed the audience behind him, the rows of plebs and nobodies who lacked his infallible talent for networking.

'How did he wangle that?' my friend Antonio Guastafeste said in my right ear, his eyes following my gaze. 'A creep like him.'

'Serafin has friends in low places,' I replied.

'Very low, if the person sitting next to him is anything to go by,' Margherita said.

I turned my head, looking at the elegant figure to my left, silver earrings glinting beneath her short dark hair. Margherita was also a friend, a close friend — my girlfriend, I suppose some people might have said, if that weren't such a ridiculous term for someone of her years. Margherita was almost sixty, but you wouldn't have known it.

The crisp cream jacket and black trousers she was wearing had an ageless simplicity. Only the traces of grey in her hair, the faint lines round her eyes and mouth gave any hint of her real age.

'The woman, you mean? Maddalena?' I said.

'No, the other side. Vittorio Castellani.'

'Oh, yes, I see him. You know the professor?'

'Professor?' Margherita said caustically. 'You flatter him. I'm surprised the university hasn't taken away his title, he's there so infrequently.'

'Do I detect a trace of *academic* jealousy?' I said, smiling at her.

'You do indeed. Some of us at the university are very old-fashioned. We believe in actually

33

showing up every once in a while and teaching students. I doubt Castellani knows what a student looks like. Well, apart from the pretty female ones he tries to bed.'

'Maybe not just academic jealousy,' I said.

'Oh, *please*. Have you seen him? That ridiculous bouffant hair, the manicured nails, those leather jackets he wears. He's nearly fifty, for goodness sake.'

'He looks familiar,' Guastafeste said.

'You've probably seen him on television,' I said. 'RAI's resident intellectual. Politics, current affairs, culture, even sport — he seems to be able to talk about them all.'

'Talking about a subject and actually knowing something about it are two very different things,' Margherita said. 'Not that a television producer would recognise the distinction.'

I laughed. Margherita took my hand and gave it an affectionate squeeze.

'But we won't let an arrogant loudmouth like Vittorio Castellani spoil our evening out, will we?' she said. 'Even if he does have a better seat than we do.'

'He won't hear any better,' I said. 'Probably worse, in fact. The sound will travel over his head and be at its best . . . oh . . . about here, I'd say. Right above us. That's why I chose these seats. I've been to concerts here before.'

'You must let us pay you for the tickets, Gianni,' Margherita said.

'I wouldn't hear of it.'

'No, I insist.'

'So do I. I'm delighted you both could come.

34

Listening to music with friends, that is my idea of a perfect night out.'

'It could be a disaster, you know,' Guastafeste said. 'That new bridge you fitted. What if it collapses halfway through?'

I'd told them about my experiences of the afternoon, though I hadn't revealed Yevgeny Ivanov's secret. Guastafeste is a detective with the Cremona police. I would trust him with my life, but not a juicy titbit of gossip.

'Don't worry, Gianni,' Margherita said. 'If anything goes wrong, you can put my jacket over your head and sneak out the side exit. And I'm sure Antonio can fix up a police escort to stop the mob from lynching you.'

'Nothing is going to go wrong,' I said. 'You wait till you hear Ivanov. He is sensational.'

The soloist appeared moments later. He walked quickly out from one of the transepts, almost scuttling across to the front of the nave, as if he didn't want to be noticed. He had his head down, his eyes fixed on the floor, the Cannon clutched in his left hand. Most of the cathedral was in shadow — it is simply too vast a space to illuminate effectively — but that only added to the spine-tingling atmosphere of the occasion. There was a single spotlight focused on the area below the altar steps, where Yevgeny Ivanov was standing. Reflected light glinted off the gilt surround of the organ loft to his right, penetrating back into the apse to play round the edges of Boccaccino's sixteenth-century fresco of Christ flanked by four saints, including Omobono, the patron saint of Cremona. Nearly all

35

the other frescoes that decorate the interior of the cathedral were hidden in darkness, the only exceptions being the ones by the entrance, where rows of votive candles cast a dim, flickering light over the walls.

Yevgeny gave a perfunctory bow to acknowledge the audience's applause; then he lifted the violin to his chin and the transformation I'd seen earlier in my workshop took place again. Ivanov the introverted man became Ivanov the extrovert performer. The shyness fell away like a cloak dropping to the ground, and a new, more assured person stepped out into the limelight.

He began with the Bach B-minor unaccompanied partita, and I felt the audience sit back, as if they had been physically buffeted by the wave of sound that rolled down the nave. I heard sharp intakes of breath all round me, little gasps like explosions. Even I, who had heard the Cannon only an hour or two before, was stunned by the intensity of the sound. The acoustics in the cathedral are superb, but I had never heard anything like this. It was awe-inspiring — a barrage that knocked you out with its power, then resuscitated you with its passion and ardour.

I'd been nervous before Yevgeny started playing. Margherita had been joking about the lynch mob, but it was my reputation that was on the line here as well as Ivanov's. If something did go wrong with *il Cannone*, something physical, then the finger of blame would be pointed at me. All my years of hard work, the name I'd built for myself in Cremona and beyond would count for nothing. I would become infamous as the luthier who ruined the Cannon.

But as Yevgeny's beautiful playing washed over me, I relaxed. The violin sounded magnificent. I'm not conceited enough to think that I could take credit for that, but I was quietly pleased that — if nothing else — my new bridge was allowing Giuseppe Guarneri's infinitely superior craftsmanship to be enjoyed by a throng of enthralled listeners.

It was an unforgettable recital — one of those evenings that you know will linger in your memory forever. Yevgeny played Bach; then he was joined by a pianist and together they played Paganini: some of the caprices with Schumann's accompaniment, followed by the 'Moto Perpetuo' and three of the virtuoso variations on operatic arias that allow a soloist to let loose the fireworks — 'I Palpiti,' 'Nel cor più non mi sento,' and the 'Moses Fantasy.'

At the end, I doubt that even Paganini himself would have received a more tumultuous ovation. The entire audience leaped to its feet, clapping and cheering in what must surely have been the wildest, most unrestrained celebration the cathedral had ever seen. But it didn't seem inappropriate, given the circumstances. *Il Cannone* was back where it had been created. Like the prodigal son, it had been forgiven and restored to the affectionate bosom of its family.

Three encores followed before it became obvious that Yevgeny wasn't going to reappear, whereupon the audience began, reluctantly, to disperse. Margherita, Guastafeste, and I left the

37

cathedral and walked across the Piazza del Comune to the town hall. The square was floodlit, almost as bright as day, and crowded with concertgoers making their way home or to restaurants for a late dinner. We crossed the courtyard in the centre of the Comune and paused by a door, where an official checked off our names on a list — struggling to find them until he located a supplementary sheet of late additions.

A long flight of stone stairs took us up to the Salone degli Alabardieri on the first floor; then we passed through an arch into the Salone dei Quadri — the Salon of the Paintings — a long, narrow room with a high ceiling and walls hung with paintings by Boccaccino, Miradori, Cossali, Cattapane, and others, some of them four metres high and five or six metres wide. A doorway on the far side of the salon led to the most famous room in the town hall, the Sala dei Violini, where the city's collection of fine string instruments is kept, including violins by Stradivari, Guarneri, and Amati. The room was closed this evening, a uniformed security guard standing outside it to keep people away.

We helped ourselves to glasses of wine from a table and retreated into a corner. I glanced longingly at the door to the Sala dei Violini. I would far rather have been in there, studying the great luthiers' inspiring creations, than out here at a civic reception. I generally do everything I can to avoid formal functions like this. I loathe the shallowness of them, the tedium of the small talk, all these people I do not know twittering on at me like tepid water dripping from a tap. But I wanted to see Yevgeny. Our encounter that afternoon, our confidential discussions, had made me feel close to him. I wanted to tell him how much I'd enjoyed his playing.

'Gate-crashing, eh, Gianni?' a voice said beside me.

I turned, to see Vincenzo Serafin gazing up at me, his mouth twisted into a grimace that I think was meant to be a sardonic smile.

'I thought this party was for movers and shakers only,' he continued. 'If I'd known they were letting anyone in, I wouldn't have bothered coming.'

He gave a harsh, humourless laugh and glanced at the two people accompanying him.

'You know Maddalena, of course.'

I nodded politely at his mistress, a stick-thin fake blonde with the sharp face and angular body of a fashion model. She sniffed disdainfully at me, then looked round the room, her eyes bored and vacuous.

'And this is a friend of mine from Paris,' Serafin said. 'François Villeneuve. This is Gianni Castiglione. He does work for me from time to time. When I can't find anyone better.'

I ignored the slight — I think it was a joke, but with Serafin, you can never be sure — and shook hands with Villeneuve.

He was a short, goatlike man with crooked, slightly buck teeth, a shock of untidy grey hair, and a covering of pale fluff on his chin that was too insubstantial to warrant the term *beard*. He gave the impression of good-natured affability, until you looked into his eyes. His eyes were cold and cloudy, like chips of frosted glass.

'How do you do?' I said. 'Are you here for long?'

'Just a few days,' Villeneuve replied in hesitant Italian.

'You are staying in Cremona?'

'At the Hotel San Michele.'

'God knows why,' Serafin said sourly. 'A provincial little backwater like this. He could be in Milan with me, a real city. But he wanted to see how the yokels live.'

'I hope you enjoy your stay,' I said. 'Have you been here before?'

Villeneuve shook his head.

'This is my first time. But it seems an attractive city.'

'First impressions can be deceptive,' Serafin said. He tapped me on the chest with his forefinger. 'I've got a violin I want you to look at for me. It might be a Bergonzi, but then again, it might not.'

'I'm a bit busy at the moment. I'll have to check my diary,' I said coolly.

'Busy?' Serafin said, his lip curling. 'What, scraping away at bits of wood? I don't know why you modern violin makers bother. You heard that sound tonight. Doesn't it make you want to go away and slash your wrists?'

'Not everyone can be a Guarneri,' I said.

'No, thank goodness. If Guarneris were two a penny, where would dealers like me be? I sat there this evening and, you know, I was strongly tempted to dash out, snatch *il Cannone* from

40

Ivanov's hands, and make a run for the exit.'

'Yes, but you're not really built for running, are you, Vincenzo?' I said dryly.

He gave me a sharp look, then forced a thin smile.

'What I wouldn't give to own a violin like that,' he said. 'What's it worth, twenty million? I have clients who would pay fifty million for it. Probably more.'

'We'll bear that in mind,' Guastafeste said. 'Should anything unfortunate happen to the Cannon.'

'Oh, yes?' Serafin said. 'And you are?'

'This is Antonio Guastafeste. Of the Cremona police,' I said, enjoying the moment.

Serafin's eyes narrowed. His tongue flicked out and touched his lips nervously. Then he recovered himself, waving an arm in the air expansively.

'I'm just talking, of course. Who wouldn't want the Cannon? I'm sure Gianni here would, wouldn't you, given the chance?'

'What for?' I said. 'To shut away in a bank vault or a private collection? It belongs to the people. It should be heard; it should be played. The last thing I want is to own it.'

Serafin patted my arm in an exaggerated gesture of sympathy.

'That's why you're just a simple luthier, Gianni, and I'm a millionaire.'

He took Maddalena by the arm.

'Come on, darling. Let's see who else is here.'

They moved away across the room, weaving in and out of the groups of people, searching for

41

someone more worthy of their attention.

'What a horrible little man,' Margherita said. 'Is he always like that?'

'Not always,' I replied. 'Sometimes he can be quite unpleasant.'

'How on earth do you work with him?'

'He's a very successful dealer, very well connected. And occasionally — very occasionally, when he wants something — he can be perfectly charming.'

'Who's the blonde with him, the clotheshorse? His wife?'

'I love it when you're catty,' I said. 'No, Serafin's wife is kept hidden away in the country, like one of those madwomen in gothic novels. I'm sure it suits her as much as him. Maddalena is his mistress.'

'She's a bit young for him, isn't she?'

'Mistresses of rich men tend to be,' I said.

A white-coated waiter came past with a tray of canapés. We helped ourselves, then spent an amusing few minutes trying to spot the celebrities at the reception. The footballer was there, of course, accompanied by a woman who was even blonder and thinner than Maddalena — if such a thing were possible. Guastafeste pointed out a couple of flashy local businessmen who, he claimed, had links with organised crime, and Margherita thought the man holding court at the other side of the room was a well-known fashion designer from Milan, or possibly a film actor — she couldn't be sure which. For Cremona, it was an impressive turnout. We are not quite the provincial little backwater Serafin

42

sneered at to his French friend, but neither are we a sophisticated, cosmopolitan city like Milan, our close neighbour to the northwest, in whose preening shadow we have always lived. We like it that way, of course. We are quiet people, without great pretensions. We are happy to remain watching from the wings while the Milanese shout and strut about on the stage.

I sensed a sudden movement in the room, the guests shifting sideways, repositioning themselves as a phalanx of men in suits swept into the chamber. The group marched to the far end and broke apart to reveal Ludmilla and Yevgeny Ivanov and the mayor of Cremona in their centre. The room fell silent. The mayor held out his arms, as if to embrace us all, and launched into a speech of great length and even greater tedium. He welcomed the Ivanovs to the city, then veered off at various irrelevant tangents, clearly under the delusion that someone other than his fawning acolytes was interested in what he had to say.

Throughout the whole rambling address, Ludmilla stood straight and attentive, obviously relishing being the centre of attention. But at her side, Yevgeny was a picture of embarrassment, shoulders hunched, eyes locked on the floor, which, unfortunately for him, showed no signs of opening up and swallowing him.

Finally, the speech came to an end. There was a brief round of applause and then the guests got back to the more pressing business of talking and drinking and being seen.

43

'What a load of drivel,' Guastafeste said in disgust.

'The fellow's a politician,' I said. 'He can't help it.'

'Can we go now?' Margherita asked.

'In a minute,' I said.

I'd just noticed a skinny figure in a black dress suit creeping stealthily round the perimeter of the room. Yevgeny Ivanov stopped next to us, his back pressed to the wall like a cornered animal. Margherita, Guastafeste, and I closed in round him, sensing instinctively that he needed our protection. He seemed lost for words, so I congratulated him on his performance.

'Thank you,' he said in English. 'But it was not just me. It was the violin, too.'

'You have *il Cannone* with you?' I asked.

'The insurance company men take it away from me. It is on its way back to Genoa now.'

'It must have been quite an experience, playing Paganini's violin.'

'Yes, amazing. My own violin is Stradivari, but it is nothing compared to the Cannon. The sound, it will seem very thin now.'

He looked anxiously round the room, keeping his head down, as if he didn't want to be spotted.

'I am glad you are here,' he said in a low voice. 'These things, I hate them. Strange people talking to me, saying nothing. It is good to see a face I know.'

'Thank you for inviting us,' I said. 'These are my friends, Margherita Severini and Antonio Guastafeste. Antonio is the cellist in the quartet I told you about earlier.'

'Ah, yes.'

Yevgeny shook their hands. He thought for a moment, then said to Margherita in Italian, 'Please excuse my Italian; it is not good. But you are in Gianni's quartet, too?'

'Oh, no,' Margherita replied.

'She plays the piano, though,' I said. 'Rather well.'

'Not at all well, actually,' Margherita said. 'I'm strictly an amateur.'

'But amateur does not mean bad,' Yevgeny said. 'To play for pleasure only, that is good. Sometimes I wish I was amateur, too.'

'Your Italian is very good,' I said. 'Your mother said you didn't speak much.'

'Yes, well, my mother. She does not believe I do anything well.'

'Except play the violin,' Guastafeste said.

'Sometimes not even that,' Yevgeny said, and laughed uneasily.

'When do you leave Cremona?' Margherita asked.

'On Tuesday,' Yevgeny replied. 'Then I have concerts in Venice and Florence and Bologna. After that, I fly to New York, then Japan and Australia. At the end of next month, I am back in Italy — Milan and Turin.'

'It's an exciting life.'

Yevgeny gave a sad little smile.

'Exciting? No, I don't think so.'

'You have plans for the next two days?' I asked.

Yevgeny shook his head.

'Some practice. A lot of looking out of hotel

window. Hotels, airports — that is where I live these days.'

'Come for lunch tomorrow,' I said on impulse. 'You and your mother.'

'For lunch?'

'If you have no other plans. It would be my pleasure.'

Yevgeny hesitated.

'Well . . . if you are sure?'

'I would like nothing better.'

'That is nice. I will have to ask my mother, of course. I do not get invite to lunch much.'

'You astound me.'

'People think I am too busy, too grand. They keep distance from me. I spend my life travelling, but I never meet anyone.' He paused; then his eyes lit up. 'I could bring my violin. We could play quartets. What do you think?'

'Oh, no,' I said. 'We are not good enough for you.'

'What does that matter? We do not perform.'

I looked at Guastafeste.

'I'm not on duty tomorrow,' he said.

'It will be a shock for you,' I said to Yevgeny. 'We really aren't very good.'

'I would like it.'

'Then I'll phone our viola player and see if he's free. Shall we say — '

I broke off as a figure loomed up beside me, almost barging me out of the way to get to Yevgeny.

'Signor Ivanov, a truly memorable performance. Superlative playing. Allow me to congratulate you. Vittorio Castellani, professor of

46

music at the University of Milan.'

Castellani reached out, grasped Yevgeny's hand, and pumped it up and down. Yevgeny stared at him with the terrified look of a man accosted in the street who fears he's about to be mugged.

'I'm something of an authority on Paganini, you know,' Castellani went on. 'I'm doing a piece for the *Corriere della Sera*. *Il Cannone* coming back to Cremona, that kind of thing. So what did you think to the violin?'

Castellani pushed me sideways with his arm, treading on my toes in the process.

'Excuse me, would you mind?'

I stepped back. Not that I had much choice. Castellani wasn't the type of man to let anyone stand in his way. He swung round, giving me a close-up view of his leather jacket and thick swept-back hair. The pungent scent of his aftershave filled my nostrils.

'I particularly liked your interpretation of 'Nel cor più non mi sento,'' Castellani said to Yevgeny. 'Of course, Paisiello has fallen out of fashion these days, even in Italy. I saw a production of *La Bella Molinara* at Spoleto a few years ago and, frankly, I can see why. 'Nel cor' is just about the only half-decent thing in the whole opera ...'

I looked across at Margherita and she rolled her eyes at me. 'An arrogant loudmouth' was what she'd called Castellani earlier, and though she wasn't far off the mark, there was more to him than just his mouth. He'd been a hardworking academic once, a respected musicologist who had written several well-received books on music, including a biography of Paganini, which I had on my shelves at home. But somewhere in his late thirties, he'd branched out and started a parallel career in journalism, writing initially only about classical music but soon becoming a self-proclaimed authority on rock and pop, too. Endowed with the glossy good looks and superficial charm that the broadcasting industry requires in its presenters, it wasn't long before he was making guest appearances as a pundit on television, giving his opinions on a wide variety of subjects, from archaeology to Zen Buddhism. It was true — as Margherita had said — that he knew very little about most of these topics, but that was immaterial, for his audiences knew even less. What counted was his viewer-friendly demeanour, trendy clothes, and ability to talk in sound bites of no more than the twenty seconds deemed by television producers to be the maximum attention span of the average Italian couch potato.

Castellani had become the acceptable face of the intellectual classes, an academic who could hide his learning beneath a veneer of populism but still maintain some credibility. Producers liked him because he added a touch of gravitas to their lazy, shallow programmes, and Castellani liked them because of the fame and adulation that came with a broadcasting career. Once you have answered the call of the television siren, there is no escaping her pernicious embrace. He was no longer a musicologist and university teacher; he was a 'personality,' and in becoming one, he had lost his identity.

'I must say, I've rarely heard 'I Palpiti' played better,' he was saying to Yevgeny. 'You know the story behind it, of course, that Rossini wrote the original aria in the time it took him to boil a plate of rice for his supper. Utter rubbish. I don't believe a word of it. Rossini enjoyed that kind of dissimulation — portraying himself as an indolent *bon viveur* who knocked off his operas in a couple of weeks . . . '

Castellani paused and turned to the hangers-on who had accompanied him across the room. As celebrity entourages go, it was fairly modest, consisting of just two people — a dark, saturnine young man and a slim, attractive girl who looked like a student.

'Marco,' he said to the young man. 'Bring me another glass of wine, and something to eat. I'm starving. And some wine for Signor Ivanov, too.'

'No, no, I can get it myself,' Yevgeny protested, trying to edge away along the wall.

'Nonsense. Marco will bring it. That's what he's for. Chop, chop, Marco, I'm dying of thirst here.'

Marco turned and I saw a cloud of resentment pass across his face as he walked away. Castellani reached out to the pretty young woman.

'Mirella, dear, come over here. I'm sure you'd like to meet Signor Ivanov.'

Castellani grasped the girl by the hand and pulled her to him, slipping his arm round her

shoulders in a manner that was more proprieto-
rial than affectionate. I took advantage of the
moment to squeeze myself between Yevgeny and
Castellani.

'My apologies,' I murmured, 'but Signor
Ivanov is wanted elsewhere.'

'What? What do you mean . . . ' Castellani
began, but by then I had taken Yevgeny by the
arm and was leading him firmly away.

I didn't stop until we were across the room, at
least fifty other people between us and
Castellani. Guastafeste and Margherita had
followed, Margherita unable to contain her glee
at my audacious manoeuvre.

'You should have seen Castellani's face,' she
said. 'Bravo, Gianni. I wish more people had the
nerve to do that to him.'

'Thank you,' Yevgeny said. 'Who was that
awful man?'

'Nobody,' I said. 'We have to go now, I'm
afraid. But I will expect you tomorrow, one
o'clock.'

'I will have to check with my mother first,'
Yevgeny said.

'Please do. But come alone, if you have to.'

It was a relief to step out of the reception
chamber, to get away from all the people, the
heat, and the noise. The landing at the top of the
stairs was cool and quiet. It seemed deserted
until I heard voices coming from somewhere
over to my right. I turned and saw two people
standing in a shadowy corner, conversing in low
but intense tones. I was surprised to see that one
of them was Ludmilla Ivanova. The other was a

thickset man with a fleshy face and shiny bald pate that caught the light as he moved his head. They were speaking in Russian, but I could tell from their voices, and from their gestures, that they were arguing about something. Neither of them noticed us watching; they were too preoccupied with their dispute, which was becoming increasingly heated. Ludmilla raised her voice, angry now. The bald man shrugged and tried to walk away. This seemed to incense Ludmilla further, for she grabbed hold of the man's shoulder and pulled him back, leaning close and snarling furiously into his face.

The scene made me uncomfortable. It felt as if we were spying on them, eavesdropping on a private, and very personal, conversation. I looked at Margherita and Guastafeste, sensing they felt the same. We crept softly across the landing and down the stairs. Above us, Ludmilla Ivanova was still shouting, her incomprehensible Russian words reverberating menacingly round the stone walls of the town hall.

4

I half-expected Yevgeny to phone me the next morning to cancel our lunch appointment. He was so much in thrall to his mother that I feared she would refuse to let him come, particularly as she had not been a party to the arrangement. But in the event, they both turned up on the dot of one o'clock.

I went out to greet them on the forecourt. Ludmilla was paying the taxi driver who had brought them from Cremona, Yevgeny standing beside her with his violin case. I smiled at him warmly and shook his hand.

'Yevgeny, how nice to see you again. How are you? You have recovered from last night's reception?'

'Yes, thank you.'

'Did you stay long?'

'Awhile. Mama enjoys these things.'

'One can't leave too soon; it would be rude,' Ludmilla said, turning away from the taxi. 'These civic receptions are an honour, Yevgeny. You have a duty to attend them.' She held out her hand. 'Dottore Castiglione, it is kind of you to invite us.'

'Please call me Gianni.'

'Then you must call me Ludmilla,' she said graciously.

If she harboured any resentment towards me for insisting that she leave my workshop the previous afternoon, it certainly wasn't obvious.

She seemed in a good humour, her face relaxed and benign. She was wearing another low-cut dress — a tight royal blue one that clung to her full figure — and matching shoes. Her long black hair hung loose over her shoulders, and round her neck was a silver chain from which a sapphire cluster dangled.

'We are playing quartets?' Yevgeny asked.

'If you still wish to,' I replied.

'Of course. That is why I bring my violin. Are the others here?'

'Antonio is. Our viola player, Father Arrighi, will be here shortly.'

'Father? He is a priest?'

'When you play quartets the way we do,' I said, 'it helps to have God on your side.'

We went into the house. I settled Yevgeny and Ludmilla in the sitting room, then walked through into the kitchen, where Margherita was preparing a tray of antipasti, Guastafeste loitering awkwardly in the vicinity, trying to appear willing but not actually doing anything useful. I asked him to make some aperitifs for everyone and he accepted with alacrity, rummaging in my cupboards and bringing forth all manner of spirit bottles, some of which I'd forgotten I had. Antonio's drink-mixing skills are legendary. His aperitifs, a potent concoction of gin and vodka and anything else he can lay hands on, are guaranteed to whet your appetite — if they don't knock you out first.

He was arranging the drinks on a tray when — with the impeccable timing for which he was renowned — Father Ignazio Arrighi arrived.

53

'He knows,' Guastafeste whispered to me as the priest came into the kitchen. 'Somehow he always knows. He must be able to smell booze on the wind or something.'

'Ah, just what I need,' Father Arrighi said, helping himself to one of the glasses.

He was wearing his dark suit and dog collar, his soft pink face glowing with good health. I knew he'd had a busy morning — Mass at seven-thirty for the early risers, then another at ten for the laggards — but he was free now until the evening. The Catholic Church is a civilised institution. It realised long ago that the well-being of a congregation, and its priests, is dependent on a long lunch and a nap on a Sunday afternoon.

I took him through into the sitting room and introduced him to the Ivanovs. Guastafeste followed with the aperitifs. I helped distribute the drinks, then excused myself and returned to the kitchen. Margherita was at the sink, busying herself with some washing up.

'Leave that,' I said.

'I'm just clearing a few things out of the way,' she replied.

'Go and sit down with a drink.'

'I will. But I'll just — '

'Now,' I said firmly. 'I didn't invite you here to do the washing up.'

'You can't do it all yourself, Gianni.'

'No arguments,' I said. 'Out.'

'What about the pasta sauce?'

'*Out!*'

I shooed her out of the kitchen. She went, but

54

only reluctantly. We are both of a generation that grew up with entrenched views about the respective roles of men and women. My wife, when she was alive, did all the cooking and virtually all the other household chores. It was how things were. The world has changed since then, though perhaps not as much as we would like to think. Margherita is an independent, liberated woman who, by her own admission, loathes the drudgery of domesticity, but the traces of convention are hard to throw off. There was something in her that would not allow her to put her feet up and do nothing when there was work to be done in the kitchen.

I checked the tomato sauce that was simmering on the hob, then the pork escalopes in the oven. I am a latecomer to the art of cooking and my repertoire is relatively limited. I have learnt a few new dishes in the seven years that I've been a widower, but my staple diet is still essentially the same food that Caterina cooked for us during the thirty-five years we were married — pasta, chicken and pork, plenty of fresh vegetables. It is a simple, unfussy regimen, but then, I am a simple, unfussy person. The food suits me well enough, and I am not embarrassed to serve it to my guests. I am a sixty-four-year-old man who lives alone. People do not expect me to provide cordon bleu meals. They are generally amazed that I can even boil an egg.

We ate in my small, rather cramped dining room. In summer, I like to eat al fresco on the terrace, but it was now October and too chilly to sit outside. It was a pleasant, sociable meal. Guastafeste, Father Arrighi, and I have known one another for many years. Margherita has been a feature of my life for only twelve months, but already she is comfortable with my friends, and they with her. The Ivanovs were easy guests. Yevgeny said very little, but Ludmilla more than made up for his reticence.

'Tell me,' I said to her at the end of the meal. 'How did you learn to speak such excellent Italian?'

We had finished the cake that Margherita had brought with her from Milan and I was passing round some torrone, the honey and almond nougat that is a Cremonese speciality. Guastafeste was topping up our glasses from a fresh bottle of wine and carefully leaving the half-full bottle next to Father Arrighi.

'I studied here,' Ludmilla said. 'When I was younger. I was a student at the conservatoire in Moscow, but I came to Milan for a year, to the conservatorio.'

'You play an instrument?' Guastafeste asked.

'I was a singer.'

So I had guessed correctly the day before.

'You sang professionally?' I said.

'For a short time. Then I met my husband and had Yevgeny and' — she smiled tenderly at her son — 'suddenly my career was not so important.'

'Your husband is travelling with you?' Father Arrighi asked.

'My ex-husband,' Ludmilla said carefully, 'is living in Moscow with his second wife.'

'Ah, I'm sorry I asked.'

'Not at all. Fyodor and I were divorced a long time ago, when Yevgeny was only a child. It is all in the past.'

I made coffee for everyone; then we went through into the back room to play quartets.

'Let me apologise now for our poor standard,' I said to Yevgeny as we took out our instruments. 'If at any time it all becomes too excruciatingly awful for you, you must say so and we will stop. We do not want to torture you.'

'We do this for fun,' Yevgeny said. 'I do not care how you play.'

He was holding his Stradivari in his hand.

'May I?' I said.

He passed the violin to me and I ran my eyes over it. I could tell at once — from the warm dark colour, the long corners, the handsome two-piece maple back — that it dated from the early 1700s, the beginning of Stradivari's 'Golden Period.' He was in his late fifties then, not much younger than I was. Like me, he'd been making violins for more than forty years, although there the comparison ends. This was an exquisite violin, far surpassing anything I have been able to create in my own, not entirely undistinguished, career. I have examined many Stradivari violins and I have never once felt jealous of his unique skill as a luthier. He is such a world apart from everyone else that it would be like a mortal envying a god. I am just glad that he lived, and that his work has survived for new generations of violin makers to enjoy and attempt to emulate.

I couldn't help comparing this instrument with Paganini's, the Cannon was so fresh in my mind. Guarneri del Gesù — literally, 'of Jesus,' because of the cross he inscribed on his labels — and Stradivari were very different characters as men, and those differences are readily apparent in their violins. Stradivari was a perfectionist, an austere, serious sort of man who led a life of hard work and sober propriety. Guarneri was a wilder, less focused character — much like the rest of us — who got drunk on a Saturday night and didn't give a damn if some of his work was slipshod. Stradivari's instruments are meticulously crafted, every detail given care and attention. Guarneri's — particularly *il Cannone* — are rougher, louder, but don't be fooled by appearances. The trappings may be different, but underneath they both sing like angels.

I peered inside the f-hole, tilting the violin towards the light so I could read the maker's label: *Antonius Stradivarius Cremonensis Faciebat Anno 1701.*

'It is not mine,' Yevgeny said. 'I could not afford a violin like that. It is on loan from the Moscow Conservatoire.'

'It's a fine instrument,' I said, handing it back reluctantly, then picking up my own violin — one I made myself, of course — dating from what I like to think of as my own 'Golden Period,' which lasted for about a fortnight in 1985.

'What shall we play?' Guastafeste asked. He was already seated in front of his music stand, his cello between his legs.

'Let Yevgeny decide,' I said. 'What would you like?'

'I do not know,' Yevgeny said. 'There is so much to choose from. Help me, Gianni. Where do I begin?'

'At the beginning,' I said.

So we played Haydn, the father of the string quartet, then moved on to his heirs, Mozart and Beethoven, sometimes just playing single movements rather than whole works. Yevgeny was happy to dip in and out, sampling a range of composers. He was like a child opening birthday presents, delighted to find something else to unwrap and enjoy.

I was relieved that he didn't want to work on the pieces, to practise the tricky passages. Over my years as an amateur quartet player, I have come to realise that practising the difficult bits doesn't really make you play them any better; it just hammers home the depressing conclusion that you'll never be able to play them.

The string quartet is, in theory, a unified musical form comprised of four equal parts, each as important as the next. In practice, the first violin is more equal than the others, which suited Guastafeste, Father Arrighi, and me perfectly. We could sit back and allow Yevgeny to dominate. We could listen and relish his wonderful sound. Never before had we played with a violinist of his stature. He was accustomed to being a soloist, to being the star, but he was too good a musician to swamp the ensemble with his superior technique. He did his best to blend in, to avoid humiliating us, though the vast gap between us was patently obvious to everyone in the room.

Margherita and Ludmilla sat in the armchairs against the back wall, listening raptly. When we played the cavatina from one of Beethoven's late quartets — one of the most beautiful pieces of chamber music ever written — I glanced at Margherita and saw she had tears in her eyes. Antonio and Father Arrighi were also showing signs of emotion, not just at the music but at the memories it brought back. The cavatina was one of Tomaso Rainaldi's favourite pieces, and this was the first time we had played it together since his death. This was the first time, in fact, that we had played quartets at all.

Losing our first violinist had been a traumatic experience. Having Yevgeny filling the gap was musically rewarding, but Tomaso had been a friend since childhood; we had made music together for fifty years. No one could take his place, either in my life or in our quartet. I found my own eyes watering as I remembered him, remembered all those happy moments we'd had together, and at the end of the movement I made my excuses and hurried from the room.

Margherita found me in the kitchen a few minutes later, dabbing at my eyes with a handkerchief. She didn't say anything, just put her arms round me and drew me close, holding me until I'd composed myself.

'It was Tomaso, wasn't it?' she said, pulling back from me.

I nodded. Margherita had never met Tomaso,

but I'd told her stories about him.

'That piece in particular,' I said. 'Tomaso loved it so much. We used to joke about it. 'Not the cavatina *again*,' we used to say when Tomaso suggested it.'

'It's a very moving piece of music. And you played it so well.'

'I know. Yevgeny is terrific, isn't he? I'm sure he played it better than Tomaso ever did, but the funny thing is, it didn't feel as if he did. Do you know what I mean? It didn't feel right, didn't sound right, because it wasn't Tomaso playing it.' I wiped my eyes again with my handkerchief. 'All the time, I was thinking, I am never going to hear Tomaso play this again. I am never going to see him, speak to him, make music with him. He's gone.'

Margherita hugged me again.

'I know,' she said gently. 'It's hard, isn't it? Memories are painful, but they're also uplifting. He's still with you, Gianni. You have to look at it like that. Tomaso has gone, but a part of him is still here with you, and always will be.'

She smiled at me.

'Why don't you take a break now? You've played enough. I'll make tea for us all.'

I took her hand and held it tight.

'Thank you. I'm glad you're here.'

'You can always talk to me, Gianni. You know that.'

I went out into the garden for a time to let the fresh air clear my head. It had been many months since I'd shed tears for Tomaso, but grief is like that. It's not a continuous process; it

61

comes in waves. You can keep it at bay for a time, like a dam holding back a lake, but then something triggers an explosion inside you, shattering the wall and letting loose a flood. With me, that trigger is so often music. Music, more than anything, has memories, associations, and it works on a subliminal level that is somehow more powerful than more overt influences. Photographs, remembered conversations, geographic locations — they can all release that torrent of emotion. But music seems to probe deeper, to find the most raw, sensitive part of me, and the resulting deluge is all the more overwhelming.

The afternoon sunshine, the breeze gusting across the plain soothed me, dried my damp cheeks. I picked a few late French beans and a courgette from my vegetable patch, then heard footsteps behind me. I turned and saw Yevgeny approaching.

'You are all right?' he asked, his face concerned.

'I'm fine.'

'I have not tired you too much?'

'Not at all.'

'I know we play a lot. But it has been such fun. All this wonderful music I never play before. Thank you.'

'Thank you for joining us,' I said. 'To play with a violinist like you has been a great privilege. I'm sorry we can't match you.'

'You play well, all of you. And I see you love playing. That is good. In my world, the professional world, it is not always fun.'

He looked round the garden, at the shrubs and trees, the surrounding fields rolling away into the distance.

'It is very peaceful,' he said. 'You always live here?'

I shook my head.

'I lived in the city for many years. I like the countryside, but it was better for my children to be in Cremona. That was where their schools were, their friends.'

'You have children?'

'Two sons and a daughter. All grown up and settled elsewhere now. I have three grandchildren, too.'

'In Cremona?'

'Mantua. Not far away.'

'It must be nice to have family,' Yevgeny said. 'Friends, too,' he added with a pensive frown.

'You have friends, surely?' I said.

'Not really,' he replied. 'My life, from age four, has been violin and nothing else — lessons, practice, concerts. Those things boys do — playing football, going to parties, cinema — I do none of them.'

I felt sorry for him, but I wasn't surprised by his revelation. I have encountered a large number of gifted musicians in my time as a luthier, and none of them has had what I would regard as a proper childhood.

Childhood and musical excellence are not compatible with each other — you have to make a choice between the two. I could sense the loneliness in Yevgeny. I could imagine the isolated kind of life he'd led — the years of

63

single-minded practice he'd had to put in to reach his current position. And he was one of the lucky ones. He'd survived, come through it all to establish himself as a soloist, but I knew there were thousands more just like him who had fallen by the wayside. They had sacrificed their youth to music and then found there was no place for them in the adult world.

There are rewards in being a child prodigy, but it is not a life I would wish on anyone, and it is probably not a life many children would choose for themselves if they weren't forced into it by an ambitious parent. And there is usually a pushy mother or father in the background somewhere. Most children do not willingly practise a musical instrument for the many hours a day required to reach a virtuoso standard. I know this from my own three, all of whom learned instruments, and all of whom resisted my attempts to persuade them to practise. I was not inclined to force them and I never had any doubts that that was the right course of action to take. Music should be a pleasure, not a chore. I have seen too many disillusioned, embittered professionals to want my children to become like them. Yevgeny was not yet disillusioned — he was, after all, a prizewinning soloist with a glittering career ahead of him — but he clearly had regrets and was beginning to wonder what he had missed out on for all those years.

'Maybe you should slow down a bit,' I said. 'Do something else as well as music.'

He smiled ruefully.

'Slow down? My mother, she never allow it. I

just win the Premio Paganini. My life, it will get faster and faster. Lots of people already invite me to play. Mama says I must say yes to them all.'

'You're no longer a child, Yevgeny,' I said. 'You can make your own decisions now.'

He looked at me thoughtfully. Then he nodded and started to say something, but the words were cut off by a sudden shout from the terrace. Guastafeste was walking across the lawn towards us. His mobile phone was in his hand.

'I'm sorry, Gianni, I've got to go,' he said. 'I've had a call from the *questura*.'

'Bad news?' I said.

'It's François Villeneuve — Vincenzo Serafin's friend from Paris. He's been found dead in his hotel room. And he didn't die of natural causes.

5

Murder investigations are usually so time-consuming and absorbing that Guastafeste effectively disappears from my life for several days, sometimes several weeks, on end. I was therefore surprised to get a phone call from him the following morning. I was in my workshop, cutting out the front plate for a new violin from a two-piece sheet of spruce.

'Are you busy?' he asked.

'Nothing that can't wait,' I replied.

'I need your help. Can I come out and see you?'

'Of course. But what about the Villeneuve case? Aren't you working on that?'

'This is to do with the case,' he said.

Twenty minutes later, I heard his car pull into the drive, the tyres crunching on the gravel. I put down my saw, removed my apron, and went out onto the terrace to meet him. He was unshaven and bleary-eyed. His clothes looked as if he'd slept in them, though — from past experience — I knew he'd probably been up most of the night. As one of the senior detectives at the *questura* he'd have borne the brunt of the homicide enquiry, working flat out during those first few hours, while the trail was still fresh.

'Coffee?' I said. 'You look as if you could use one.'

'Thanks.'

We went into the kitchen and I filled the espresso pot and put it on the stove. Guastafeste sat down at the table. He rubbed the dark shadow along his jawline and yawned.

'You want to borrow a razor?' I asked.

'I'll stick with the designer stubble for the moment.'

'When we've finished, you can come into the workshop and sand down some maple for me with your chin.'

He gave a lopsided grin.

'You wouldn't like the finish. It'd be too rough.'

I took a couple of coffee cups out of a cupboard and put them on the table.

'So what about Villeneuve?' I said. 'What happened to him?'

'He was hit over the head. There was blood, as well as a few hairs, on a table lamp in his room. We haven't got the forensics back yet, but the lamp was almost certainly the murder weapon.'

I winced.

'Poor fellow. You have any leads?'

'Nothing significant so far. The hotel staff, the other guests, none of them saw or heard anything. Someone obviously came to see him. It looks as if they had an argument or a fight — there were signs of a struggle in the room — then the visitor, whoever it was, picked up the table lamp and hit Villeneuve over the head with it. The pathologist who did the autopsy said Villeneuve had unusually thin skull plates. It wouldn't have taken much of a blow to kill him.'

'This was when, exactly — yesterday afternoon?'

'The doctor puts the time of death as yesterday morning, between ten A.M. and noon.'

'But you weren't called until — what time was it? Five-thirty six o'clock?'

'That's when the body was discovered. There was a DO NOT DISTURB sign on the door, so the hotel cleaning staff didn't go in yesterday morning. It was only when Villeneuve's wife phoned the duty manager from Paris later in the day that anyone went to check the room. She'd been trying to reach her husband all day, on both his mobile and the hotel land line. She was worried. The manager used his pass key to open the door, and he found Villeneuve on the floor.'

Guastafeste yawned again. I studied his haggard face.

'Have you had breakfast?'

'No,' he said. 'But, Gianni, you don't need to — '

'Someone has to look after you,' I said, interrupting him. 'If you won't do it yourself.'

I found bread and butter and apricot jam and placed them in front of him.

'There is always time for a proper breakfast,' I said, aware that I sounded like a bossy parent. But I knew Guastafeste would take no notice if I didn't insist. He is in his mid-forties, twenty years younger than I am, and sometimes I worry about him as if he were my son. He's lived alone for several years since his divorce, and his irregular working hours and careless lifestyle have taken a toll on his health. Police work is

68

stressful. The least I could do was ensure he fed himself properly.

Guastafeste sighed. He spread butter and jam on a slice of bread and ate it. I poured coffee into our cups and sat down at the table with him.

'You said that you needed my help.'

Guastafeste felt in the pocket of his jacket and brought out a small transparent plastic bag, about fifteen centimetres square. I saw from the official stamp along the bottom that it was a police evidence bag. Guastafeste placed the bag on the table and turned it round so that I could see clearly what was inside — a small fragment of sheet music.

'We found this in Villeneuve's wallet,' he said. 'People don't usually carry bits of music round with them, so it intrigued us. The name of the piece and that of the composer are missing. Your knowledge of music is immense. Do you have any idea what it is?'

I peered more closely at the bag. The fragment of music was roughly square in shape, with one straight edge and three jagged edges where it had been torn off a larger sheet of paper. It was obviously the top left-hand corner of a piece of classical music, but the title and composer had been left behind with the remainder of the page.

Only the opening two bars of the piece were there. It was a single stave of music, so it wasn't for a keyboard instrument. It had a treble clef, the time signature 4/4, key signature of three flats, and the tempo marking adagio. I pitched the notes in my head and hummed them silently — crotchet G, double-dotted crotchet C, semiquaver D, double-dotted crotchet E flat, semiquaver F. That was it.

'You know what it is?' Guastafeste asked.

'I need to make sure,' I replied.

I went through into my back room and played the notes on the piano.

'Do you recognise it?'

Guastafeste gazed at me blankly. 'Should I?'

'You heard it very recently. You need more help?'

'Just tell me what it is, Gianni,' Guastafeste said irritably.

I pulled out the drawers of one of my many music cabinets and rummaged through the piles of sheet music inside until I found what I was looking for — a piece of violin music with piano accompaniment. I discarded the piano score and held out the violin part with the evidence bag alongside it. The fragment of music inside the bag was the same as the opening bars of my own music.

'It's even the same Schott edition,' I said. 'The 'Moses Fantasy,' by Paganini.'

Guastafeste took the music and the evidence bag from me and made his own comparison.

'This is one of the pieces Yevgeny Ivanov played on Saturday night.'

'I said you'd heard it recently.'

Guastafeste suddenly stiffened. He stared at me, his eyes narrowing, but I could tell his mind was elsewhere.

'What's the matter?'

'Moses,' he said. 'Villeneuve had an item in the hotel safe. He deposited it there on Friday evening. A gold box, about the size of a book, only thicker. Looks like an antique to me, well made, expensive. And on the lid of the box is an engraving of Moses on Mount Sinai receiving the tablets bearing the Ten Commandments.'

'A gold box?' I said. 'Is there anything in it?'

'We don't know. It has an unusual lock on it. A four-dial combination lock, but instead of numbers on the dials, there are letters.'

'You've attempted to open it?'

Guastafeste nodded.

'Just tried a few random combinations. But there are seven letters on each dial. That means probably thousands of different permutations. We're not going to open it by chance, and we don't want to force it open.'

'You think Villeneuve's murder is linked to this box?'

'Who knows. It's the only valuable thing he seemed to have with him. But we haven't established yet whether he came to Cremona to sell the box, or whether he acquired it here. I spoke to his wife on the phone. She wasn't much help. She didn't know anything about the box. She didn't even know what her husband was doing in Cremona, except that it was a business trip.'

'What business was he in?'

'He was a fine-arts and antiques dealer.'

'How about Serafin? Have you spoken to him?'

'About an hour ago. He claims to know nothing, either.'

'You believe him?'

Guastafeste smiled wryly.

'You've told me enough about Serafin to know not to trust him.'

'Was he doing business with Villeneuve?'

'He says not, but' — Guastafeste paused — 'I had the feeling he wasn't being absolutely straight with me.'

'With Serafin, that's an easy feeling to get,' I said. 'Did Villeneuve deal in violins?'

'I don't know. Fine arts and antiques, that's a pretty broad area, isn't it? Does Serafin buy and sell only violins?'

'He'd buy and sell anything if it made him money.'

I stirred my coffee and took a sip.

'That fragment of music and this gold box are connected?' I said.

'Why else would Villeneuve have a corner of the 'Moses Fantasy' in his wallet? But connected in what way?' Guastafeste was silent for a moment; then he stood up and began pacing restlessly round the kitchen. 'It's odd, don't you think? Villeneuve is killed, and in his wallet is a scrap of music that just happens to have been played at a recital he attended the day before. Is that a coincidence?'

'There's only one way to find out,' I said.

★ ★ ★

We heard the faint sound of a violin being played as we walked along the corridor. I recognised the music immediately — the last, and most famous, of Paganini's twenty-four caprices, the one on which Brahms, Liszt, and Rachmaninov later wrote variations. We stopped outside the door. Guastafeste didn't knock immediately. Like me, he was listening to the beautiful sound seeping out from the room. It had a striking quality that made you go still, that made you hold your breath in case you missed a single note. Only when the final chord had been played and there was a moment's silence did Guastafeste raise his hand and rap on the door.

Ludmilla Ivanova answered. We'd phoned in advance, so she was expecting us.

'*Buon giorno*,' she said in her rich, dark voice, her body filling the doorway. 'Come in.'

She pulled back the door to let us enter. We were in one of the Hotel Emanuele's larger and more luxurious suites, a spacious sitting room with two bedrooms and two bathrooms off it, all located at the end of a wing, where Yevgeny's practice wouldn't disturb the other guests too much.

Yevgeny was standing by his music stand in the middle of the room. He put down his violin and smiled at us.

'It is good to see you again,' he said in his accented Italian. 'I enjoy our quartets yesterday.'

'I'm sorry I had to cut them short,' Guastafeste said. 'It would have been nice to play more.'

'You have job to do. I understand,' Yevgeny said. 'And a thing like this — a murder — it is important, no?'

'You cannot have many murders in a place like Cremona,' Ludmilla said.

'No, they are fairly rare, fortunately,' Guastafeste replied.

'It was in the newspaper this morning. An antiques dealer from Paris, they said.'

'That is correct.'

'Do you know why he was killed?'

'Not yet.'

Ludmilla sat down on a chair and crossed her legs, decorously adjusting her dress so that it covered her knees.

'So, how can we help you?' she asked.

Guastafeste turned to Yevgeny.

'Your recital on Saturday evening,' he said. 'I know you played from memory, but presumably you have the sheet music with you, as well?'

'Of course. I always have the music,' Yevgeny said. 'To practise from, to . . . ' He paused and said something in Russian to his mother.

'To refresh his memory,' Ludmilla said. 'He didn't know the word in Italian. Yevgeny knows a lot of the repertoire by heart, particularly the big concertos, but he still always travels with the music. For unusual pieces — like Saturday's programme — pieces he doesn't play very often, having the music is even more important.'

'Could we see the music for the 'Moses Fantasy,' please?' Guastafeste said.

'The 'Moses Fantasy'? Certainly.'

Yevgeny started towards the corner of the room, where there was an elegant mahogany

74

desk covered with stacks of music. Guastafeste moved swiftly, cutting Yevgeny off before he reached the desk.

'It's all right, Signor Ivanov. It's better if you let me find it.'

Yevgeny backed off, looking surprised.

'What? . . . Yes, as you wish.'

Guastafeste searched through the piles of music, taking care to touch only the edges of each piece, to preserve any fingerprints that might have been present. Then he extracted a double sheet of paper. I could see at once that the top left-hand corner of the first page had been torn off.

Guastafeste showed the music to Yevgeny, holding it gingerly by the top right-hand corner. Yevgeny stared at the piece, his brow furrowing.

'But that . . . what happen to it?' he said.

'When did you last look at this?' Guastafeste asked.

Yevgeny shrugged.

'I do not remember. I think Saturday afternoon — when I play through it with pianist.'

'You haven't looked at it since?'

'No.'

'You didn't realise the corner was missing?'

'It was not missing. Not on Saturday.'

'After you'd played the piece with your pianist, what did you do with the music?' Guastafeste asked.

'I put it with other music in dressing room.'

'In the cathedral?'

'Yes.'

'You just left it lying about? It wasn't in a case, or a bag?'

'It was on chair, I think. Why you interested in my music?'

Guastafeste removed the plastic evidence bag from his pocket and held it next to Yevgeny's copy of the 'Moses Fantasy.' The jagged edges on the two pieces of paper matched perfectly.

'Where did you get that?' Ludmilla asked.

She'd got up from her chair and walked across the room to take a closer look.

'François Villeneuve had it,' Guastafeste said.

Ludmilla gaped at him.

'*Villeneuve?* The dead man, you mean? But how?'

'I was hoping you might be able to help me on that,' Guastafeste said.

'Us? We didn't know him. We never met him, never even saw him, as far as I'm aware. Yevgeny?'

Yevgeny shook his head.

'I never meet him, either.'

'Yet clearly, at some point, he got hold of your music and ripped the corner off it,' Guastafeste said. 'Was your dressing room left unattended at any time on Saturday?'

'Unattended? I do not understand,' Yevgeny said.

'Was there always someone in it, or close by?'

'Let me think. After we come back from Gianni's, I rehearse a bit more with my accompanist. Then I go to dressing room with music and stay there until concert.'

'You never left the room?' Guastafeste said.

'Maybe once, to go to toilet. But insurance company men are there the whole time, standing guard outside. No one could have gone inside room.'

'What about during the recital? Did the insurance company men stay by the room?'

'No,' Yevgeny said. 'They come with me, out into the cathedral. They are guarding the Cannon, not my music. They stand at side, behind pillar, throughout recital.'

'So your dressing room was unguarded? It wasn't locked?'

'No, it was not locked.'

'And at the end of the concert, what happened?'

'I finish my encores and return to dressing room. The insurance company men are with me. I put the Cannon back in its case and they take it away from me immediately. Put it on van and take back to Genoa.'

'And your music?'

'I leave in dressing room while we go to reception. Then I go back after and take music with me to hotel.'

'Thank you, Signor Ivanov,' Guastafeste said. 'You've been very helpful.'

'Do we get that back?' Ludmilla asked, pointing at the fragment of music in the evidence bag.

'I'm sorry,' Guastafeste said. 'But I have to keep it for the time being. The rest of the 'Moses Fantasy,' too. There may be fingerprints on it.'

'Does not matter,' Yevgeny said. 'I do not need it.'

* * *

'What do you think?' Guastafeste said, checking his mirror and pulling away from the kerb outside the Hotel Emanuele. 'When did Villeneuve tear off the corner?'

'Not during the concert,' I said.

'You think not?'

'He was in the audience. The cathedral was packed with people. The nave is very open. If he'd slipped away while Yevgeny was playing, someone would have noticed. It had to have been after the concert.'

'That would be my guess, too. When the audience was on its feet, everybody milling round. He sneaked back into the vestry area, waited for Yevgeny to leave his dressing room, then nipped in. A few seconds would have been all he needed. Or perhaps he went back later, when Yevgeny was at the reception.'

'But why only the corner of the music? Why not the whole thing?'

'Maybe he wanted only the corner. Maybe he was interrupted. You know, someone startled him and he accidentally ripped off the corner.'

'It's a very odd thing to do,' I said. 'Why did he want *any* of the music in the first place?'

'I have an idea about that,' Guastafeste replied. 'Have you time for a detour? I want to show you something.'

He headed west along the Corso Vittorio Emanuele, then turned right after the Teatro Ponchielli and doubled back along the Via Tribunali. Blue-and-white police patrol cars were

78

parked along both sides of the road outside the *questura*. Guastafeste found a space and pulled in.

'You want me to wait here?' I said.

'No, come inside.'

We went through the arched entrance of the *questura*. Guastafeste signed me in at the front desk, I was issued a visitor's pass, and we went upstairs into a large open-plan office crammed with desks and computers and intense-looking men in shirtsleeves. Guastafeste introduced me to his colleagues and pulled out a chair for me.

'I won't be a minute.'

He crossed the room and disappeared through a door. I looked round. The other detectives were all on the phone or tapping away at keyboards. On the wall at the far side of the office was a large whiteboard covered in writing — words and phrases in black boxes, with arrows connecting them all together. I saw Villeneuve's name at the top, then other names and bits of information sprouting out below, like a family tree.

When Guastafeste returned a few minutes later, he was carrying another transparent plastic evidence bag. He put the bag down on the desk, unsealed it, and took out a rectangular gold box about thirty centimetres long, fifteen wide, and perhaps five or six deep. It looked to me like a woman's jewellery box or perhaps a man's cigar box. It was a beautifully made item and obviously an expensive one. I know very little about metalworking, particularly gold — and silver-smithing, but I have an eye for quality, and

79

this was undoubtedly the work of a master craftsman.

'You can touch it,' Guastafeste said. 'It's been dusted for fingerprints.'

I picked up the box and examined it. The edges were finely tooled, and engraved round the sides was a geometrical pattern of lines and squares. On the lid, as Guastafeste had mentioned, was an engraving of Moses on Mount Sinai. That, too, was a superlative piece of work. The figure of Moses, with his long, flowing hair and beard, was particularly well done. His wrinkled face seemed alive, his eyes burning with fervour. The gold was slightly dirty, in need of a polish. There were specks of white dust in some of the grooves, which I guessed had been left behind by the police forensics people.

'It's a nice piece,' I said.

I turned it over and saw the hallmark on the bottom.

'Do you know who made it, and when?' I asked.

'Not yet. We'll have to get an expert in for that. Have you seen the lock?'

'Yes, it's interesting, isn't it? I don't think I've ever seen a combination lock that uses letters rather than numbers.'

The lock was along the front edge of the box. It was a sturdy-looking mechanism with four circular dials set into the metal so that only a fraction of their circumferences protruded. Engraved into the dials, the grooves filled with some kind of black mastic to make them more legible, were a series of letters. I turned each of the dials in turn with my thumb. They rotated smoothly, as if they'd been recently oiled.

'You noticed the letters?' Guastafeste said.

'Yes. A to G on each dial. Only seven letters.'

'Any ideas?'

'They could spell out someone's name.'

'I thought of that, but I didn't get very far. I couldn't think of a single four-letter Christian name that used only the letters A to G. Surnames weren't much easier.'

'Someone's initials, then?'

'That's possible. But I've been wondering: What was it that prompted Villeneuve to steal a fragment of the 'Moses Fantasy'? The music is in print and available, so he could easily have got hold of his own copy. Yet he had to tear off a bit of Yevgeny Ivanov's copy. Why?'

'He needed it there and then,' I said. 'He was in a hurry and couldn't wait.'

'Exactly. He heard the 'Moses Fantasy' being played and something suddenly occurred to him. There was an engraving of Moses on the gold box — that's an obvious link with the music. But there was another link, too. The combination lock on the box uses the letters A to G. And A to G . . .'

'Are the letters of the musical scale,' I said.

Guastafeste grinned.

'You see where I'm heading? The Hotel San Michele's night manager told me that on Saturday evening, about eleven-thirty, Villeneuve took the gold box from the hotel safe. He went up to his room with it, then returned the box to the safe half an hour later.'

'You think he opened the box? That he'd discovered the combination?' I said.

'Seems a plausible guess.'

'Why would anyone use the opening notes of Paganini's 'Moses Fantasy' as the combination for a lock? It's pretty far-fetched, you have to admit.'

'Let's give it a try.'

Guastafeste produced the torn-off corner of music and put it down on the desk next to the box.

'Do you want the honours?' I said.

'No, you do it. I'll read out the notes.'

Guastafeste peered at the music. 'G.'

I turned the top dial of the combination lock to G.

'C, D, E flat.'

I turned the other three dials. Then I tried the lid. It didn't budge.

'Try them from the bottom up,' Guastafeste said.

I reversed the order of letters and tugged on the lid again. It was still firmly locked.

'Let me see,' Guastafeste said.

He took the box from me and rotated the dials himself, trying out several combinations of those four letters. None of them worked.

'*Merda!*' he said.

'I told you it was far-fetched,' I said.

Guastafeste gave a low growl of annoyance.

'I was hoping to avoid it, but it looks now as if I'll have to break it open.'

'Surely not,' I said, aghast. 'It's such a splendid box. You would ruin it.'

'What choice do I have? I'll need permission, of course. It's a valuable item. Technically, it belongs to Villeneuve's estate, to his wife or heirs. I'll have to apply for a warrant from the investigating magistrate.'

'How long will that take?'

'The bureaucracy round here, at least twenty-four hours.'

I picked up the box and looked at the engraving on the lid again: Moses clutching a stone tablet in each arm, a range of mountains in the background, and a break in the clouds above, through which a heavenly ray of light was shining — presumably to signify the divine revelation of ancient Jewish law, the Decalogue, whose sixth commandment, in François Villeneuve's tragic case, had recently been broken.

'It doesn't feel very heavy,' I said. 'It would be a shame to force it open and then discover it was empty.'

'I don't believe it is empty,' Guastafeste said with quiet conviction. 'There's something inside it; I'm sure of it. And whatever it is, it's important.'

6

I spent the rest of the day in my workshop, quietly getting on with my violins. I have made violas and cellos in the past — and would do so again if asked — but luthiers tend to specialise, and my output now is predominantly violins. People sometimes ask me how many instruments I have made. I keep a record of each one, so the exact figure is available in the dog-eared logbook in my safe, but off the top of my head it is probably somewhere in the low three hundreds. That is a respectable number, but modest compared to some of the great makers of the past. Stradivari produced twelve hundred, Jean-Baptiste Vuillaume an astonishing three thousand.

Making the violins is not the problem, though producing a good one is difficult. It is selling them that is the tricky part. When I was a young man, I struggled to find buyers for my instruments. Why would anyone want a new violin by the unknown Giovanni Battista Castiglione when they could get a serviceable secondhand instrument for half the price? But making violins was my calling, so I persisted, determined to succeed, although most of my income in those early years came from repairs and overhauls and bow rehairing.

As I grew more experienced and began to acquire a reputation as a good craftsman, I started to sell more instruments. Word of mouth from satisfied customers, particularly among the professional musicians who formed my main clientele, led to more sales, until I no longer had to make violins on spec, but was working to commission only. At my peak, I was probably producing ten or more instruments a year, and that was entirely on my own. Stradivari and the others, it must be remembered, had apprentices doing a lot of the less skilled work, but I have never employed anyone else. I have thought about it occasionally, but I like working on my own, like doing all the tasks myself. It adds variety to the day, but it also means that every part of the violin-making process is completed to my own exacting standards. I am a perfectionist, and not ashamed to be one. I would find it very difficult to entrust anything but the most menial tasks to an apprentice, and that would make little sense for either of us.

I have never felt lonely in my workshop. I have always worked either at home or close to home. When my wife was alive, we had lunch together every day, friends or other luthiers would pop in for a chat, and the children would always come in to see me when they came home from school. Now that my wife has gone and my children have grown up and left, I have my music for company. I never work in silence. I always have a CD or an old LP on my player, an orchestral or vocal piece, or something from my extensive collection of violin music.

I do not make so many instruments now — probably no more than five a year, and all to order. I could make many more than that — I have a waiting list of commissions that is several years long — but I like to take my time, and I still like to do some repair work, though only at the upper end of the market, Stradivaris and Guarneris and the like.

My job is necessarily repetitive, but very rarely do I get bored. There are many different stages in the making of an instrument, and as I always have more than one in progress at any given time, if I get tired of one task on one violin, I can simply move on to another task on a second instrument, or a third. In an average day, I might be sawing a piece of maple, or gluing ribs, or carving a back, or fitting a neck, or one of a hundred other jobs. I am a mini-production line, but I can move round it as much as I choose.

There is something deeply satisfying about working with your hands, particularly with wood. I think it meets a basic, almost atavistic need in all of us — a throwback to more primitive times, when building a shelter or fashioning a hunting tool was essential to one's survival. I find it soothing and therapeutic and would recommend it to anyone who is suffering from stress. The world would be a more peaceful place if we were all craftsmen. At those international conferences, when our belligerent leaders get together to squabble and plot but never manage to resolve their differences, I would take them all into a room, give them each a knife and a block of wood to carve, and by the end of the day they would be calmer and more willing to compromise. Problems would not be solved overnight, but the odds on agreement would certainly be improved. I am being naïve, perhaps. More likely, given the nature of our leaders, they would ignore the block of wood and just apply their knives to one another's backs.

At half-past six, I stopped work and went into the kitchen to make dinner — a cheese omelette and some of the French beans I'd picked the previous day, with a glass of red wine to go with them. I'd finished eating and was drinking my coffee when the phone rang. To my surprise, it was Ludmilla Ivanova.

She wasted no time on social courtesies, but said bluntly, 'Is Yevgeny there?'

I could hear an undertone of worry in her voice.

'No, why should he be here?' I said.

'You're the only person he knows in Cremona. I thought he might be visiting you again.'

'No, signora, he hasn't been here. Is everything all right?'

'No, it isn't all right.'

The undertone surfaced and there was open anxiety in her voice now.

'He's disappeared. I don't know where he is. Yevgeny has disappeared. Something's happened to him.'

'What do you mean, 'disappeared'?' I said.

'He's not here. I went out shopping this afternoon, and when I got back, he was gone.'

'What time was this?'

'About half an hour ago.'

'Signora, relax. He's probably just gone for a walk.'

'Yevgeny doesn't go for walks. And if he did, he'd leave me a note.'

'Half an hour isn't long. Have you checked downstairs? Maybe he's in the hotel restaurant or lounge.'

'No, he isn't there; I've looked. He's nowhere in the hotel. Something's wrong, I can tell. Something's very wrong.'

'I'm sure there's nothing to worry about,' I said reassuringly.

'You think so?'

'It's not late. He's a grown man. My guess is he's out sight-seeing or something like that. Give it more time; he'll probably be back very soon.'

'And if he's not?'

'Call me again, and we'll decide what to do then.'

'Yes, okay. I'll wait a bit. Thank you. You are very kind.'

She rang off. I put down the receiver and shook my head. Parents will always worry about their children, which is only natural, but sometimes you can be overprotective. Ludmilla really needed to let Yevgeny go a bit. It would do them both good.

I washed up my plate and cup, then pondered what to do next. Sometimes in the evenings I return to my workshop and tidy up a bit, or I sharpen my tools or take care of the routine administration relating to my business — invoices, accounts, that kind of thing. Occasionally, I watch television, though there is seldom much on worth watching. This evening, I didn't feel like any of those activities. I felt like playing my violin.

I went through into the back room and opened my violin case. I cast a critical eye over the instrument inside. When confronted with excellence in a field of endeavour to which we ourselves aspire, we tend to have two instinctive responses: It inspires us to try even harder to match that excellence, or it dispirits us so much that we throw up our hands in defeat and say, Why bother? Some people are temperamentally more inclined towards one of these responses than the other. I tend towards the first. When I examined *il Cannone*, I was aware that it was a much finer violin than anything I have produced, or will probably produce in the future. But that realisation didn't fill me with despair. The reality of life is that we are all second-rate. Mediocrity is the norm in human existence, which is why when an individual transcends that mediocrity, we stand back and gaze on their achievement with awe. We cannot quite believe that they have done it.

How did Guarneri make such sublime instruments? I don't know. Probably he himself didn't know. He learnt his craft and worked at it for years, of course. But I have also worked at my craft for years, yet my violins are crude wooden boxes compared to Guarneri's. The sad truth is that he had something that I do not, something special, something innate. He was born with the gift, and no matter how hard I work, how hard I dedicate myself to the task of equalling him, I will never succeed. That does not mean I should not try, however. I may not be a Giuseppe

Guarneri, but I can certainly be a better Giovanni Battista Castiglione.

The same applies to playing the violin. I had heard Yevgeny Ivanov, and been overwhelmed by his astonishing virtuosity. But it didn't make me despondent; it didn't make me want to give up the instrument myself. It made me want to play better, to strive that little bit harder to improve my own standard. I will never be anything more than a good amateur; I know that. But there is satisfaction and fulfilment to be found in pushing the barriers, in seeing just how far you can take your limited talents.

I attached the shoulder rest to my violin and tightened my bow. I warmed my fingers up with a few scales and arpeggios, then looked round for some music to play. The 'Moses Fantasy' was still out on top of the piano. I would not normally attempt a piece by Paganini — the technical demands are too great for me — but this evening I thought, What the hell. Why not?

I put the music on my stand and studied it. There is a pattern to these great bravura variations on operatic arias that Paganini wrote. The opening few bars generally state the theme in its simplest form; then the variations that follow get progressively harder, utilising double and triple stops, running demi-semiquavers, left-hand pizzicato, and artificial harmonics of quite fiendish difficulty. The piano accompaniments to these dazzling pyrotechnics are always basic in the extreme. I used to attempt a few of them with my wife — who was a far better pianist than I am a violinist — and she found them unbearably dull. The accompaniment to 'Le Carnaval de Venise,' for instance, consists of the same sixteen-bar sequence repeated twenty times. The 'Moses Fantasy' is similar — a showy, near-impossible violin part, and a piano accompaniment that a moderately dexterous chimpanzee could probably manage.

There is a pattern to the way I play these pieces, too. I start off boldly, giving a rendition of the opening bars that is close to what Paganini actually wrote — the notes are generally in tune and in the right order. But as I get farther into the piece, the accuracy begins to disintegrate. I miss notes, I miss chords, and sometimes I miss whole bars, until what I am playing is only a vague approximation of the music. By bar twenty, I am out of my depth, by bar thirty I am sinking, by bar forty I am drowning, and by bar fifty I have had to be dragged out and given artificial resuscitation.

The 'Moses Fantasy' is a particularly sadistic piece of composition, for not only is it devilishly difficult but it all has to be played on just one string of the violin — the lowest string, the G, which is the hardest of all to play on because of the contortions the left hand must go through to get to the notes.

I put my violin under my chin and lifted the bow.

Then I paused, the bow in midair.

I stared at the music on the stand before me. I'd just noticed the small line of text that was printed beneath the title.

Of course. *Of course.* How unforgiveably

stupid of me. I couldn't believe I'd forgotten.

I put the violin and bow back down in the case and went to the telephone. It was gone half-past seven, but I knew Guastafeste would still be at the *questura*. I dialled his direct line.

'It's me,' I said when he answered. 'The gold box, I think I might know how to open it.'

'You do? How?'

'*Scordatura*,' I said.

★ ★ ★

Nicolò Paganini was nothing if not a showman. He realised very early on in his career that if he was going to make a mark on the musical world, he needed an image. He wouldn't have used that word, of course, but he would have known that he had to do something to make himself stand out from the crowd. Music then, as now, was an intensely competitive business. Instrumentalists, in particular, found it hard to establish themselves. The voice, certainly in Italy, was king — or, more often, queen, for the female voice had an especial appeal to audiences. The great sopranos of the day commanded huge fees for their appearances, a tradition that continued throughout the nineteenth century and, indeed, still holds sway today. Adelina Patti, the most celebrated vocalist of the late-Victorian era, was once famously engaged to give a recital at the White House, in Washington. When it was pointed out to her that her fee for one evening's entertainment was greater than the annual salary of the U.S. president, she replied pointedly, 'Can he sing?'

The singers of Paganini's time had a similarly exalted status. This must have been firmly imprinted on young Nicolò's consciousness when, as a ten-year-old prodigy, he appeared as the supporting act to Teresa Bertinotti and Luigi Marchese, who had come to Genoa to perform a concert. Bertinotti was a famous, and very expensive, soprano, but Marchese was, if anything, even more renowned because he was a castrato. In that final decade of the eighteenth century, castrati were still immensely popular. Handel, Mozart, and Rossini all wrote for that voice, and audiences seemed to find castrati both musically and sexually fascinating. They were already a dying breed — volunteers to join their dwindling number were understandably thin on the ground — but by the beginning of the nineteenth century, the practice of castration had virtually ceased, though a pocket of resistance was maintained in the Papal States, where at least one castrato still sang in the Sistine Chapel Choir up to the age of the gramophone.

Paganini must have gazed on these two superstar celebrities with awe and perhaps wondered how he was going to emulate them in the field of violin playing. There had been great virtuosi violinists before — men like Corelli and Tartini, whose names have endured more as composers than players — but it was difficult for a young instrumentalist, even one as gifted as Paganini, to make a name for himself.

There was no easy route to the top. There

were no national newspapers in Italy — indeed, at that time it wasn't even a nation at all — and there were no radio stations or recording companies to promote an artist. A young player had to travel round from town to town organising his own concerts — hiring the venue, booking the orchestra, organising the publicity, as well as actually getting up on the stage and performing. Attracting an audience required shrewd and effective marketing — the soloist had to sell himself, create a persona that would bring the punters through the doors — and Paganini proved himself an adept self-publicist right from the beginning.

The 'Moses Fantasy' was written in 1819, when Paganini was in his late thirties, but many of its key features date from much earlier in his career. It wasn't the first piece he'd composed for the G string alone. Playing on one string had been a speciality of his for many years — one of the ways in which he distinguished himself from his competitors. Violin strings in those days, being made of gut, frequently broke, and they sometimes snapped in the middle of a concert. The highest string — the E — because of its greater tension, was particularly prone to giving way. In such circumstances, most soloists would stop and replace the broken string. Paganini, however, would continue playing on the remaining three strings, going higher and higher on the A string to produce the notes normally played on the E. If his A string snapped, he kept going on the D; then if that broke, the G. This was such an impressive party piece that Paganini was rumoured to begin his concerts with deliberately frayed strings, or that he even kept a knife concealed about him to cut through a string while he was actually playing. Whether this was true or not it is impossible to say, but Paganini did little to dispel these kinds of stories at any stage in his career. In the short term, this made a kind of perverse professional sense — the rumours added to the controversy that seemed to follow him round like a shadow, boosting audiences for his concerts — but in the longer term, it earned him a reputation for charlatanry.

Another technique he used in many of his compositions was *scordatura* — changing the tuning of the strings on his violin. He wasn't the first musician to do this, but he certainly put it to greater use than any of his contemporaries. His first concerto, for example, was written in E-flat major, but the violin part is in D major, with the strings all tuned up a semitone so the instrument sounds as if it is playing in E flat. This makes the solo part easier to play, but it also adds to the brilliance of the violin, enabling it to stand out better against the orchestral accompaniment. Paganini used the same trick in other compositions, 'I Palpiti' and 'Le Carnaval de Venise' among them. And he also used it in the 'Moses Fantasy.'

'We were trying the wrong notes,' I said to Guastafeste.

He'd driven out from Cremona and was sitting at my kitchen table with a glass of red wine in his hand. He'd brought the engraved gold box with him, which must have breached at least half a dozen official regulations, but he seemed to have a clear conscience. The Italian police, like police forces everywhere, are sticklers for rules when applied to the general population, but they are not nearly so rigorous in applying those same rules to themselves.

'The wrong notes?' he said.

I showed him my copy of the 'Moses Fantasy.'

'The first four notes appear to be G, C, D, and E flat,' I said. 'That's how they're written. But look up here, under the title.' I pointed to the line of text — written in German, because this was a Schott edition. '*Die G Saite nach B umstimmen.*'

'Which means?' Guastafeste said.

'Tune the G string up a minor third to a B flat,' I said.

'B flat? It says B.'

'This is German, remember,' I said, then explained to him the mysteries of Teutonic musical notation; how their chromatic scale, for reasons best known to themselves, didn't go A, B flat, B, C, as ours did, but, A, B, H, C.

'The violin part is written in C minor,' I said. 'But look here at the piano accompaniment. It's in E-flat minor. So you have to retune your violin so that it sounds in the same key as the piano.'

Guastafeste peered at the music, transposing the first four notes in his head.

'So what we really have is B flat, E flat, F, and G flat.'

'That's right,' I said.

Guastafeste removed the gold box from its

96

plastic evidence bag and placed it in the middle of the table.

'Let's give it a go.'

He turned the first dial on the combination lock to B, then the second to E. He rotated the third dial to F, then paused. He looked up at me. 'You'd better be right, Gianni, or I'm going to have to take a crowbar to this.'

He turned the fourth dial to G. There was an audible click as the lock disengaged. Guastafeste glanced at me again.

'You have your uses, you know.'

He took hold of the top of the box and pulled gently. Nothing happened. He pulled harder. The lid swung open, the hinges sticking a little. The first thing we saw inside the box was a folded piece of paper. Guastafeste lifted the paper out by a corner and put it to one side, obviously hoping to find something else underneath. But there was nothing. Apart from the paper, the box was empty.

'Oh,' Guastafeste said, unable to conceal his disappointment. 'I thought . . . I didn't expect anything at all.'

'It's empty now,' I said. 'But it hasn't always been empty. Look at it.'

The internal dimensions of the box were smaller than the external. The length and width were more or less the same, but the depth was different — shallower by about three centimetres because a false bottom had been inserted. It was like a platform across the whole base of the box — a platform covered in soft navy blue velvet, with a recess cut out in the centre, which was

97

also lined with velvet.

'What the . . . ' Guastafeste began. 'But that looks like . . . '

'Doesn't it?' I said.

The recess was the exact shape of a violin. The gold box wasn't just a gold box. It was a golden violin case.

'But not a real violin, surely?' Guastafeste said. 'It's too small.'

I looked more closely at the recess. It was about twenty centimetres long and ten centimetres across at the widest point. Violins come in many sizes. You can get half- and quarter- and even eighth-size instruments for very young children to begin on, but I'd never seen one that would have been small enough to fit into this recess.

'I don't know,' I said. 'It would be quite possible to make a violin that size, though it wouldn't have much of a sound.'

'Then why do it?'

I shrugged.

'As an ornament? As a joke? Who knows? The challenge, maybe. It would be a test of any luthier's skill to make an instrument that tiny.'

'Have you ever tried?'

'No.'

'Has anyone else? You know, the greats. Did Stradivari ever make any violins that size?'

'Not to my knowledge. Certainly none has ever been discovered.'

'You're sure about that?'

'Quite sure. Why do you think Stradivari might have been involved?'

Guastafeste ran his fingers over the outside of the box.

'It can't have been an ordinary violin that went in here,' he said. 'This box must have cost a fortune. Look at the craftsmanship, the quality of the gold. It was made for a very special violin. But whose?'

'Why don't you look at the letter?' I said.

'Letter? What letter?'

His eyes followed my gaze.

'You mean . . .'

He saw it now. The piece of paper he'd removed from the box had come unfolded slightly. Traces of handwriting were just visible on the reverse side.

'Don't touch it,' Guastafeste said. 'I'll be right back.'

He went out of the kitchen and round the side of the house. I heard the distant, very faint sound of his car door opening and closing. When he returned, he was wearing a pair of thin latex gloves. He sat back down at the table and carefully examined the letter.

It was written on a thick ivory-coloured sheet of notepaper that had been folded in half and sealed with red wax. The seal was still attached to the paper. It was an ornate affair — an elaborate coat of arms that only a nobleman or person of some consequence would have used, with the initials E.B. stamped in the centre.

'E.B.?' Guastafeste said. 'Does that mean anything to you?'

I shook my head.

'Who's it addressed to?' I asked.

Guastafeste turned the paper over and looked at the writing on the front. The ink had faded to a faint grey colour and wasn't easy to read. Guastafeste studied the words for a moment, then let out a low exclamation.

'Nicolò Paganini. The letter is addressed to Paganini.'

He held the sheet up to the light to show me. There were three lines of writing, but the bottom two were so smudged, they were indecipherable. Only the top line was legible. 'Sg. N. Paganini,' it read.

Guastafeste unfolded the sheet and held it flat on the table, using only the tips of his gloved fingers. The letter itself was clearer than the address. The ink had faded a little and the paper had yellowed with age, but the writing was legible enough. At the top, in a bold feminine hand, were the words 'Villa Vicentina, Trieste, September 1819.' Below that was the text of the letter.

My dear Nicolò,

I am distressed to have received no reply to my letter of June last. Have I done something to offend you? Have you forgotten your poor Elisa, languishing here in this dull, godforsaken little hole? Have pity on me and send me news of your adventures.

I have been looking again at the wonderful 'Moses Fantasy' you sent me in the summer. I have yet to see Signor Rossini's Mosè in Egitto, but if it is half as beautiful as your variations, it must indeed be a masterpiece. I am *honoured by your kind dedication, which brings back so many happy memories of our time in Lucca, not least that other piece — your Serenata Appassionata — that you wrote for me. I can still hear that haunting melody in my head. I think of it as your ghost, a spirit that is constantly with me though so many years have elapsed since we last saw each other.*

I am sending you this box as a gift, a token of my affection and my gratitude for your variations. I hope you like it. I had it specially commissioned to go with the other gift I gave you in Lucca — you will know the one I mean. You will be intrigued by the lock, but with your sharp mind I am sure you will quickly work out how to open it.

Felice has attempted your variations and you have never seen or heard anything so comical in your life. I would dearly love to hear them played properly, to hear them the way you would play them, dearest Nicolò. Visit us, if you can, for nothing would make me happier. And if you cannot, and I must forgo the pleasure of hearing you play, then write so that I may have the pleasure of your thoughts instead.

Your affectionate friend, Elisa

Guastafeste took his fingers off the letter and looked at me.

'Elisa? Do you know who she was?'

'Elisa Baciocchi,' I said. 'The princess of Piombino and Lucca.'

'A princess? She was a friend of Paganini's?'

'Not just a friend. They were lovers.'

Guastafeste glanced back at the letter.

'He moved in high circles, didn't he? Having an affair with a princess.'

'No ordinary princess, either,' I said. 'Baciocchi was her married name. Her maiden name was Elisa Bonaparte. She was Napoléon's sister.'

7

I do not regard myself as an expert on Paganini, but I have read enough about him to know something of his life. If you are interested in violins, it is impossible not to be fascinated by this complex, troubled man, the most celebrated — and notorious — virtuoso in history.

I know that he was born in Genoa in 1782, and from an early age showed a prodigious talent for the violin. His father, Antonio, a feckless porter at the harbour, realised quickly that his son's gift had the potential to relieve the family's poverty and maybe even bring great riches to them, so he encouraged Nicolò's playing, finding him teachers and enforcing a brutal regime of practice, which undermined the boy's already-fragile health.

In later life, Paganini claimed that his father starved him in order to make him practise harder. This may be an exaggeration. Successful people have a tendency to play up the hardships of their youth, but it was certainly true that Antonio Paganini was a demanding taskmaster.

His efforts paid off, however, for Nicolò was soon performing in public and astounding audiences with his technical prowess. Just as important to his father, he was also beginning to earn money — so much so that by the time he was sixteen, Nicolò's parents could afford to buy themselves a retirement home in the countryside outside Genoa.

Throughout that period, Antonio Paganini was a constant presence at his son's side — supervising his practice, organising his concerts, accompanying him on tour, and pocketing the proceeds. Nicolò, like any other teenage boy, must have found his father's attentions oppressive and longed to break away. His opportunity came in 1801, when he was permitted to travel to Lucca for the annual music festival of Santa Croce, accompanied not by his father this time but by his elder brother, Carlo. When the festival finished, Carlo returned home to Genoa. Nicolò didn't. He went to Pisa instead and organised a concert himself. Then he went to Livorno and Florence and Sienna, putting on more concerts. Never again would he have his life controlled by his grasping father.

Little is known about Paganini's activities immediately after that. The period from 1801 to 1804 is often referred to as his 'missing years.' Much later, when Paganini was established as a soloist of international renown, stories circulated about what he had actually been doing during that time. One had him falling in love with a wealthy widow and retreating with her to her country estate, where he taught himself the guitar and whiled away the hours eating lotus and serenading his lady love. Another story claimed that he had been in prison for murder, having killed his mistress or — in a slightly different version — a rival for a woman's affections. While in prison, the story went, his

104

jailer's daughter — that essential ingredient of all these kinds of tales — had taken pity on him and smuggled in his violin. Confined to a cell for several years — the period expanding depending on who was telling the story — Paganini had used the time to perfect his technique.

Interestingly enough, an almost identical story once circulated about Giuseppe Guarneri del Gesù, the maker of Paganini's Cannon. Guarneri was also said to have spent a few years in prison for killing a man. The obliging jailer's daughter in that case supposedly smuggled in wood and tools, giving Guarneri the opportunity to hone his craft as a luthier. Disappointingly for lovers of romantic fiction, the Cremona annual censuses show Guarneri to have been living at home throughout the period in question.

The rather dull, prosaic truth is that Paganini was indeed perfecting his violin technique during those missing years, but not on a country estate or in prison, but as the leader of the city orchestra in Lucca. He was still there in 1805, when Elisa Baciocchi, née Bonaparte, came into his life.

Elisa was the eldest of Napoléon's three sisters, and the one most like him in both appearance and temperament. She was not a beautiful woman, but she had a good figure, small feet and hands, and seductive dark eyes, which did much to compensate for her rather plain looks. She was intelligent and cultivated, with a sharp mind and strong character, which did not always endear her to those round her.

Elisa and her brother didn't really get on.

Napoléon liked his siblings to be passive and malleable — two characteristics that were entirely alien to Elisa — and he handed out titles and kingdoms to them like birthday presents. Joseph became king of Spain, Louis was made king of Holland, Jérôme king of Westphalia, and Lucien prince of Canino. The husband of Napoléon's youngest sister, Caroline, whose name was Joachim Murat, was given the kingdom of Naples, and Bonaparte's other sister, Pauline, became a princess by marrying into the Borghese family, though her greatest claim to fame was posing topless for a statue by Canova.

Elisa had long wanted a title and a principality to rule over, so to placate her, Napoléon gave her Piombino and Lucca, an insignificant little corner of Tuscany. The title wasn't just symbolic. Elisa had a penchant for government and her effect on the sleepy province was dramatic.

Lucca, a quiet, dreary backwater, was transformed into a brilliant capital, full of life and culture. Two theatres were opened, a casino and bathing centre were built, schools, libraries, and other educational institutions were set up, and wealthy visitors poured in from all over Italy to enjoy the diversions on offer.

Elisa had artistic and literary pretensions, once shocking Napoléon by appearing onstage in a Voltaire play in pink silk tights, and she quickly established a salon at which writers and artists could meet and show off to one another. Music was also high on her list of interests. Her dim-witted husband, Felice, whose main role in life was to do what Elisa told him, was a keen amateur violinist, and it was not long before Elisa began to take an interest in the leader of what, by now, had become the court orchestra.

Paganini was then twenty-three years old. Portraits of the time show him as a handsome young man with a shock of curly dark hair. His face had none of the ravaged, unhealthy look that we have come to associate with him, though the seeds of that physical deterioration had already been sown. Paganini had almost certainly contracted syphilis by this stage — but then, who hadn't? Practically every young man of the day would have been exposed to the disease if he were sexually active. You were either chaste or you had VD. There wasn't much in between.

Elisa was five years older than Paganini and a woman accustomed to getting what she wanted. Within a short space of time, the two of them were lovers. Paganini was given the job of violin teacher to Felice and, because Elisa wanted him to appear at court functions in splendid uniform, the additional roles of captain of the royal gendarmerie and a member of her personal bodyguard — this last post providing a convenient cover for their assignations, which frequently took place when Felice had been sent away to do his violin practice.

This much about Paganini and Elisa I remembered from the books and articles I'd read. I gave Guastafeste the general picture, but the details of their time together in Lucca were hazier. For those, I would need to jog my memory a little.

Going through into my back room, I removed

107

a biography of Paganini from one of the shelves and returned to the kitchen. Guastafeste saw the author's name on the front of the book and gave a start of surprise.

'Vittorio Castellani? He's written a book?'

'Several,' I said. 'He was really quite a serious academic before he became a television poodle.'

I looked through the index at the back of the book, then turned to the chapter dealing with Paganini's relationship with Elisa. Guastafeste watched me scanning the pages.

'Does it say anything about gifts Elisa made?' he said.

'Nothing specific,' I replied. 'But she was a generous woman — and she had a very powerful, wealthy brother behind her.'

'She didn't give Paganini a tiny violin?'

'I can't see any mention of it here, though that doesn't mean she didn't, of course. There are quite a few grey areas in Paganini's life.'

' 'Grey areas'?'

'Well, there are the 'missing years' I told you about just now. Then his time in Lucca is something of a puzzle. He had just escaped from his father's clutches and was building a reputation for himself as a soloist, so why did he go to Lucca and accept the relatively lowly post of leader of a court orchestra?'

'Security?' Guastafeste suggested. 'Maybe he was scared of going it alone.'

'There could have been an element of that,' I said. 'He wasn't known for his lack of confidence — at least not later in his career. But maybe at the beginning he had his insecurities. Breaking with his father must have aroused mixed feelings. He was glad to get away, but it must also have been a worrying time. His father had organised his life for him, taken care of all the peripheral details. All Paganini had to do was play his violin. Establishing a career entirely on his own must have been a daunting prospect.'

'A woman?' Guastafeste said. 'The wealthy widow you mentioned. Maybe that story was true.'

'Maybe. There's so much nonsense surrounding Paganini that it's hard to separate the truth from the myth.'

'Then perhaps he fell in love with Elisa and that kept him in Lucca?'

'Perhaps.'

'You sound doubtful. *Wasn't* he in love with Elisa?'

'Who knows,' I said. 'He was certainly her lover, but that doesn't mean he was in love with her. He was in a difficult position. Elisa was his employer — and a princess. No doubt he was flattered by her attentions, but he was hardly going to turn her down, was he? That wouldn't have been wise.'

'You make it sound very dispassionate. That isn't like you, Gianni.'

'I'm being realistic. Paganini was a womaniser. He would have had affairs with other women during that period. Elisa, too, probably had other lovers. Adultery was a pastime among the ruling classes of the day — still is today. They would no more have thought of being faithful to their spouses than they would have considered dining out at only one restaurant.'

'That's quite a warm letter she wrote him,' Guastafeste said. He checked the date on the notepaper. 'September 1819. She obviously still had feelings for him, though their affair must have been long over.'

'Yes, they were lovers for only a couple of years,' I said.

I consulted Castellani's biography again to check the facts. Elisa arrived in Lucca in July 1805. By early 1808, Paganini was obviously growing restless, for he asked for, and was granted, permission to go on a concert tour of northern Italy. The tour took him to Turin and the court of Elisa's sister, Pauline Borghese, who had a fondness for jewels and rich living, famously receiving visitors in baths of milk, to which she was carried by a huge black manservant. Pauline's husband, Prince Camillo Borghese, was an ineffectual lover with transvestite tendencies, so Pauline satisfied her considerable sexual appetite by bedding almost any man who happened her way, Paganini included. It was while he was in Turin that Paganini came down with some unspecified illness, which was misdiagnosed by an incompetent doctor. The treatment made the illness worse and Paganini's health — always poor — became even more precarious thereafter.

Summoned back to Lucca by Elisa, Paganini resumed his duties with the court orchestra, but relations between the two of them were clearly beginning to cool. In the spring of 1809, Elisa was made grand duchess of Tuscany by her brother and moved her court to Florence. Paganini accompanied her, but there were rumours of a rift, which finally came to a head later in the year at a court gala concert.

Paganini conducted the concert dressed in his uniform as captain of the royal gendarmerie, when Elisa had expected him to wear plain black court dress. She sent instructions for him to change, but he ignored her, appearing at the ball that followed the concert still dressed in his captain's uniform. Elisa again instructed him to change. Paganini refused and was dismissed on the spot. He packed his bags, ordered a coach, and was gone from the palace by dawn.

Elisa, it seems, relented immediately and pleaded with him to stay, but Paganini was having none of it. Given his unscrupulous character, it was more than likely that he engineered this confrontation so as to ensure his dismissal. He was tired of being an orchestral player and a servant of a demanding princess. His tour the previous year had brought back his taste for the life of a wandering soloist. From then on, he was his own master, setting out on the long, arduous path that would take him to international acclaim.

'Did he see Elisa again?' Guastafeste asked.

'I don't know,' I replied.

'He was evidently still in touch with her in 1819. And he dedicated the 'Moses Fantasy' to her. That shows he was still thinking of her. What was Elisa doing in Trieste?'

'Very little, I should think. Napoléon had fallen from power by then, exiled to St. Helena by the British. Elisa had lost the duchy of Tuscany and her palaces and was presumably living a quiet life of provincial obscurity.'

'And Paganini?'

'He was maintaining his exhausting round of concerts all over Italy, always on the move, never settling anywhere. A bit like a modern-day concert soloist, in fact.'

Guastafeste read through the letter again.

'So Elisa sent him the gold box as a thank-you for the 'Moses Fantasy,'' he said.

''To go with the other gift I gave you in Lucca,' she says. That has to be a violin. That's what the box is made for. But what happened to it? What happened to that violin?'

I was spared the need to answer by the sudden ring of the telephone. It was Ludmilla Ivanova again, sounding even more worried than earlier.

'Yevgeny hasn't come back,' she said. 'I've waited in all evening. Something has definitely happened to him.'

I glanced at my wristwatch.

'It's not even nine o'clock, signora. It isn't late.'

'He should be back by now. Or he should have rung me.'

'Does he have a mobile phone?'

'Yes. I've tried calling him, but all I get is his voice mail. I'm going to go to the police.'

'Signora, perhaps you're — '

'No, I must go to the police. That friend of yours, Antonio, he will help me. What's his number?'

'He's here with me now.'

112

'Let me speak to him.'

'One moment.'

I put my hand over the receiver and explained the situation to Guastafeste. He pulled a face.

'Why me? I've better things to do than hold Ludmilla Ivanova's hand. Yevgeny has probably gone to some bar to get drunk. If you had a mother like her, wouldn't you?'

'Sssh,' I said. 'She might hear you.'

'What does she expect me to do?'

'Reassure her. Have a word with her, Antonio. Tell her she has nothing to worry about.'

Guastafeste sighed and held out his hand. I passed him the phone. He put it to his ear and started to say something, but Ludmilla interrupted before he'd finished his sentence. I could hear her voice gabbling faintly, but insistently, at the other end of the line. Guastafeste looked at me and rolled his eyes.

'Yes, signora, but . . . yes . . . if you'd just . . . ' he said. 'Signora . . . I'm sure that . . . yes, I understand . . . but, if you'd let me . . . '

He gave up and listened until Ludmilla had run out of steam.

'Okay,' he said finally. 'Okay.'

He hung up.

'I said we'd go over and see her,' he said.

'We?'

'I need backup, Gianni. She sounds hysterical. You're better with distraught women than I am.'

Guastafeste picked up Elisa's letter by the corners and put it back in the gold box. Then he

113

returned the box to the plastic evidence bag and tucked it under his arm. We went out to his car and drove to the Hotel Emanuele.

★　★　★

Ludmilla Ivanova was clearly in a state. She whipped open the door to her suite before we'd even knocked, as if she'd been listening out for our footsteps in the corridor, then launched into an incoherent tirade, pacing up and down across the sitting room. She seemed angry rather than distressed.

'How could he do this to me? It's not like him. It's so selfish, so inconsiderate. You know what I think has happened? He's kidnapped him; he's taken him away somewhere and is brainwashing him, turning him against me. That's what it is; it's the only explanation.'

'Signora — ' I began.

'No, I'm sure of it. He's kidnapped him. That's an offence, isn't it? You must find him, arrest him, lock him away. Yevgeny is very weak. He will give in; I know he will.'

'Signora . . . *signora*,' I said.

Ludmilla turned and gazed at me. Her eyes were moist, her jaw trembling with emotion.

'You're not making sense,' I said. 'Who are you talking about? Are you saying Yevgeny has been *kidnapped?*'

'What else could have happened? Where is he? He's been away for hours. He's never gone off and left me like this before.'

'Kidnapped by *whom?*' Guastafeste said.

114

'By Kousnetzoff, of course. Who did you think I meant?'

'Kousnetzoff? Who is Kousnetzoff?'

Ludmilla didn't reply. She had resumed her pacing, tearing at her long black hair with her fingers.

'Signora,' I said. 'Who is this Kousnetzoff?'

She stopped walking and frowned at me.

'What?'

'Kousnetzoff. We don't know who he is.'

'Vladimir Kousnetzoff. I knew he was up to no good when I saw him in the cathedral, then caught him sneaking round the place afterwards. The man is a despicable rogue.'

'Signora Ivanova,' Guastafeste said impatiently. 'We cannot help you unless you tell us who this man is.'

Ludmilla seemed surprised by our ignorance.

'He is an agent,' she said. 'A lying, dishonest villain, like all of them.'

'An agent? A secret agent? A spy, you mean?' Guastafeste said.

Ludmilla stared at him incredulously.

'A spy? Well, yes, he is a spy, I suppose. He's been following us round for months, waiting for the opportunity to snatch Yevgeny away from me.'

'I think she means a classical-music agent,' I said. 'Who represents artists. That's right, isn't it, signora?'

'Yes, that's what I said.'

'Is he a stocky man with a bald head?'

'So you *do* know him. How do you know him?' Her eyes narrowed, suspicious now. '*How?*

You have seen him? Where?'

'At the town hall, after the reception on Saturday night,' I said. 'You were talking to him outside the state room.'

'Ah, yes, that. You see what he was up to? He had no business being there except to come between me and Yevgeny.'

'You are accusing this man of kidnapping your son?' Guastafeste said. 'Do you have any evidence to back that up?'

'Evidence?' Ludmilla said. 'Isn't it obvious? He's been after him for a long time. That's what they do, these agents. They do nothing when you might need them, when you're an unknown, struggling musician trying to get a break. But the minute you make it, they're all round you like vultures round a carcass, all fighting to get a piece of meat. They're parasites. They take twenty-five percent of your earnings, and for what? For nothing, that's what. That's why he wants Yevgeny. Yevgeny is a star. He's going to be one of the great violinists. Kousnetzoff will lure him away; I know it. He'll tempt him with promises of recording contracts, world tours, riches, glory, and Yevgeny will give in. He's young, soft. Kousnetzoff will brainwash him. All these years I've supported Yevgeny, been there when he needed me. I have given up everything for him. I gave up my career — and I could have had a glittering career as a singer. And now he's going to walk out on me.'

Her face crumpled and she burst into tears. It took me unawares. She had seemed so strong. I had never imagined her breaking down like that.

116

Guastafeste and I looked at each other. I could see the horror in his eyes. He'd been a police officer for twenty-five years, seen all manner of crimes and victims, but a woman crying could still unsettle him. I knew he was relying on me to sort this out. I was better with distraught women, he'd said. That wasn't true. I had had no more experience of emotional breakdown than he had. But I'd been married for more than three decades, so I had more personal experience of female moods. I knew that soothing words would do nothing right now. Exasperation or irritation — the common male response that I could sense in Guastafeste's demeanour — would be even worse. Physical contact was what Ludmilla needed. Guastafeste was too young for the task. There would have been something inappropriate about his involvement. But I am an old man, a grandfather. Ludmilla would not take offence if I comforted her. I went across and put my arms round her. I didn't say anything. She buried her head in my shoulder and I held her until she stopped crying.

'I'm sorry,' she said when she broke away, wiping her eyes with the back of her hand. She looked at the smear of mascara on her knuckles. 'Excuse me.'

She hurried into the bathroom and shut the door behind her. Guastafeste and I waited in silence. It was five minutes before Ludmilla came back out, the damage to her makeup repaired.

'I'm sorry,' she said again. 'I'm just very upset.'

'We understand,' I said. I gave her a brief reassuring smile. 'But I think you're worrying about nothing. Yevgeny isn't going to walk away. He doesn't strike me as that kind of man.'

'You don't know him. You don't know how easily he can be influenced. He's just a boy.'

'He's twenty-three,' I said gently. 'Have more faith in him. I'm sure he's tougher than you seem to think.'

Guastafeste took his notebook and pen from his pocket.

'Let's start at the beginning, shall we?' he said, relieved to get back to professional matters. 'When did you last see your son?'

Ludmilla sat down on the lyre-backed chair beside the desk and crossed her legs, composed now, though her eyes were still bloodshot.

'After lunch,' she said. 'Yevgeny was practising. I left him to go shopping — not much, just some shoes, a few clothes.'

'And you came back to the hotel at what time?'

'About six o'clock. Yevgeny wasn't here. I checked downstairs, in the hotel lounge and dining room, but he wasn't there, either. That's when I phoned Dottore Castiglione. I thought Yevgeny might have gone to see him.'

'He left no note?'

'No. He's with Kousnetzoff; I'm sure of it. Where else could he be?'

'Let's not jump to conclusions,' Guastafeste said. 'There are many places he could be.'

'Oh, yes? Such as?'

'He could be in a bar having a drink.'

118

'Yevgeny doesn't drink.'

'Not at all?'

'No.'

'He could have gone to a restaurant.'

'By himself? I don't think so.'

'Or just be wandering round the city.'

'Yevgeny never goes anywhere without me,' Ludmilla said.

'Never? He must go out with friends, surely?'

'He doesn't have any friends. He is too dedicated to his music. He doesn't have time for friends.'

'But there is nothing to indicate that he has been abducted against his will.'

'I'm not suggesting Kousnetzoff threw a bag over his head and bundled him into the back of a car. He's far too clever for that. He'll have taken Yevgeny somewhere quiet, where they won't be disturbed. He'll be using his charm on him, trying to ensnare him. I know how these agents work.'

'Even if you're correct,' Guastafeste said, 'what do you expect me to do? There is nothing unlawful about what you describe.'

'Kousnetzoff is a crook,' Ludmilla said fiercely. 'A devious, cunning crook who is interested in Yevgeny only for the money my son can bring him. Nothing else, just the money.'

'That's how all business works, signora.'

'Yevgeny is not a businessman. He is an innocent, inexperienced boy. Kousnetzoff will take advantage of him. He will — what's the word? — con him. He will persuade Yevgeny to sign a contract, to become one of his clients. He

119

may have done so already. He has to be stopped. Don't you see that? Yevgeny is my son. He needs me to look after him.'

Guastafeste ran a hand along his jawline, rubbing the rough strip of stubble. He caught my eye, then sighed wearily.

'Do you know where Kousnetzoff is staying?' he asked Ludmilla.

'No. If I did, I would have gone round there.'

'I'll track him down and see if he knows anything about Yevgeny's whereabouts. Okay?'

'Yes. Thank you. That would be good.'

'Good night, signora.'

Guastafeste took out his phone as we walked away along the corridor and called the *questura*. He asked someone to check the hotels, find out if Kousnetzoff was registered anywhere.

'A complete waste of time,' he said, putting the phone back in his pocket. 'What a life that kid has, eh? A different city every couple of days, no friends, only his suffocating mother for company. He's probably gone down to the station and picked up a prostitute.'

'He's not the type,' I said.

'People change. A highly strung, nervous boy like him — anything could happen.'

We were at the car when the *questura* phoned back. Guastafeste listened for a moment, asked a couple of questions, then rang off.

'Vladimir Kousnetzoff was staying at the Hotel San Michele,' he said.

'Was?' I said.

'He checked out earlier this evening. No forwarding address.'

'The San Michele? The same hotel as François Villeneuve.'

'There aren't many to choose from in Cremona. But I'll look into it anyway.'

Guastafeste slid in behind the wheel of the car. I got in beside him.

'We'll go to the *questura* and I'll get someone to run you home, Gianni. Thanks for your help.'

'Anytime.'

Guastafeste turned the key in the ignition and looked across at me.

'Will you do me a favour? This is your area of expertise — violins and violinists. Check all those books you've got. See if you can find out exactly what gift Princess Elisa gave Paganini in Lucca. That's what our killer was after.'

8

After breakfast the following morning, I didn't go across to my workshop as usual, but went into my back room and browsed through my collection of music books. I have a small library of biographies and reference books, built up over many years. I say 'small' because by comparison with a municipal or university library, it *is* very small, but by most domestic standards, it is quite extensive — there are several hundred books downstairs and many more upstairs. My wife, Caterina, when she was alive, used to complain good-naturedly about the way in which my books were slowly colonising the entire house. From a few shelves in the back room, they had gradually spread to the sitting room and then, as the children grew up and left home, to all of the bedrooms. It was like a disease, she said, or mould on a damp wall. It started small; then, before you knew it, every surface was covered with a virulent fungus that had no known cure.

I have a number of books on Paganini. As I dipped into them, searching for information about the violinist's relationship with Elisa Baciocchi, I was reminded of a famous quote — from Stravinsky, I believe, though I may be wrong. 'Good composers borrow; great composers steal.' The same could be said of biographers. When you read a few books about the same subject one after the other, you come to realise that biography is essentially plagiarism disguised as originality. The same information, the same phrases, the same quotes, even the same mistakes keep cropping up, and it's hard to avoid the suspicion — no, the certainty — that the writers have simply copied a previous biographer's work. With popular biographies you expect this — the ropy 'celebrity' profiles that have been cobbled together by a hack from newspaper cuttings and a couple of interviews — but it is disappointing to find the same shoddy secondhand writing in supposedly academic tomes.

I checked through five books and discovered that the sections about Paganini and Elisa were virtually identical in each case. There could, of course, have been a legitimate explanation for that. Maybe the authors had all consulted exactly the same source material, visited the same archives, studied the same documents. But I was inclined to be sceptical. It was just too much of a coincidence that all five books — making due allowance for differences in style and emphasis — could easily have been written by the same person. Vittorio Castellani's version, its title as unoriginal as its contents, was called *Paganini: The Man and the Myth*. It was the most recent of the biographies, having been written only ten years earlier, and the most readable of the five, though given the turgid prose of the earlier books, that wasn't saying much.

I reread his chapter on Elisa, then checked the index for any reference to gifts Paganini had received, or instruments he had owned. There was nothing to indicate that Elisa had ever given him a violin small enough to fit in the gold box. I thought about what Guastafeste had said. Why commission someone to make an expensive gold violin case if the violin you were going to put in it was a run-of-the-mill instrument? It had to be something special, something valuable. Was Guastafeste right? Had one of the great luthiers, Stradivari or perhaps Guarneri del Gesù, made a tiny violin at some point, a violin that Elisa later acquired and gave to Paganini? I had never heard of such an instrument, but that didn't mean it didn't exist. Much of Stradivari's and Guarneri's lives is still a mystery, and neither of them left behind records of the instruments they made.

I took a short break to make myself a cup of coffee, then went back to Castellani's biography of Paganini. Something else about Elisa's letter to the violinist was bothering me. I tried to recall exactly what she'd written. Something about another piece of music Paganini had composed for her. 'I think of it as your ghost, a spirit that is constantly with me . . . ' Had I remembered that correctly? Paganini's ghost. A 'Serenata *Appassionata*,' she'd called it. I didn't know the piece, and that troubled me. I had piles of sheet music of Paganini's works and dozens of recordings — by Salvatore Accardo, Ruggiero Ricci, Arthur Grumiaux, Itzhak Perlman, Zino Francescatti, and others. I had all the concertos, three or four different versions of the caprices, and several LPs and CDs of his lesser-known works for violin. But I didn't recall a Serenata *Appassionata*.

I studied the list of compositions in one of the appendices in Castellani's book. There was no mention of a Serenata *Appassionata*. That was strange. I took out my sheet music and recordings and started to go through them one by one. Maybe there was some obscure track on a CD I'd forgotten about.

I was still checking when the phone rang. It was Guastafeste.

'Ludmilla Ivanova has been in to see me,' he said. 'Yevgeny didn't come back to the hotel last night. Or this morning. She's worried sick. She didn't burst into tears again, thank God, but she wouldn't leave the *questura* until I'd promised to find him.'

'You think he really has been kidnapped?'

'We're ruling nothing out.'

'Kousnetzoff?'

'We don't know where he is. He was on his own when he left the San Michele yesterday evening, according to the receptionist on duty. We have the number of his office in Saint Petersburg. We've tried it, but there's no reply.'

'So where do you go from here?'

'Kousnetzoff had a hire car. He picked it up from Malpensa when he flew in last week. We've got the registration number.'

'He could be anywhere by now. He could even have left the country. Did Yevgeny have his passport with him?'

'No, he left everything behind. Passport, clothes, his Stradivari.'

'It doesn't sound good to me.'

'Nor me. If he didn't leave with Kousnetzoff,

then either he must still be in Cremona or he left another way. We're checking the railway station, the bus and taxi companies.'

'He might have hired a car, I suppose.'

'He doesn't have a credit card.'

'What about cash?'

'Or much cash. Mama takes care of all the money. Pays the hotel and restaurant bills, books the plane tickets. She even buys all Yevgeny's clothes. He gets a small monthly allowance and that's all. Pocket money. She really does treat him like a kid.'

'What's your gut feeling?'

'I don't know. He's a prominent international concert violinist. It's possible he's with Kousnetzoff. It's also possible someone else has abducted him.'

'Like who?'

'Some crank. Maybe organised criminals. We've had no ransom demand, but it could be on the way. On the other hand, he might simply have got on a train and gone to Venice, or Florence, or somewhere for a couple of days. If he were a child, we'd have a full-scale national search under way. But with a twenty-three-year-old man, things aren't quite so cut-and-dried.'

Guastafeste broke off. I heard him talking to one of his colleagues in the background.

'Sorry,' he said when he came back on the line. 'This is all we need. A high-profile missing person case when we're right in the middle of a murder enquiry.'

'How's it going?'

'Villeneuve? Nowhere. I have to go, Gianni. I'll keep you posted.'

I resumed the search through my music collection without success. If there'd ever been a recording made of the Serenata *Appassionata*, I certainly didn't have a copy of it. I put my CDs and LPs back on the shelves and sat in an armchair for a while, wondering what to do next. I'd consulted all my books on Paganini and found no useful new information. I could go into Cremona, to the public library, and see what I could find, but I knew from past experience that the music section there was limited. I doubted I'd find anything I didn't already know. A scholar, of course, would have gone back to original sources — sifted through the archives, examined old letters and records — but I didn't have either the time or the resources to do that. Besides, Paganini's personal papers were in Genoa and at the Library of Congress in Washington, and I had no idea where Elisa Baciocchi's were, if indeed they had survived at all. That left me with one other possibility: finding someone else to ask, someone who knew more about Paganini than I did.

★ ★ ★

The dark, brooding young man I knew only as Marco was waiting to greet me in the foyer of the University of Milan's music department. His face looked drawn and tired, and he had shadows beneath his eyes. We shook hands and he looked at me curiously.

'Haven't we met before?' he said. 'Ah, yes, of course. The reception in Cremona. You were the one who . . . Mirella told me.' He paused, smiling slightly.

'Well, yes, that was unfortunate,' I said, filling in the uncomfortable silence.

'You don't need to worry about it. He won't remember you.'

'He won't?'

'Vittorio doesn't notice anyone or anything round him,' Marco said. 'Except when he looks in the mirror,' he added tartly. 'Come on, I'll show you to his office.'

We went up a broad flight of stone steps to the first floor and along a corridor lined with notice boards covered in concert posters, timetables, and other departmental information. As we reached a door halfway along the corridor, we had to step aside to let a man in dirty overalls pass. He had a lightweight aluminium ladder in one hand, a toolbox in the other. I glanced into the room he'd just left and saw a second man perched on a trestle platform, plastering the ceiling.

'There's a toilet on the floor above,' Marco explained. 'A pipe burst over the summer, brought the whole ceiling down.'

'Over the *summer*?'

'University maintenance people — they live in a different time zone to the rest of us. With any luck, it might be finished for Christmas.'

We kept going along the corridor. A group of students came towards us, most of them carrying instrument cases. They broke apart in the middle to let us through. Somewhere in the distance I could hear the faint sound of a piano, someone practising scales and arpeggios.

'You are Professor Castellani's assistant?' I said.

I sensed Marco bristle a little at the suggestion.

'I'm technically an associate lecturer,' he said stiffly. 'I've just finished my doctorate, but I'm doing bits of research for Vittorio, as well.'

He stopped outside a panelled oak door that had Vittorio Castellani's name stencilled on it in white paint. He knocked once and pushed open the door without waiting for a reply. Castellani was seated behind his desk on the far side of the office. It was a big room, as befitted his status as a professor of music, but a large part of it was occupied by a Steinway grand piano. There were shelves crammed with books and scores on three of the walls and a high window on the fourth, through which a chestnut tree could be seen, its bare branches silhouetted against the sky. It was late afternoon and it was growing dark. The panes of the window were spotted with raindrops.

'Signor Castiglione for you,' Marco said.

I walked towards the desk, but Castellani made no attempt to acknowledge my arrival. He looked straight past me at Marco.

'Have you typed up that article yet?' he demanded.

'Almost finished,' Marco replied defensively.

'It's taking you a long time. What about the stuff for Friday? The briefing.'

129

'The *Culture Show?* It's in progress.'

'I want it tonight.'

'You said tomorrow.'

'I want it tonight, okay? Get it done. And call Gilberto's. Book me a table for two for Saturday night. Nine o'clock. You seen Mirella about?'

'No.'

'You do, tell her I want to see her.'

Castellani waved a hand, dismissing Marco from the room. I waited for the young man to go, then approached the desk.

'Professor, it was good of you to see me at such short notice.'

I held out my hand. Castellani gave it a perfunctory shake.

'What is it you want?' he asked brusquely. 'I haven't got long.'

He looked at me, and I was relieved to see no flicker of recognition in his eyes. Marco was right: Castellani didn't remember me.

I sat down in a chair that was positioned to one side of the desk and placed the light raincoat I'd brought with me on the carpet underneath the chair. There was a limited amount of legroom because the floor was taken up with cardboard boxes of books for which, presumably, there was no space on the shelves.

I told him I was looking for information about Paganini and Elisa Baciocchi, remaining vague about my reasons for seeking it.

'I've read your biography of Paganini,' I said. 'A most enjoyable book, by the way,' I added, judging that a little flattery would do me no harm.

130

Castellani ran a hand through his long hair, sweeping it back behind his ears. He was wearing an open-necked black shirt — doubtless of designer origin, though I was too out of touch with fashion even to hazard a guess at the label — faded blue jeans and hand-sewn black leather shoes, which I knew were Gucci, but only because there was a discreet logo on them advertising that fact.

'Yes, the reviewers thought so, too,' he said. ''Undoubtedly the most complete biography of Paganini that has ever been written,' was what *La Stampa* said about it. And I don't even write for them. Well, I didn't then anyway.'

'You were very good on the relationship between Paganini and Elisa. But I imagine there was a lot of material you left out of the book.'

'Of course, there always is. One is limited by space, by the requirements of the publisher. One has to make a judgement about what is important and what is not. Those years in Lucca were only a small part of Paganini's career.'

'But very significant years,' I said.

He gave me a sharp stare, seeming to question my credentials for making such a statement.

'Not in the context of his whole life,' he said. 'Lucca was something of a distraction, a sideshow. He was really only marking time there. All his major achievements came later.'

'I meant significant in his personal life. His affair with Elisa.'

Castellani laughed scornfully.

'Don't be taken in by all the romantic bullshit that surrounds Paganini. He used Elisa, and she

131

used him. That's pretty much the norm in relations between men and women.'

'Not in my experience,' I said.

Castellani's gaze was pitying now.

'You seem very naïve. What did you say you were on the phone? Your occupation?'

'I am a violin maker.'

'Ah, yes, a craftsman. Well, I imagine your experience of the world — and women — is probably fairly narrow. Paganini, when he was in Lucca, was young, handsome, charismatic. It was only natural that Elisa would want to sleep with him. Talent is a wonderful aphrodisiac to a woman. It's no different today.'

Castellani smoothed back his hair again, a man speaking from experience — or trying to give the impression of it.

'Don't think for a moment that Paganini cared a damn about Elisa,' he went on. 'She was just a passing conquest to him, one of many.'

'But he dedicated compositions to her,' I said.

'That means nothing. Elisa was his patroness. Composing works dedicated to her was expected of him.'

'Do you know exactly what he wrote while he was in Lucca?'

'You say you've read my book. I give a full list in an appendix at the back.'

'You are sure it is a full list?'

Castellani didn't like that. His mouth tightened.

'You are implying that I might have missed something?'

'No, no, professor. But it's not unknown for

132

new works to be discovered. Did Paganini, for example, ever write a Serenata *Appassionata* for Elisa?'

'A Serenata *Appassionata*?' Castellani frowned. 'It's a long time since I wrote that biography. I can't remember every detail. Let me find a copy.'

He pushed back his chair, stood up, and scanned the shelves behind his desk. I looked down at the cardboard boxes beside my feet, wondering if I could help locate the book. The boxes had open lids. The books spilling out from them were different shapes and sizes, all about music. I saw Beethoven's name on the spine of one, a dog-eared dust jacket bearing the face of Richard Wagner on another. Then I glanced in a second box and noticed something else. I reached down.

'Here we are,' Castellani said.

He turned, his biography of Paganini in his hand. I straightened up and gave him my attention.

'He wrote the twenty-four caprices in Lucca, of course,' he said, leafing through to the end of the book. 'Undoubtedly his greatest, and most lasting, contribution to the violin repertoire.'

'But he didn't write them for Elisa,' I said.

'No, the caprices are dedicated 'To the Artists.' They were his Opus One. His Opus Two, six sonatas for violin and guitar, were dedicated to Signor Delle Piane, and his Opus Three, another six sonatas for violin and guitar, were for Eleonora Quilici, a childhood friend. He left her money in his will, too. His Opus Four, three quartets for violin, viola, guitar, and cello, were dedicated 'To the Amateurs, from Nicolò Paganini,' and so was his Opus Five, another set of three quartets for the same instruments.

'Of his published works, that's about it as far as Lucca goes. We know he wrote an unpublished 'Scène Amoreuse' for the G and E strings — a sort of duet between a lady and her lover, the E representing the lady's voice, the G the lover's. And he wrote a sonata entitled *Napoleone* for the G string only, but that was dedicated to Elisa's brother, and has never been published, either.'

'No Serenata *Appassionata*?'

'I have never heard of such a piece. What makes you think it exists?'

'A reference I read somewhere,' I said vaguely.

'You must be mistaken. I did a huge amount of research for this book and never came across a Serenata *Appassionata*.'

'Perhaps I'm wrong,' I said. 'What about presents? Did Elisa give many gifts to Paganini?'

'She was famously extravagant, yes. She gave him jewels, money.'

'What about violins? Did she ever give him a violin?'

'Quite possibly. Paganini accumulated violins throughout his life, though he played almost exclusively on *il Cannone*.'

'You don't know for certain?'

'It was two hundred years ago. I have seen no mention of a violin in the papers I've read. Like any biographer, I had to work with the records that were available to me. Where there were gaps, I had to do my best to fill them in, but it could only have been educated guesswork.'

Castellani replaced his biography on the shelves and sat down again at the desk, tilting back his padded leather chair and watching me attentively.

'This reference to a Serenata *Appassionata* you mentioned,' he said. 'Where did you see it?'

'I'm not sure,' I said evasively.

'In a book?'

'I don't know. I'm interested in Paganini, that's all. Perhaps I've got hold of the wrong end of the stick.'

'Paganini *did* write a Sonata *Appassionata*,' Castellani said. 'You could be thinking of that.'

'Yes, that must be it.'

'But that was much later than Lucca. Perhaps as late as 1829. He parted from Elisa nearly twenty years before that.'

'And never saw her again?'

'I wouldn't like to say with any certainty.'

'He dedicated his 'Moses Fantasy' to her. And that was written in 1819.'

Castellani nodded slowly.

'You've read — and remembered — my book well.'

'Not just your book. I've read others, too.'

'Pah,' Castellani said contemptuously. 'They are all inferior works. None of them has the depth or ambition of my biography.'

I didn't contradict him. I needed to keep him sweet for my next question.

'If Paganini had written something for Elisa, a piece of music that later disappeared, what do you think might have happened to it?'

135

'That's a ludicrous question, impossible to answer. Anything could have happened to it.'

'What if Elisa kept it until her death?'

'She died in 1820. That's a very long time ago.'

'Do you know what became of her possessions, her estate?'

'I have no idea. I wrote a book about Paganini, not Elisa Baciocchi. She had no interest to me beyond her relationship with Paganini. And she still has no interest to me.'

Castellani looked at his watch.

'Now, if you'll excuse me, I have a lot to do.'

'Of course, professor. Thank you for your time. You have been most helpful.'

I reached down and picked up my raincoat. It slipped from my fingers on to one of the boxes of books and I had to fumble to retrieve it. Castellani, meanwhile, had lifted up the telephone and was talking to Marco.

'Signor, Signor' — he couldn't remember my name — 'my *visitor* is ready to leave. Show him out, will you?'

I went back downstairs with Marco. The young man was quiet, seemingly preoccupied with his own thoughts.

'Professor Castellani can't be an easy man to work for,' I said.

'What? Oh, no, he isn't easy,' Marco replied. 'But if I'm to get a tenured post, having him on my side is essential. He carries a lot of weight in the department.'

In the foyer, I shook hands with Marco and thanked him. Then I went out onto the street.

The spots of rain had turned into a light drizzle. I unfolded my raincoat, carefully extracting the book that I'd concealed inside it, then slipped the coat over my shoulders, put the book in a side pocket, and walked away along the pavement.

★ ★ ★

It was only a short distance to the university's department of economics, but by the time I got there, my hair was gleaming wet and the rain was dripping off the hem of my coat onto my shoes. I found Margherita in her office, reading through a large pile of papers.

'I'm a little early,' I said. 'Shall I go away for half an hour, then come back?'

Margherita gave me a look of incredulity.

'Are you kidding? It's raining out there. You're drenched.'

'It's only a shower. It'll blow over soon.'

'Take off your coat. Put it on the radiator.'

'But I'm disturbing you.'

'You're rescuing me, Gianni. You haven't come a moment too soon. I've had just about enough of this rubbish.'

She pushed the pile of papers to one side and sighed with relief.

'Final-year students' assignments,' she said. 'If this is the future of Italian economics, then God help us all.'

I shook the water off my coat and hung it over the radiator.

'Bad?' I said.

'*Bad* is an understatement. These are supposed to be the cream of our young people, yet half of them can't even spell properly. One or two don't seem able to use a calculator, either. I don't dare to think about it, but in ten years' time, they'll be running the country.'

'They can hardly be worse than the bunch we've got in at the moment. Or the ones before that.'

'Yes, that's reassuring, I suppose. But the worrying thing is, I taught some of *them* economics, too. Is it all *my* fault?'

I smiled.

'I expect so. After all, politicians never take responsibility for anything, do they? *They* can't possibly be to blame, so it must be you.'

Margherita pushed back her chair and looked round the floor underneath her desk.

'Can you see my shoes anywhere?'

'They're over here.'

'How did they get there? I'm sure they move round the room of their own accord.'

I picked up the shoes and passed them over the desk. Margherita put them on and started to pack away her student assignments in a briefcase.

'You're taking those home?' I said.

'I know, it's masochistic, but someone has to mark them.'

'I thought we were going for dinner.'

'We are.'

'And you're going to work afterwards?'

She paused.

'Yes, it's a bit silly, isn't it? Am I realistically

going to start marking at eleven o'clock?'

'Leave them here. They'll wait another day.'

Margherita nodded. She pulled the papers from the briefcase and dumped them on a corner of her desk.

'You're so good for me, Gianni,' she said.

She was good for me, too, I reflected as we left her office and walked through the drizzle to a nearby trattoria. We have not known each other long. We met just over a year ago in traumatic circumstances — when her uncle, an eccentric collector of violins, was murdered in Venice. The death, and its aftermath, brought us together, and we have continued seeing each other since. It was strange, at first, to have her in my life. When my wife died, seven years ago now, I did not think I would ever form another close bond with a woman. I had seen other men recover quickly from bereavement, even marry again within a short space of time, but I couldn't understand them. I couldn't understand how they could shake off their grief so easily, how their first wives could so swiftly be supplanted.

There is a pattern to our sexual lives that is almost universal. We all have those intense adolescent infatuations that end in tears; then most of us fall prey to that temporary chemical imbalance in the brain that we call 'falling in love' — nature's way of pairing us off. We marry, we have children — an exhaustingly absorbing outlet for our love — and we find an equilibrium, a harmony that, if we are lucky, will last until the pair bond is severed by death. That, at any rate, has been my experience. Caterina

139

and I were together for thirty-five years. I married her when I was twenty-two and I was fifty-seven when she was taken from me. I did not expect to lose her so soon. She was truly the light of my life, and when she died, the whole world went dark. For a long time it remained in blackness; then gradually the night began to pass and a new light crept over the horizon. At first it was just a flicker, like a candle in the wilderness, but slowly it became brighter, until there was enough for me to see my way, to light the path through my remaining years. It will never be a dazzling summer day again, but I have found much to comfort me in the glow of an autumn afternoon, to keep me warm until my own inevitable darkness comes to claim me.

I have my work. I have my friends. I have my children and grandchildren. And now I have Margherita. I didn't think anything like this would happen. I didn't go looking for it. It just came about. I felt guilty in the early months, wondering whether I was betraying my dead wife. Then I realised that in questioning this new relationship I was inadvertently insulting Caterina, ascribing to her a jealousy, an ill nature that was not part of her makeup. She was a generous, good-hearted woman. She loved me as I loved her. She is gone, but she would not begrudge me a little happiness in the years I have left.

Margherita has not taken her place — no one could do that. I have not fallen in love with her. I am too old and experienced for infatuation. This is not a hormonal relationship; it is a

140

meeting of minds, an attachment that is still young, still relatively unformed, but which may, in time, become something deeper.

'Would you like a drink?' I said after we were settled at our table.

'Please. Just a glass of wine will do me fine.'

I ordered a bottle of red and glanced round the restaurant. It was still early in the evening. People were drifting in — couples, a few business executives in suits — but several tables were unoccupied.

'How was your meeting with the professor?' Margherita said, the last word subtly emphasised.

I'd told her earlier on the phone that I was going to see Castellani, told her also about the gold box and the letter inside it.

'He was very civil to me,' I said.

'Really?'

'Which is more than he is to his staff. He has this assistant — Marco something — whom he treats like a servant.'

'An associate lecturer?'

'How did you know?'

'It's very common. The university is full of them. Able young postgraduates doing the most menial tasks for people like Castellani in the hope of preferment.'

'That's what Marco said. He needs Castellani's support if he's to get a tenured post.'

'That's how the system works. In theory, all lectureships are decided by competitive examination, open to anyone from anywhere in the country. In practice, the jobs are all stitched up

141

beforehand by the departmental power brokers — people like Castellani. If this young man crosses Castellani, his academic career will be over before it's started.'

'Nasty.'

'Oh yes, very. Universities are like the Papal court — cabals of ruthless schemers plotting against one another. If you want a job, you play the game. Spend a few years on the periphery, kissing the backsides of your superiors, swallowing your pride. It's unavoidable.'

'Did you have to do it?'

Margherita smiled dryly.

'I'm a woman in a man's world. I used my feminine wiles, of course, and slept my way to the middle. Isn't that what we all do? No, I'm joking. But I did my share of dogsbody work before I got a secure post. Fortunately, the head of department at the time was a decent, enlightened man. He loathed the system of patronage and had the revolutionary idea that posts should be allocated according to ability. He was clearly insane. He wouldn't last two minutes in today's world.'

We paused while the waiter brought the wine and filled our glasses. Then we looked at the menu and ordered our food. Margherita drank some of her wine.

'So, was Castellani helpful?' she asked.

'Not very,' I replied.

I gave her a brief summary of my conversation with the professor. 'He was pretty patronising, really. Talked down at me most of the time.'

'That's his style,' Margherita said. 'Have you

142

ever seen him on the *Culture Show*, that trashy piece of froth RAI puts out on a Friday night? The way he talks to some of the guests. If I were on it, I'd give him a good slap.'

'That would help the ratings,' I said.

'The whole programme infuriates me.'

'Why do you watch it, then?'

'It's good for my blood pressure. Every time I see Castellani's blow-dried hair and those skintight jeans, I want to hurl something at the television. I'm all in favour of popular culture, but why on earth does it have to be so vulgar, so crass? And don't even get me started on those stupid blondes who escort the guests into the studio. Can people really take culture only if it's served up by a reptilian narcissist like Castellani, with a few scantily clad bimbettes to keep him company?'

'Steady on,' I said. 'This is supposed to be a relaxing evening out.'

'Am I moaning? Sorry. My daughter says that's all I do. Is it an age thing, or is there really a lot to be disgruntled about?'

'It's not an age thing,' I said.

'I interrupted you. Go on. What did he say?'

'Not much more than is in his biography of Paganini. He didn't know anything about any gifts Elisa Baciocchi might have given Paganini, and he'd never heard of the Serenata *Appassionata*. I can find no mention of it in any of the other books, either.'

'But you think it exists?'

'Elisa mentions it by name in her letter. It

143

definitely exists — or it did then. Whether it's still round now, that's a different question.'

'So what might have become of it?'

'That's what I need to find out.' I looked at her. 'I have a confession to make. I've done something rather disgraceful, particularly for a respectable man of my mature years.'

'My God, now you've got me interested,' Margherita said. 'Come on, don't keep me in suspense.'

I reached across to my raincoat, which was draped over the back of a spare chair, and pulled the book from the pocket.

'I took this from Castellani's office.'

'You *stole* it?' Margherita said.

'Borrowed it. I have every intention of returning it.'

'What is it?'

I showed her the title.

'*Napoléon's Sisters: Caroline, Pauline, and Elisa.* There may be something useful in it,' I said.

'Won't Castellani miss it?'

'It was gathering dust in a cardboard box on the floor. I couldn't believe it when I looked down and saw it. He obviously doesn't need it for anything. I'll keep it for a few days, then hand it back to Marco. He won't give me away.'

I leafed quickly through the book. I saw passages underlined, notes scrawled in the margins, but I didn't look closer. Now wasn't the time.

'And what about the violin you think may

once have been in the gold box?' Margherita said.

'I've got no further with that.'

'You think François Villeneuve opened the box and removed it?'

'That's one possibility.'

'If he did, what happened to it?'

'It wasn't in his hotel room. Either he disposed of it before he was murdered or his killer took it.'

Margherita shuddered.

'Someone would kill for a violin?' She paused. 'Stupid of me. Of course they would,' she said, and I knew she was remembering her uncle. 'Didn't you say it must be a very small violin?'

'The smallest I can imagine, yes. But if it were a Stradivari, it could be worth a lot of money.'

'And the other possibilities?'

'Villeneuve opened the box and found it empty. Or he never opened it at all.'

'Empty? You mean the violin had already been taken from it? When? By whom?'

'I couldn't say. There are an awful lot of unanswered questions.'

I put the book back in my coat pocket and topped up our wineglasses as the waiter brought us our first course — wild mushroom risotto for Margherita, spinach and ricotta cannelloni for me. For the rest of the meal, we kept away from Paganini and Elisa and François Villeneuve and talked of other things — about Margherita's work, about my work, about our families. We had so much in common, so many shared interests, that conversation was never difficult.

Afterwards, I walked Margherita back to her apartment. She invited me in for coffee, but I declined. It was getting late and I had my train to Cremona to catch. Margherita kissed me lightly on the lips and stepped back.

'Thank you for a wonderful evening, Gianni.'

'It was my pleasure. I'll call you soon.'

'I'd like that. Good night.'

I watched her go in through the door of the apartment block, then found a taxi to take me to the station. I never drive my car into Milan if I can help it, especially at night. The traffic is insufferable and the parking even worse.

An hour and a half later, I was home. The red light on my answering machine was flashing. I had two messages. The first was from Vincenzo Serafin, though he didn't bother to identify himself, just left a peremptory command on the tape.

'That violin I mentioned on Saturday. I need you to look at it. I'll expect you in my office tomorrow morning, eleven o'clock. Okay?'

I was used to Serafin's lordly arrogance, but even so, the message annoyed me. How dare he address me in such a discourteous fashion. I wasn't one of his employees, a minion at his beck and call. I was an independent artisan with an international reputation in my field. I was damned if I was going to let him push me about. I'd ring his office in the morning and say I couldn't come.

The second message was from Guastafeste, simply asking me to give him a call. It was half-past eleven. I wouldn't normally phone anyone at such a late hour, but I knew that Guastafeste would still be up. He rarely goes to bed before midnight, and often much later, particularly when he's working on a major investigation.

'Thanks for calling, Gianni,' he said when he heard my voice on the line.

'Sorry, I was out,' I said. 'I've been in Milan, asking Vittorio Castellani about Paganini and Elisa Baciocchi.'

'And?'

'Nothing of any interest, I'm afraid. But I'll keep looking. You?'

'I had the forensics people go over the inside of the gold box and the letter from Elisa. They found no trace of Villeneuve's fingerprints. It doesn't look to me as if he managed to open the box.'

'Unless he wore gloves,' I said.

'Why would he do that? He was a fine-arts dealer, not a safecracker. His prints were all over the outside of the box. If he'd opened it, his prints would have been inside, too.'

'He didn't work out the *scordatura*?'

'I think not. He wasn't a violin specialist like you. It would never have occurred to him that the actual notes of the 'Moses Fantasy' weren't what was written on the page.'

'So the violin had already been removed. Villeneuve didn't touch it.'

'It looks that way to me.'

'Have you found out where he acquired the box?'

'Not yet. A jeweller is coming in tomorrow to inspect it. But I have a suspicion your friend Vincenzo Serafin knows more than he's letting on.'

'Serafin? Don't talk to me about Serafin. I got a message from him on my answering machine this evening, practically ordering me to go to his office tomorrow morning. The man is an obnoxious bully.'

Guastafeste was silent for a moment. Then he said, 'Are you going to go?'

'I wasn't intending to. I thought I'd assert my independence. Why?'

'What does he want to see you about?'

'Just a violin.'

Guastafeste was silent again.

'Antonio?' I said. 'What is this?'

'Go and see him, Gianni,' Guastafeste said. 'I'll come with you. I'd like a word with him, and face-to-face will be better than on the phone.'

'A word with him about Villeneuve?'

'I spoke to him yesterday morning, if you remember. He said he knew nothing about why Villeneuve was in Cremona, said he wasn't doing business with him.'

'And he was?'

'I don't know for sure. But we've got the phone records from the Hotel San Michele now. François Villeneuve phoned Serafin on Thursday evening, and again on Friday morning. I'd like to know what they talked about. Oh, and while we're on the subject, we checked the phone

148

records at the Hotel Emanuele. A call was put through to Yevgeny Ivanov's suite yesterday afternoon, at three-forty-six, when Ludmilla was out shopping.'

'You know who the call was from?' I asked.

'It came from the Hotel San Michele,' Guastafeste replied. 'From Vladimir Kousnetzoff.'

9

We drove into Milan in an unmarked police car. Guastafeste has none of my qualms about big-city traffic and, as far as parking is concerned, he has the policeman's careless disregard for what he sees as minor inconveniences. He leaves his car wherever he pleases, in Cremona and elsewhere — and not just his police vehicle but his private car, too. He gets parking tickets, of course, but never pays them — and never gets fined for not paying them. His colleagues are all the same. Somewhere in the *questura*, I imagine, there is a room that is knee-deep in paper, all the various tickets and summonses that officers have accumulated over the years and ignored.

We headed across the River Po to the A21, then joined the A1 outside Piacenza and went northwest towards Milan at a steady 140 kilometres an hour — greater than the speed limit to satisfy Guastafeste's professional pride, but moderately restrained in deference to the nervous, elderly passenger by his side.

'Any news of Yevgeny Ivanov?' I asked.

Guastafeste banged on the horn and flashed his head-lights at the van in front of us, then sped past as the van pulled over into the inside lane.

'Not a thing. We've circulated an alert to every police force in the country, telling them to watch

150

out for him. Airports, seaports, and border posts have been notified, too.'

'And Kousnetzoff?'

'No sign of him, either.'

'You think Yevgeny's with him?'

'That phone call on Monday makes it more likely. Kousnetzoff phones the Emanuele. Ludmilla is out. He speaks to Yevgeny; maybe they arrange to meet. But if Yevgeny is with him, he's there of his own free will. All that stuff about abductions, that's just Ludmilla getting overexcited. An agent wouldn't kidnap a potential client; that would be ludicrous.'

'And if he's not with Kousnetzoff?'

'That's trickier. We have to decide whether we go public, notify the media, get Yevgeny's photo in the press, on television. Fortunately, that's not my decision. The *questore* will have to make that call.'

Guastafeste eased on the brakes as we came up behind a small Fiat Panda. He hammered on the horn again, but the Panda stayed where it was, crawling past the lorries in the inside lanes before finally pulling over to let us pass.

'I've been thinking overnight,' I said. 'About the gold box, the violin it must once have contained, Elisa's letter to Paganini. What happened to the violin? Villeneuve didn't manage to open the box, but someone must have taken the violin. Who?'

'The box could have been empty for years,' Guastafeste said. 'Maybe Paganini himself disposed of the violin.'

'There's another mystery, too,' I said. 'The

151

piece of music Elisa refers to in her letter, the piece of music that Paganini wrote for her in Lucca. His 'ghost,' she called it.'

'I remember.'

'A Serenata *Appassionata*. I can't find any mention of it in any books on Paganini. Castellani didn't know anything about it, either. It appears to have gone missing, too.'

'Is that significant?'

'I don't know. But it's intriguing. What if someone were looking for this 'ghost'?'

Guastafeste looked across at me sharply.

'You think Villeneuve's killer may have been after a piece of music?'

I shrugged.

'It's possible.'

'A missing composition by Paganini. Would that be valuable?'

'Maybe.'

'How valuable? Thousands? Tens of thousands?'

'Certainly thousands,' I said.

'But not more?'

'Paganini wasn't a great composer. A long-lost composition by Mozart or Beethoven, now that might fetch a fortune at auction. But a Paganini? I'm not sure. His name alone is worth something. He seems to fascinate people. There may well be collectors of Paganiniana — and there are quite a few of those — who would pay a lot of money to own one of his compositions.'

'But would they kill for it?'

I didn't reply. We were on the outskirts of Milan now. The road into the city centre was solid with slow-moving or stationary traffic, but Guastafeste had no intention of waiting patiently in line. He rolled down his window, took a portable flashing light from a clip under the dashboard, and hooked it out through the window, attaching it to the car roof by its magnetic base. He flipped the switch to turn the light on and another to activate the siren, pulled over on to the wrong side of the carriageway, and accelerated. I hung on to the door handle, watching the scenery flash past outside.

Guastafeste turned his head and grinned at me.

'I know it's childish, but I always get a kick out of this.'

'Try to keep your eyes on the road, Antonio,' I said a little hoarsely.

'This the first time you've done this?'

'Yes, but it's never too late to get killed in a multiple-car crash.'

'Relax, I know what I'm doing.'

'You may be right. But does everyone else know what you're doing?'

Guastafeste braked hard and veered back to the right side of the road as a huge articulated lorry loomed up in front of us.

'Are you allowed to do this in Milan?' I asked. 'Being a policeman from Cremona.'

'Strictly speaking, no, it's outside my jurisdiction.'

'What if the Milanese police catch you?'

Guastafeste winked at me.

'Be serious. The Milanese police *catch* me?'

He lurched back out across the carriageway

and overtook a few more crawling cars before swerving back in time to skip a red light through the Porta Romana. He slowed down then and removed the flashing light from the car roof. We negotiated the inner ring road at a sedate twenty kilometres an hour and turned down the Via Manzoni towards Vincenzo Serafin's office.

The narrow side street near La Scala on which the office is situated is technically a no-parking zone, but Guastafeste interpreted the regulations as not so much a prohibition as a tentative suggestion. He pulled to the side of the road, then, to compound his transgression, drove up over the kerb and stopped the car with the two nearside wheels on the pavement, blocking the path of pedestrians.

'Here's how I want to play it, Gianni,' he said. 'You go in by yourself. How long do you reckon you need to complete your business with Serafin?'

'Fifteen minutes, maybe twenty. It depends on how much he talks.'

'Okay, I'll give you twenty minutes, then come in. He'll be more at ease with you there. I might catch him off guard.'

I opened my door and climbed out. Serafin's violin-dealing business has a shop frontage at street level, but there is nothing in the shop except a desk and chair occupied by his haughty blonde receptionist, Annalisa. She glanced at me without interest as I walked in, then turned her attention back to the glossy fashion magazine she was idly flicking through. She has worked for Serafin — and I use the term *work* loosely — for several years, but I have yet to figure out exactly what she does. She has no computer. She does not appear to write letters or file invoices. She seems to be a sort of 'trophy' receptionist, a status symbol that affirms Serafin's position as a successful businessman. She is certainly a decorative addition to his establishment, but then, so would be a vase of flowers — and the vase would probably be more productive.

'I'm expected,' I said.

Annalisa looked up again, as if she were surprised that I was still there.

'Your name?'

I choked back the curt retort that was rising in my throat. I'd been there dozens of times. She knew perfectly well who I was, but this was her way of bolstering her self-esteem, of reassuring herself that others could be as insignificant as she was.

'Gianni Castiglione,' I said with icy politeness.

'Ah, yes, you may go up.'

'Thank you.'

She reached under the desk and pressed the hidden button with one of her varnished talons. A door at the back of the room clicked open and I walked through into the small hall, where a security man in a suit sat on guard outside Serafin's inner sanctum — the soundproofed music room where he keeps his stock of violins. I nodded at the man and went upstairs to Serafin's office.

Serafin wasn't alone. His mistress, Maddalena, was with him, perched on the corner of his desk, her bright pink lips pulled together in an angry pucker.

'But you always let me, Vincenzo,' she was whining. 'Why not today?'

'I can give you a number of reasons. Two thousand six hundred reasons, to be precise,' Serafin replied.

'It wasn't that much.'

'I have the bill in a drawer. I can show you it, if you like.'

Serafin waved me into the room, then continued his conversation with Maddalena.

'And the one before that wasn't much less. Fifteen hundred euros, if I remember correctly.'

'It was less than that,' Maddalena protested.

'I have that bill, too.'

Maddalena leant back over the desk, showing off her willowy figure. Her voice took on a more conciliatory tone.

'All right, maybe it *was* that much. But you can afford it, darling. What's the problem? You like me to look nice, don't you?'

'You look nice in the clothes you already have,' Serafin said. 'Why do you need more?'

'Just this once. I promise I'll be a good girl. I'll get only a few things.'

'No.'

'Aw, Vincenzo, don't be such a spoilsport.'

Maddalena slipped off the desk and went round behind Serafin's chair. She put her arms round him, her face nuzzling the side of his neck. I turned away in embarrassment and went to the window and looked out. Guastafeste's car was directly below me, though I couldn't see

Antonio. How much time has passed? I wondered. Five minutes? Another fifteen and he'd be coming in. I tried to shut out the voices behind me, Maddalena's coy and wheedling, Serafin's holding firm. I've negotiated fees with him often enough to know that once his mind is made up, he is utterly intractable. Maddalena must have known that, too, but she continued to niggle away at him until, frustrated by his intransigence, she lost her temper and started hurling abuse at him, completely oblivious to my presence in the room.

I looked over my shoulder. Maddalena was snatching up her leather handbag from the desk and walking away in a rage. She threw open the door, paused to fire one last parting insult at Serafin, then stalked out, slamming the door behind her so hard, I could feel the vibrations through the floor.

Serafin waited a few seconds, then said dryly, 'Hell hath no fury like a woman refused a credit card.'

'I came at the wrong moment. I'm sorry,' I said.

'You weren't to know. Never get yourself a high-maintenance woman, Gianni. Sometimes they're more trouble than they're worth.'

'You wanted me to look at a violin,' I said.

'It's on the table over there.'

I took the violin out of its case and held it in my hands for a while. When you've been examining and authenticating string instruments for as long as I have, you develop an instinct for a fake. That sounds like arrogance, but it's really simply experience. All violins have a 'feel' to them. You pick them up and you sense at once whether they are genuine or not. I say 'sense' because it's very much an intuitive process. You cannot know for certain whether a particular instrument is by, say, Stradivari, or anyone else. You were not present, after all, when it was made. But you can nevertheless be pretty sure of its provenance. You can give your opinion of a violin's authenticity with a clear conscience, and that is all I am required to do. To give my *opinion*, based on knowledge and experience. My nose for a fake is not infallible, but I use it as a starting point — an initial impression, which a closer examination will either confirm or refute.

'It's labelled Bergonzi,' Serafin said. 'But you know how unreliable that can be.'

I nodded, tilting the instrument towards the light so that I could peer through the bass sound hole. The label was grey and dirty, but I could make out the words '*Anno 1732, Carlo Bergonzi fece in Cremona.*'

Bergonzi's labels varied during his career. That particular wording was certainly one he used on many of his instruments, but a label, of course, does not make a violin genuine. It is probably the least reliable indicator of an instrument's provenance, because it can be so easily faked — and I'd seen a lot of fakes labelled as Bergonzis.

I turned my attention to the rest of the instrument, to the plates, the scroll, the varnish. It was a fine-looking violin. I would expect nothing less if it were a genuine Bergonzi. Carlo was the first, and best, of three generations of luthiers. He lived and worked in Cremona during the last two decades of the seventeenth century and the first half of the eighteenth. He was a contemporary of Stradivari and Guarneri del Gesù and, not surprisingly, has always been overshadowed by those two great craftsmen.

At one time, it was thought that he had been a pupil of Stradivari, who was almost forty years his senior, but now it is believed he may have been taught by the Giuseppe Guarneri who is always known as 'filius Andreae,' to distinguish him from his more famous namesake, his son, Giuseppe del Gesù. Bergonzi certainly had close relations with Stradivari and Guarneri del Gesù — in a city as small as Cremona, where violin making was an important established business, it would have been unthinkable that he didn't — and his instruments show their influences. His f-holes are very like Stradivari's and his sound boxes have narrow waists and squarish upper corners similar to del Gesù's. But his craftsmanship is much more refined than Guarneri's. His scrolls, in particular, have a symmetry and delicacy that few other luthiers, Stradivari included, have ever managed to achieve.

'What do you think?' Serafin said.

'Where did you acquire it?' I asked.

Serafin didn't reply immediately. I lowered the violin and looked at him. He was squirming slightly in his chair, his arms bent, elbows tucked into his sides, his palms out flat, a pose that, I knew from long experience, preluded some kind of evasive answer.

'Well, you know how these things are,' he said vaguely.

'No, I don't,' I said. 'Where did you get it?'

'Is that really relevant?'

'Of course it is. Did it come with any paperwork, any provenance? Where's it been for the last three hundred — odd years?'

'Is it genuine? That's all I want to know,' Serafin said. 'You're the expert; just give me your opinion.'

I said nothing, just kept gazing at him. Serafin squirmed a bit more, then looked away. I waited.

'You don't need to know the details, Gianni,' he said.

'That's exactly what I need to know. Bergonzi is one of the forger's favourite makers.'

'Is it a forgery?'

'The provenance first, Vincenzo. Then I'll give you my opinion.'

Serafin sniffed. He stroked his sleek black beard with his fingertips.

'It belonged to an old lady,' he said.

I'd heard Serafin's 'old lady' story before, but I was prepared to hear it again. You never knew; this time it might actually be true.

'Yes?' I said.

'She died a few weeks ago, leaving all her possessions to her nephew. It was the nephew who contacted me, asked me to go and look at the violin.'

'Go where?'

'To her house, in Stresa.'

'On Lake Maggiore?'

'Yes. You know I have a country place out

160

there. Someone had told the nephew that I was a violin dealer. He thought I might be able to help.'

'And?'

'That's it. I went out to the house. The nephew showed me the violin. I said I'd have to take it away and get a full assessment before I could give him a valuation.'

'You haven't bought it, then?'

'Not yet. I need to know if it's genuine first.'

'What was the old lady's name?'

'Look, Gianni, we're wasting time.'

'Her name?'

Serafin sighed.

'Nicoletta Ferrara.'

'And what did the nephew tell you about the violin? Where did his aunt get it?'

'He said it had been in the family for generations. He thought his great-grandfather might have acquired it back in the nineteenth century, but he didn't know from whom.'

'There was no paperwork? No bill of sale or invoice? No dealer's certificate of authenticity?'

'No, nothing. That's all he knew, Gianni. Now, can we get on? Don't keep me on tenterhooks. Is it a genuine Bergonzi?'

'You've looked at it. What do you think?'

'I'm not an expert like you. I can't be sure.'

'Well, the scroll looks like one of Bergonzi's.' I took the violin across to the desk and showed him. 'See how beautifully it's carved. Those clean lines, that perfect spiral. Then the f-holes and the archings, they're consistent with it being by Bergonzi.'

161

'Yes, that's all very well. But all I really want to know is — '

Serafin broke off as the telephone rang. He picked up the receiver and listened for a moment. Then he said, 'Now? I'm engaged . . . Very well, send him up.'

He replaced the receiver and looked at me. He was frowning, his manner distracted. The violin seemed to have slipped from his thoughts.

'The police want to talk to me.'

'Shall I . . . ' I put the violin back in its case.

'No, stay. It won't take long,' Serafin said.

The door opened and Guastafeste came in. His double take as he saw me was worthy of some kind of acting award. Even I could believe that this meeting was entirely coincidental.

'Gianni . . . what're you doing here?'

'Business,' I said.

Guastafeste turned to Serafin.

'My apologies, Signor Serafin. Am I interrupting?'

'No, we were just finishing.'

Serafin peered at Guastafeste.

'Aren't you . . . You were at the reception in Cremona, weren't you?'

'Yes, I met you there.'

Serafin's eyes went from Guastafeste to me, then back to Guastafeste, suspicious but not absolutely sure whether his suspicion was justified.

'You're Gianni's friend?' he said.

'That's right,' Guastafeste replied. 'I hope I won't take up too much of your time. I wanted to ask you about François Villeneuve.'

162

'Villeneuve? What about him?'

Guastafeste pulled up a chair and sat down in front of the desk. He took out his notebook and pen.

'We spoke about him on the phone two days ago. You remember?'

'Yes, I remember.'

'I just want to check one or two details. You'd known François Villeneuve how long?'

'A few years.'

'Can you be more specific?'

'Two years, maybe three.'

'And you met him how?'

'I believe it was at a fine-arts convention.'

'In France?'

'No, it was here in Milan. I was one of the speakers. François was a delegate from Paris.'

'But you kept in touch with him?'

'We got on well. We shared a common interest in the arts.'

'Was he a close friend?'

'I wouldn't say close, no. He was more a business contact. Globalisation is shrinking the world. Nothing is purely local any longer; we all operate on an international stage. François found it useful to have a person he could trust in Milan and I found it useful to have someone in Paris. It was as simple as that.'

'So you did business together?'

'Yes.'

'Often?'

'Once or twice a year.'

'But you told me on the phone that you didn't do business with him.'

Serafin gave Guastafeste a narrow look.

'I told you that *on this occasion* we weren't doing business.'

'You expect me to believe that?'

'It's the truth.'

'You're saying that Villeneuve came all the way from Paris to Milan, but he wasn't doing business with you?'

'That is correct.'

'Who was he doing business with?'

'I have no idea. He didn't tell me.'

'And you didn't ask?'

'No, that wouldn't have been diplomatic. In my business, it's not polite to pry.'

'You say you do business with him once or twice a year. What kind of business?'

'It varies. I put work his way; he puts work my way.'

'What sort of work?'

'I deal in violins, as Gianni here will be able to tell you. If François came across an instrument he thought might be of interest to me, he would let me know. If I came across paintings or antiques that might be of interest to him, I would let him know. We exchanged information, I suppose you could say.'

'And shared in the proceeds of that information?'

'If the information made money for either of us, yes, we would apportion the proceeds. That is only fair.'

Guastafeste wrote something in his notebook. Serafin looked at me.

'Have you two known each other long?'

'Years,' I said.

'Is that so?' Serafin gave me a nod, filing the fact away in his head. Then he turned back to Guastafeste.

'Have you made any progress in your search for François's killer?'

Guastafeste looked up from his notes. He must have heard the question, but he didn't answer it.

'Do you know anything about a gold box that François Villeneuve had with him?' he asked.

'A gold box?' Serafin said. 'What kind of gold box?'

'About this big,' Guastafeste held up his hands. 'With an engraving of Moses on the lid.'

'*Moses?*'

'Holding the Ten Commandments. You know the ones I mean — 'Thou shalt not covet thy neighbours' goods,' 'Thou shalt not lie,' that kind of thing.'

It wasn't subtle. Even Serafin, notoriously insensitive though he was, must have got the message. He gazed coolly at Guastafeste.

'I'm afraid I don't know what you're talking about,' he said.

'Villeneuve didn't mention a gold box to you?'

'No.'

'So you don't know where he might have got it?'

'No. Is this box relevant to his murder?'

'When did you last see Villeneuve?'

'On Saturday evening, at the reception in the town hall in Cremona.'

'You didn't see him on Sunday morning?'

165

'No.'

'Can you prove that?'

Serafin stared at Guastafeste, not blinking for several seconds.

'You're asking me for an alibi? I was in my apartment all Sunday morning. I have a friend who can vouch for that.'

'And your friend's name?'

'Is this necessary? François Villeneuve was a friend. Why would I kill him?'

'It's just routine,' Guastafeste said. 'The name, please.'

'Maddalena Fraschini.'

'And her address and phone number?'

Serafin gave him the information.

'How many times did you see Villeneuve during his stay?' Guastafeste asked.

'Just on the Saturday evening. At the recital, and the reception afterwards.'

'Not before that?'

'No.'

'Did you speak to him on the phone?'

'Yes, I believe I did.'

'How many times?'

'I forget.'

'Let me refresh your memory. Villeneuve rang you on Thursday evening, shortly after he'd checked in at the Hotel San Michele. And he rang you again on Friday morning.'

'Yes, that's right. I remember now.'

'Why did he ring you?'

'To say hello, to chat. We were catching up with each other.'

'Both phone calls?'

'Certainly Thursday's. On Friday morning, I think we discussed Yevgeny Ivanov's recital and I said I'd try to get him a ticket. The concert was sold out, but there are always ways of obtaining tickets, if you know the right people.'

'And at no time did he say why he was in Cremona?'

'As I've already said, no.'

Guastafeste gave him a hard, concentrated look. Serafin gazed back with wide-eyed innocence.

'If that's all . . . ' he said.

'Yes, thank you, Signor Serafin.'

Guastafeste put away his notebook and pen and turned to me.

'Are you going back to Cremona, Gianni?'

'Yes,' I said.

'You want a lift?'

'Thank you.'

'I'll be outside.'

Guastafeste left the room. There was silence for a time; then Serafin said, 'So you mix with policemen, Gianni?' There was a steely edge to his tone.

'Antonio and I go back a long way,' I said.

'Do you, now?'

'He'll be waiting for me.'

'Let him wait. We haven't finished our business yet. The violin? Your verdict?'

A part of me would have enjoyed telling him that the Bergonzi was a fake. I knew he'd cheat Nicoletta Ferrara's nephew, offer him much less than the instrument was worth, then sell it on at a huge profit to one of the many rich collectors

167

he had on his list. That was how the violin-dealing world worked — how all buying and selling worked. Serafin had the contacts; he controlled access to the customers. If I had one piece of advice to give anyone thinking of venturing into business, it would be 'Become the middleman.' They're always the ones who do the least work for the greatest reward.

'It's genuine,' I said.

'You're sure?'

'Yes, I'm sure.'

I took my leave then and went out to Guastafeste's car. He was sitting behind the wheel, scribbling more notes in his notebook. I glanced up as I climbed into the car. Serafin was watching me from the window of his office.

Guastafeste finished his notes. He started the car and we drove off, heading for the inner ring road.

'I hope I haven't damaged your relationship with Serafin,' Guastafeste said.

'I don't care if you have,' I replied. 'I don't need him.'

'So what do you think? You've known him for years. Was he telling me the truth?'

'Some of the time, yes.'

'But not all the time?'

'Serafin is a practised liar. He's good at telling half the truth, being open about some things and hiding others. The trick is knowing which is which.'

'Which bits weren't true?'

'His claim not to know why Villeneuve was down here. That rubbish about being diplomatic.

168

What did he say? 'In my business, it's not polite to pry.' I almost burst out laughing when he said that. Not polite? Serafin has never worried about being polite, and prying is second nature to him. He can't bear to be cut out of a deal. If Villeneuve was holding out on him — and I don't believe he was — Serafin would have hammered away at him remorselessly until Villeneuve cracked.'

'You think they were, in fact, doing business together?'

'I'm not sure. If it was as simple as that, Villeneuve would have gone to Milan, maybe even stayed with Serafin. But he came to a hotel in Cremona. Why? What was he doing in Cremona?'

We turned onto the inner ring road and headed south in a line of sluggish traffic.

'Those questions you asked — about his whereabouts on Sunday morning?' I said. 'Do you seriously think he might have killed Villeneuve?'

'I wanted to see how he reacted.'

'He has an alibi.'

'From his mistress. We'll see how it stands up.'

'You think it might not?'

'An enquiry like this, we check out every-thing,' Guastafeste said. 'I'm keeping an open mind. I've got a list of potential suspects, and right now, Serafin's name is on that list.'

10

It was nearing one o'clock when Guastafeste dropped me off at my house. I tried to persuade him to come in for something to eat, but he declined my invitation — he had work to do at the *questura*. I made myself a simple lunch of spaghetti tossed in butter and Parmesan and settled down at the kitchen table with *Napoléon's Sisters: Caroline, Pauline, and Elisa*, by Maria Pellegrini, the book I'd borrowed from Vittorio Castellani's office.

I read first the chapters on Elisa's period in Lucca. I already knew a reasonable amount about those years from my biographies of Paganini, but this time I was getting the story from Elisa's perspective. A strong-willed, ambitious woman, Elisa had formidable reserves of energy, which had barely been tapped before her arrival in Tuscany. She had previously maintained a salon in Paris, at which writers like Chateaubriand and Louis de Fontanes had read from their works while their hostess reclined on a sofa, fanning herself coquettishly, but apart from that she had done very little with her life except marry Felice Baciocchi — and that was hardly a great achievement. Baciocchi was almost the exact opposite of his wife. He was weak, unambitious, and by the age of thirty-five, when he and Elisa were wed, had risen no higher than the rank of captain in the army. But he was the only suitor in sight, and Elisa was, above all else, a practical woman. She was twenty years old, a veritable geriatric in the competitive marriage stakes of the day, and any husband was better than no husband.

Elisa was twenty-eight when Napoléon made her princess of Piombino and Lucca. She and Felice had been married for eight years and had settled into the dull, passionless domesticity of a couple twice their age. Felice was an amiable consort who pottered about the place reviewing the troops and playing his violin, but exciting he wasn't. Paganini, however, most decidedly was.

'From the first moment she met the violinist, Elisa fell madly in love with him,' Maria Pellegrini had written in her book, going on to describe Paganini's 'wild good looks,' his 'charisma,' and his 'mutual passion for the princess' in prose that seemed more suited to a romantic novella than a serious biography.

La Pellegrini's language might have been a little florid, but she was right about the impact Paganini must have made on Elisa. In the small provincial arena of Lucca, populated by philistines and dullards, his talent must have seemed like a supernova, a raging ball of fire that would incinerate anyone who came too close.

'For three unforgettable years, Elisa and Nicolò conducted a torrid, all-consuming love affair,' the book said. 'Neither made any secret of their attachment, and poor Felice, the cuckolded husband, could only stand and watch as his wife gave herself body and soul to her flamboyant lover. Elisa was besotted with him, showering

171

him with jewellery and other valuable gifts, many of them confiscated from monasteries and convents round Lucca and farther afield. Napoléon was constantly short of money to fund his wars, and he forced his sister to close down these religious institutions, appropriate their property and riches, and send the proceeds to Paris.

'Paganini, for his part, showed his devotion to his mistress by composing music dedicated to her — a 'Duo Merveille,' a 'Duetto Amoroso' for violin and guitar, and several other pieces.'

I stopped reading. This last paragraph had been underlined in ink, and in the margin alongside it was a question mark and the handwritten words 'Serenata *Appassionata?*'

Strange. Vittorio Castellani had quite clearly told me that he had never heard of any Serenata *Appassionata*, and yet here he was, writing the name in the margin of one of his books.

I read on for a few pages, through the section describing the gradual drifting apart and eventual acrimonious breakup of the two lovers, then skimmed ahead to get a general idea of Elisa's life without Paganini.

Her time in Florence, after she moved there as grand duchess of Tuscany in 1809, was little different from her years in Lucca. She still kept her palaces at Piombino, Massa, Viareggio, Bagni di Lucca, and Marlia — her country estate outside Lucca, on whose gardens and furnishings she had lavished a fortune — but, in addition, she had the Pitti Palace in Florence to enjoy. She continued to work energetically on behalf of both herself and her subjects — though the former generally took precedence over the latter — and maintained her soirées with artists and writers and — very occasionally — her husband.

These were happy days for Elisa. She had given birth to a daughter, Elisa Napoléone, in Lucca and now, in Florence, she had a son. Her brother was still emperor, so her power and privilege were safe, but in 1812, after Napoléon's disastrous campaign in Russia, things began to change. Further French defeats at Vitoria and Leipzig weakened her brother's position even more, and in early 1814 the British landed at Livorno, on the Tuscan coast, and demanded that Elisa give up her principality. Impotent and humiliated, Elisa and Felice packed their bags and headed north to Genoa and exile.

In April of that year, Napoléon abdicated and was banished to the island of Elba by the allies. Elisa, meanwhile, was wandering round southern France and northern Italy, giving birth to another son, Frédéric, at the villa at Passeriano, near Venice, where in 1797 Napoléon had stayed to negotiate the Treaty of Campo Formio. She then settled in Bologna, in the Villa Caprara, a modest little residence compared to the half-dozen palaces she had once occupied. She was now calling herself the comtesse de Compignano, after one of the delightful Tuscan estates she had been forced to relinquish.

Her stay in Bologna was brief. In March the following year, four days after her brother escaped from Elba, Elisa and her older children

173

were seized by the Austrians and taken away to the fortress of Brünn. The allies' contempt for Felice was clearly shown by their allowing him to remain in Bologna with the baby, Frédéric.

Elisa never returned to Italy. In 1816, the allies decided that she was no threat to them and permitted her and her husband and children to live in Trieste. With her customary energy and determination, Elisa set about obtaining compensation for the property she had left behind in Tuscany, eventually receiving an annual income from the Austrians of some 300,000 francs. With this money, she was able to buy a house on the Campo Marzio in Trieste, and a nearby seaside residence, the Villa Vicentina. It was from here, in 1819, that she wrote the letter to Paganini that we had found inside the gold box.

Had she seen the violinist since that final angry parting in Florence a decade earlier? Maria Pellegrini's book was silent on the subject. The index made no reference to Paganini after 1809, yet there was clear evidence that the two former lovers had not lost touch with each other entirely. Paganini had, after all, dedicated the 'Moses Fantasy' to Elisa. Why should he have done that? She was no longer his employer. She was no longer a princess. Her influence and much of her wealth were gone. Paganini, throughout his life, was desperate for a title to add to his name. Elisa might once have been able to confer that title, but not now. Yet Paganini composed a piece of music for her. Surely that was indication that she still had a place in his thoughts, if not his heart.

Elisa's letter from the Villa Vicentina showed no trace of animosity towards her erstwhile lover. Quite the contrary, in fact: It was warm and affectionate and made reference to a previous letter she had written him, giving reason to believe that they were in more than occasional contact with each other. The gift she had sent him — an expensive gold box — was also a sign that she still held him in high regard. She was not exactly living in poverty, but such a present would nevertheless have made a considerable inroad into her income.

Had the two of them ever met again? The romantic in me hoped that they had, but I think it unlikely. Elisa was forbidden by the Austrians from entering Italy, and Paganini never set foot outside the country until the late 1820s, by which time Elisa was long dead.

Those final few years in Trieste were comfortable and — given the turmoil following Napoléon's defeat at Waterloo — thankfully uneventful for Elisa. Of the three Bonaparte sisters, she was the best equipped to deal with adversity. She busied herself with improving the house and gardens of the Villa Vicentina and looking after her children. The social life in Trieste was dull and monotonous. There was a daily outing in the carriage and evenings at the theatre, but in general it was a quiet existence, more suited to prosperous country gentry than a former grand duchess. Felice, the betrayed, much-ridiculed husband, ironically, was now a welcome companion. He had remained loyal to his wife through all the upheavals, and the couple were resigned, even contented, with their lot.

To occupy her time, Elisa took up archaeology, initiating a dig at the nearby Roman site of Aquileia. In hindsight, it was a tragic mistake. The excavations were on marshland, and it was while visiting them in July 1820 that Elisa caught a putrid fever, from which she died the following month. She was only forty-three.

Her husband, almost immediately, left Trieste and returned to Bologna, where he once again began to call himself Prince Felice, living in great state on the fortune that Elisa's persistence had wrested from the Austrians. Elisa's body was brought to the San Petronio Basilica in Bologna and Felice erected a monument there in her memory. He lived on for another twenty-one years, dying in 1841, at the age of seventy-eight.

The next paragraph in the book had been underlined in ink and there were more scribbled notes in the margins.

'Elisa's family line soon died out. Frédéric, the son she had borne after leaving Tuscany, died in Rome in 1833 after falling from a horse. Her other son died in 1830, at the age of twenty. Her daughter, Elisa Napoléone, married Count Camerata, an Italian nobleman, but the marriage didn't last. Elisa Napoléone's only son committed suicide in 1853.'

The notes next to the text read, 'Baciocchi, Agostino — F's cousin m. Giuseppina Ferraio. Daughter, Manuela, m. Ignazio Martinelli.' The last word — the name Martinelli — had been underlined twice.

I stared at the notes for a long time. Elisa's descendants had been cut off, but the Baciocchi line had not died out. Felice had had a cousin, Agostino, whose daughter, Manuela, had married someone named Martinelli.

Felice would have inherited Elisa's estate on her death. Her possessions, presumably including any music that Paganini had written for her, would have passed to him. And on Felice's death, those possessions would have gone where? To his cousin's daughter? Is that what these notes meant? The Serenata *Appassionata* — if it survived — had been inherited by the Martinelli family.

I thought back to my interview with Vittorio Castellani. Had he forgotten about these notes he'd made? Had the Serenata *Appassionata* genuinely slipped from his memory? He'd written his biography of Paganini ten years ago, after all. That was a long time to remember minor details.

I flicked back to the beginning of Maria Pellegrini's book, to the title verso page, where its date of publication was recorded, and was stunned by what I found. The book had been published only two years earlier. These weren't old notes in the margins; they must have been made fairly recently.

I put the book down on the table and gazed at the wall in quiet reflection. Vittorio Castellani had denied all knowledge of the Serenata *Appassionata*. He had claimed to have no interest in Elisa Baciocchi. Yet here was a two-year-old book about Elisa that he had obviously been reading, and in the margins were notes that seemed to indicate an interest in Felice Baciocchi's descendants. Now why was that?

★ ★ ★

For the rest of the afternoon and into the evening, I worked on my violins, hollowing out part of a maple back for one instrument before changing tasks and carving a little more of the scroll for another. Paganini seemed to be in my blood at the moment, so I listened to some of his violin concertos — the box set LP version recorded by Salvatore Accardo in the 1970s — on the old record player that sits in the corner of my workshop.

I was growing weary and contemplating stopping for dinner, when the telephone rang. I could hear nothing but a fuzzy crackle on the line to begin with and was about to hang up, when a voice broke through the interference.

'Hello?'

It was a man's voice, speaking in English.

'Yes?' I replied in the same language.

'Gianni?'

I realised who it was.

'Yevgeny? Is that you, Yevgeny?' I almost shouted into the phone.

'Yes, it is me.'

'Yevgeny, where are you? Are you all right?'

'Yes, I am all right.'

He sounded very faint. His voice was thin and tremulous.

'What's happened?' I said. 'Have you rung your mother?'

'No. I cannot speak to her.'

'Yevgeny, you must. She's going crazy with worry. Where are you? Why did you disappear like that?'

'Please, Gianni, speak to my mother for me. Tell her I am okay. Tell her I am sorry.'

'Why can't you speak to her yourself?'

'I just can't.'

His voice cracked and I thought he was about to burst into tears.

'What is it?' I asked. 'What's happened? Did someone take you away by force?'

'By force? No, nothing like that.'

'So where are you? People are worried. It's not just your mother. The police are involved, too.'

'The *police*?'

'You vanished, Yevgeny. No one knows where you are. Anything could have happened. Of course your mother went to the police.'

'The *police*?' he said again. 'I did not know.'

'Are you in trouble? What's going on? Can I come and collect you?'

'Speak to Mama for me. Please, Gianni. I know I can trust you. Say I am sorry for all the trouble I am causing.'

'Do you need help? Tell me where you are, and I'll come and get you. Are you in Cremona?'

'I will be back in a few days. I have to sort things out.'

'What things?'

'I will call you again. I am sorry.'

The line went dead. I pressed the recall button

179

but got only a computerised voice-mail message. He'd turned off his mobile.

I left my workshop and went across the terrace and into the house, knowing I had to call both Ludmilla and Guastafeste, but unsure whom to ring first. I chose Ludmilla. Antonio's involvement in the case was purely professional, his interest detached and objective, but Ludmilla was Yevgeny's mother. Her life, her entire emotional being, was inextricably entwined with her son's. She needed, and deserved, to be told first.

It wasn't an easy call. The initial relief in her voice was so great that she sounded as if she were about to swoon. But then she recovered and became almost indignant.

'Why did he ring you?' she demanded. 'He barely knows you. Why didn't he call me?'

'I'm not sure, signora. The important thing is, he is safe.'

'But where is he?'

'I don't know.'

'Didn't you ask?'

'Yes, I asked. He didn't say.'

'Was he alone? Was Kousnetzoff with him?'

'I don't know.'

'You should have asked. You should have found out. He has engagements, commitments. What is the stupid boy playing at?'

'He sounded distressed,' I said. 'He said to tell you he was sorry and that he'd be back in a few days.'

'A few days? When? I have already had to cancel his recital in Venice. He is destroying his

180

career. We must find him. Have you told the police?'

'I am going to ring them next.'

'They can trace the phone call. They can find out where he is. Does he not realise how foolish he is being? Call them now. They must act quickly. *Now*, you understand?'

'Yes, signora. I will call them now.'

Guastafeste was still at his desk at the *questura*. I gave him the gist of my conversations with Yevgeny and Ludmilla.

'He gave no indication at all of where he is?' Guastafeste said.

'No.'

'You didn't pick up any clues? Background noise, other voices, that kind of thing?'

'No. The line was so bad, it was hard enough hearing Yevgeny.'

'And he said nothing about why he disappeared?'

'I asked him. He wouldn't — or couldn't — answer.'

'You think there was someone with him? Someone who was monitoring what he said?'

'No. When I asked if he'd been taken away against his will, he sounded genuinely surprised. I don't know what's going on, Antonio, but he hasn't been abducted. I'm sure of that.'

'Well, that's good to know. We can scale down the search for him now.'

'Ludmilla wants you to trace the phone call. Can you do that?'

'From a mobile? It's possible. If his phone is still switched on, it will be sending out an

181

intermittent signal to the nearest base station.'

'It's not switched on. I tried to call him back.'

'Then we can get the record of the call from the phone company. They'll have the coordinates of the location from where it was made. But it's a lot of hassle, and I'll probably have to get a court order. The magistrate will want some pretty good reasons for granting the order. Did Yevgeny sound as if he was scared or in danger?'

'He sounded upset, but not scared.'

'Upset?'

'Emotional, close to tears.'

'Has he had some kind of breakdown?'

'It's possible, a highly strung artist like him.'

'But he said he was coming back in a few days?'

'That's right.'

'Then I'm inclined to leave it, do nothing for the time being. He's phoned in. He seems to be safe and well. Let's wait for him to return.'

'Ludmilla won't like that. She wants him tracked down and brought back now.'

'It's not as easy as she thinks.'

'She won't take no for an answer. You know how persistent she is. She'll be coming into your office, camping out in the foyer until you do something.'

'Fortunately, I won't be here,' Guastafeste said. 'I'm going out of town for a couple of days.'

'Oh, yes? Where?'

'Paris.'

'Paris?'

'The jewellery expert examined the gold box this morning. The hallmarks indicate that it was

182

made in Paris in 1819 by Henri le Bley Lavelle. I'm flying up there tomorrow morning. Le Bley Lavelle's business was taken over by another firm in the mid-nineteenth century, but they still have all his records dating back to the 1780s.'

'You want to check the records?' I said.

'The box was made for a specific violin. The cutout shape inside it — Le Bley Lavelle must have been supplied with the exact dimensions he had to work to. I want to know if the records give any information about the violin the box was made to fit. I need to know what we're looking for. And while I'm in Paris, I want to have a talk with François Villeneuve's business partner, Alain Robillet.'

'I didn't know he had a partner.'

'Nor did I until today. We asked our colleagues at the Sûreté for information on Villeneuve. Their report was faxed through this afternoon. He had something of a dodgy reputation: three instances of stolen property being found in his possession — and not small stuff, either. We're talking valuable furniture, old masters, antique silverware. He wriggled out of the charges each time — insufficient evidence to prosecute him for receiving — but the French police clearly think he was guilty. Villeneuve might have been a successful fine-arts dealer, but it would seem that he was also a successful fence.'

'Was the gold box stolen?'

'We're checking to see.' Guastafeste paused. 'I'm glad you rang, Gianni. I was going to call you this evening anyway. You like Paris, don't you?'

183

'Well, yes,' I said warily. 'Why?'

'I want you to look at Le Bley Lavelle's records with me.'

'You mean fly up there with you tomorrow?'

'It's all cleared with my boss. You're the violin expert. I need your help, Gianni. Having your company will be nice, too.'

'I'll have to get myself a ticket,' I said.

'That's all arranged. I'll pick you up at half eight. Our flight leaves Linate at eleven.'

11

I have happy memories of Paris. It was where my wife would have liked to have gone for our honeymoon, only we were too poor to afford it at that stage of our lives. We were in our early twenties and I was an unknown, struggling luthier. A long weekend at Bellagio, on the shores of Lake Como, was all our budget would stretch to, but when you are newly married, your honeymoon destination is ultimately immaterial. You are not there to look at scenery or wander round museums; there are other things to occupy you.

Paris would have been wasted on us back then. We would have been too absorbed with each other to take in the cultural delights the city offers. But later, when the children were off our hands, we managed a few days there. We were no longer the starry-eyed newlyweds for whom the French capital is such a draw, but Paris is not the exclusive province of the young and enamoured. The middle-aged and exhausted are also allowed to share in its sophisticated pleasures.

We did all the classic tourist things — went up the Eiffel Tower, took a boat trip on the Seine, ate out at restaurants where the imagination lavished on the food came in a poor second to the imagination lavished on the bill — and loved it. Of all the European capital cities I have visited, and I have not visited many, Paris is undoubtedly the most captivating. Berlin is grand but dull, Rome a chaotic inferno of traffic and dusty ruins, London damp and unappealing. Paris cannot compete with its rivals on many fronts. Its weather is inferior to Rome's, its public services worse than Berlin's. Its parks are not a patch on London's green open spaces, yet it has a style, a charm that the others cannot match. To live there is probably hell, but to visit for a short time is an exquisite experience, particularly with someone you love.

We have become cynical these days, and with good cause. Our lives are saturated with the lies and obfuscations of the PR and marketing industries, whose main raison d'être is to part us from our money. The image of Paris, the romance of Paris, has been filtered and distorted through so many films and glossy advertising campaigns that it is hard to tell what is reality and what is a sales pitch. But my memories of the city are not tainted by commercial misrepresentations. I know that. They are not part of a movie scenario or a tourist brochure. They are real and they are vivid and they are happy. For I was there with Caterina. I was there with her when she was well and full of life, before she succumbed to the vile, creeping sickness that was to take her from me. For that, I will always have a tender spot in my heart for Paris.

Guastafeste and I, however, were not there on holiday. We had business to transact. Our flight from Milan got into Charles de Gaulle at half-past twelve. It was nearly lunchtime, but you would have to be insane to eat by choice in an airport, so we took a taxi straight into the city centre. The offices of Molyneux et Charbon were in the Place Vendome, near the Ritz Hotel, whose well-heeled customers could stroll out of the front door and straight into the jewellers' showroom, then back to their luxury suites without being unduly worn out by the weight of all those carats round their necks and fingers.

This was no ordinary high-street jewellery store. I had seen shops like it in Milan. You couldn't simply walk in and ask to see a few diamond rings. You had to make an appointment for a 'consultation,' during which items would be brought out of a display case or the high-security safe by solicitous assistants who spoke at least half a dozen languages, including English, Arabic, and fluent flattery.

Guastafeste pressed a bell by the door and spoke our names into an intercom, a CCTV camera on the wall above us scrutinising our every move. When the lock clicked back to open the door, we stepped through into a strange artificial environment. All trace of the outside world seemed to disappear. The noise of the street was cut out altogether by the thick walls; there was a deep burgundy carpet on the floor, on which our feet made no sound. The sunlight, partially blocked by the shutters and small windows, was replaced by a constellation of spotlamps sparkling and scintillating in the ceiling. The unnatural quiet, the lighting — which was somehow both bright and subdued — made me feel as if we'd walked into a well-appointed fish tank.

A man came forward to greet us. He was in his forties, a tanned, jowly man with thick black hair and dazzling white teeth. He was wearing a dark three-piece suit, which had a gold watch chain dangling from a fob pocket, and a gold tie pin inset with tiny sapphires. He had the smooth, well-fed look of an affluent banker.

'*Buon giorno, signori,*' he said, then went on in excellent Italian. 'I am Olivier Delacourt, the assistant manager.'

We shook hands. His palm was soft and fleshy.

'It's a pleasure to meet you,' he said. 'Did you have a good journey?'

'Yes, thank you,' Guastafeste replied, his voice much quieter than usual. In the refined atmosphere of the shop, it seemed almost rude to speak above a whisper.

'Monsieur Jahinny is expecting you. Please, this way.'

Delacourt opened a door at the back of the room and led us through into a vestibule, which had several other doors leading off it. One of those doors opened and a man and a woman emerged from a private consulting room. The man was dark-skinned, with the facial features of an Arab, though he was wearing Western dress. The woman was much younger, a blonde in a low-cut haute-couture dress for whom the phrase 'dripping with jewels' might have been invented. She seemed to have diamonds on every available surface of her body — dangling from her ears, round her throat, on her fingers, and even round her ankles. Behind the couple came a second man in a three-piece suit like Delacourt's

188

— presumably another shop assistant, although that description could not possibly do justice to the young man's appearance. He was tall and dark, with the smouldering good looks of an old-fashioned French movie star, the kind of actor you might have seen in newsreels from Cannes in the 1950s. He was carrying a stack of embossed leather cases, which I guessed must have contained more newly purchased additions to the blonde's already-impressive collection.

Delacourt spoke to the Arabic-looking man in French, his manner deferential to the point of servility, then stepped aside to let the group pass. We waited a moment, the blonde's cloying perfume lingering in the air, then went through one of the other doors and up a flight of stairs to an office on the first floor.

The office was large and spacious, furnished with expensive antiques — a huge leather-topped desk, mahogany chairs, an elaborate walnut chest of drawers with a marquetry front. The floor was covered in the same rich burgundy carpet as the showroom downstairs, and there were gilt-framed paintings on the walls, one a Cézanne, which I knew would be an original. Molyneux et Charbon was not the kind of firm that would have any truck with reproductions.

Monsieur Auguste Jahinny, the general manager, was a small man in his fifties. He had greying hair, a silver moustache, and close-trimmed beard, and he was wearing the dark three-piece suit and watch chain that seemed to be the standard company uniform. Perched on the end of his nose was a pair of half-moon reading glasses.

We went through the usual introductions and courtesies; then Monsieur Jahinny offered us coffee, speaking all the time in Italian.

'We don't want to put you to any trouble,' Guastafeste said.

'It is no trouble,' Monsieur Jahinny replied.

He spoke into an intercom on his desk, and a few minutes later a middle-aged woman entered with a tray of porcelain cups and a silver pot of coffee. She, too, was wearing the requisite dark suit — in her case, a jacket and skirt — but she had been spared the need for a waistcoat and watch chain. She put the tray down on the desk and left the room. Monsieur Jahinny consulted his fob watch, glancing at us anxiously, as if he feared he was being rude.

'I am timing the coffee,' he explained. 'A good-quality arabica needs at least three and a half minutes to brew, or the flavour is impaired.'

'Of course,' Guastafeste said, nodding politely in agreement.

'I am most particular about my coffee. I'm sure you are, too, being Italian. Now, while we wait, shall we get down to business? I was very sorry to hear of François Villeneuve's death. And in such horrifying circumstances, too.'

'You knew him?' Guastafeste asked.

'A little. We had occasional business dealings, but no more than that.'

Jahinny sniffed, and I thought I could detect a

hint of distaste in his expression. That was understandable. Given Villeneuve's suspect reputation, no jeweller with Jahinny's sort of clientele would want to be associated with him.

''Business dealings'?' Guastafeste said.

'He would sometimes consult us on antique jewellery that came his way. He was most knowledgeable about paintings and furniture, but jewellery was not his strong point. I saw him only last week, as a matter of fact.'

Monsieur Jahinny looked at us over his half-moon glasses.

'Interestingly enough, he also wanted to look at the records of Henri le Bley Lavelle.'

Guastafeste caught my eye, then turned back to Jahinny.

'Is that right? Did he say why?'

'He said he'd been offered an item that appeared to have been made by Le Bley Lavelle and he wanted to check its authenticity.'

'Did he tell you what the item was?' Guastafeste asked.

'No. And, of course, I didn't ask. That would not have been discreet.'

Vincenzo Serafin had said something very similar in his office, but I was more inclined to believe Monsieur Jahinny.

'And *was* the item authentic?' Guastafeste said.

'I don't know that, either. François went down into the basement — where you will shortly be going — and examined the ledgers for a time, but that is all I can tell you, I'm afraid. I hope

191

this item, whatever it is, has no relevance to his murder.'

Guastafeste didn't answer the question. He took a colour photograph from his jacket pocket and passed it across the desk to Jahinny.

'François Villeneuve placed this gold box in his hotel safe in Cremona two days before he died. We've established from the hallmarks that Le Bley Lavelle made it in 1819. I believe this may have been the item that Monsieur Villeneuve wanted to look up in your records. When was he here?'

'Last week, as I said. I think it was the Tuesday.'

'Tuesday? That was two days before Villeneuve arrived in Cremona,' Guastafeste said. 'Do you recognise the box?'

Jahinny studied the photograph.

'That is hard to tell from a photo. I have certainly seen boxes like this before. Le Bley Lavelle made a lot of gold boxes. How big is it?'

Guastafeste demonstrated with his hands.

'It has an interesting lock on it,' he said. 'A four-dial combination lock using letters rather than numbers.'

'Letters?'

'Is that unusual?'

'The lock, no. Le Bley Lavelle put combination locks on many of his boxes. They were invariably used for storing jewellery or other valuable items. A good lock would have been essential. Number combinations are the most common, but I *have* seen letter combinations before.'

'But not this particular box?'

'No. The ones I've seen were smaller than the one you describe.'

'You say they were used for storing jewellery?'

'Generally, yes. They were often made with a partitioned interior for separating the contents — rings, necklaces, brooches, and so on.'

'What about violins?'

'*Violins?*' Jahinny stared at Guastafeste.

'Did he ever make boxes for violins?'

'A violin would be far too big for a box like this.'

'A small violin.'

'I've never heard of such a thing.'

'You've looked at Le Bley Lavelle's records yourself?'

'Not in detail, no. I've consulted them occasionally, but not for several years. François Villeneuve was the first person to check the archives in a very long time.'

Jahinny glanced at his watch again. The aroma of coffee was getting stronger, tantalising my senses. I had eaten and drunk nothing since breakfast, except for a plastic beaker of a liquid on the aeroplane — which, whatever the airline chose to call it, was certainly not coffee. I was longing for a cup of the real stuff now, but Jahinny was in no hurry to serve it. At least three and a half minutes, he'd said, and he struck me as a man who would not risk going a second too soon.

'Perhaps you could tell us a little about Henri le Bley Lavelle?' Guastafeste said.

'Yes, of course,' Jahinny replied. 'He was one

of the finest French goldsmiths of the late eighteenth and early nineteenth centuries — which is to say, he was one of the finest in the world. Paris then was the centre of the international jewellery business, the home of the greatest, most renowned jewellers.' He paused to allow himself a modest smile. '*Plus ça change* . . . He had a workshop not far from here, in the rue Saint-Honoré, and worked to commission for most of Europe's aristocracy, including a number of crowned heads.'

'We believe this box was made for Napoléon's sister Elisa Baciocchi,' Guastafeste said.

'That wouldn't surprise me. He made jewellery for all the Bonaparte family — Princess Caroline, Princess Pauline, the Empress Josephine. He was a master craftsman whose work was highly prized — and highly priced, too. You say this box is hallmarked 1819? He would have been at his peak about then. Those two decades, from about 1810 to 1830, produced his best work. After 1830, he went into decline. When he died, in 1838, his business was taken over by two other goldsmiths, Molyneux and Charbon, whose names still adorn the firm to this day.'

Jahinny made a final check on the gold watch in his fob pocket and leaned forward towards the silver coffeepot.

'Let us drink our coffee now,' he said. 'Then I will ask Monsieur Delacourt to show you the archives.'

★ ★ ★

The basement of the Molyneux et Charbon premises was a complete contrast to the rest of the building. There was no carpet on the floor, just bare stone flags, and the lighting was supplied by a couple of unshaded sixty-watt bulbs dangling from cables that were wreathed in cobwebs. Instead of the heady scent of Chanel and money, there was an unpleasant smell of damp mixed with a sharper, more noxious odour that seemed to be seeping up from the sewers.

'I'm afraid this isn't a very salubrious place,' Olivier Delacourt said apologetically. 'We rarely come down here, as you can see.'

'How do we find the records for 1819?' Guastafeste asked.

'I'll show you.'

Delacourt moved off into the stacks of shelves that ran the full length of the basement, each shelf laden with leather-bound ledgers and dusty cardboard boxes.

'There's no real filing system,' Delacourt said. 'No one has ever catalogued every item that's down here; it would be a simply enormous task. The records are arranged in a rough chronological order, but I couldn't guarantee that what you're looking for is here.'

'Monsieur Jahinny said that François Villeneuve came in last week. Do you know what he looked at?'

'I'm sorry, no. I brought him down and left him. I will have to leave you, too, if that's all right. I have clients to see.'

'Yes, thank you for your help.'

We waited until Delacourt had gone, then

turned to the shelves. There must have been hundreds of volumes to go through.

'*Dio*,' Guastafeste said. 'I'm not sure this was such a good idea now. Where do we begin?'

'Can you see any dates on these ledgers?' I asked.

'No, they all look the same to me.'

I pulled out a volume. It was heavy, too heavy to hold up for long, so I propped one end up on the edge of the shelf and opened the cover. Written on the first page in a large, elegant hand were the words 'January 1823-March 1823.'

'They look like quarterly records,' I said. 'Four books for each year.'

'How could one man produce so much stuff?' Guastafeste said.

'He wouldn't have done it all alone. He'd have been like the great violin makers or painters. He'd have had apprentices, assistants who did the bulk of the work, but it would all have had Le Bley Lavelle's name on it.'

Guastafeste walked along the stack, counting off the ledgers.

'This should be 1819.'

He pulled out a volume and opened it.

'April 1827. Wrong way,' he said. 'Try your end.'

I lifted down a ledger at random and checked inside it. 'October 1820.'

'We're in the wrong stack.'

We moved into the next row of shelves and took down various volumes, finding three that related to 1819.

'The third quarter is missing,' Guastafeste

said. 'We've got January to March, April to June, and October to December, but nothing for July to September. What was the date on the letter Elisa wrote to Paganini? Can you remember?'

'September 1819,' I said.

'That was when she sent him the gold box, but would Le Bley Lavelle have made it in that same quarter, or earlier in the year?'

'It can't have been much earlier. Paganini didn't write the 'Moses Fantasy' until the late spring. But we can check.'

We carried the ledgers to the end of the stacks, where there was a small table and a single chair. Guastafeste insisted I take the chair, while he stood beside me. I opened the volume for the second quarter of 1819 and leafed through it. The pages were yellow and curling at the edges, many of them stuck together due to the damp atmosphere in the basement. Some pages were disfigured by blotches of blue mould and all of them were thickly coated with dust.

Molyneux et Charbon's filing system may have been nonexistent, but there was nothing sloppy about the records Henri le Bley Lavelle had kept almost two hundred years before. There were meticulous entries for each item of jewellery he, or his team of assistants, had made, from small gold chains through to whole silver dinner services. Every piece of metal and every jewel was documented and costed; there were detailed drawings of each item, and every stage of the production process had been approved and signed off by Le Bley Lavelle himself. A simple gold ring might have only a couple of pages of information about it, but a larger item — a necklace or a jewel-encrusted bracelet — could have nine or ten pages devoted to its creation.

I prised apart the pages, taking care not to tear them, and went through the whole ledger. There were records for several gold boxes, but not one that matched the box François Villeneuve had placed in his hotel safe.

'It's not here,' I said.

'*Merda*!' Guastafeste said. 'So it must be in the missing volume. Do you think Villeneuve took it away with him?'

'He'd have had a job. It's not exactly something he could shove up his shirt and walk out with.'

'Maybe no one noticed.'

'A place like this? You saw the security upstairs — the locks, alarms, cameras. No, it must still be down here somewhere.'

Guastafeste looked round the basement, appalled at the prospect of having to search all the shelves.

'We could be here for weeks,' he said.

'Let's think it through,' I said. 'Work out what Villeneuve would have done. He's found the volume he's searching for, so what does he do? They're heavy books. He wouldn't stand by the shelf looking through it. He'd do what we've done. Bring the book to this table and examine it here.'

'Okay, that makes sense. But then what? Where did the book go after that?'

'He must have put it back.'

'Then why isn't it on the shelf?'

198

'But not necessarily in the exact place he found it. Let's assume he'd got what he came for and had no plans to come back. He didn't need to find that volume again. You've been in libraries. Have you never dumped a book on a table or the wrong shelf because you couldn't be bothered to return it to its proper place?'

'So Villeneuve . . .'

Guastafeste turned and scanned the nearest stack of shelves. Most of the space was given over to cardboard boxes, but on the middle shelf of the stack was a small collection of four or five ledgers, tilted over at an angle.

'One of those?' Guastafeste said.

He moved towards the stack.

'The one on the far right,' I said.

'How do you know?'

'Look at the spines. Most of them are caked in dust. They haven't been disturbed for years. But that one has finger marks in the dust. You see them? They're catching the light.'

'You should have been a detective, Gianni.'

Guastafeste removed the ledger from the shelf and flipped back the cover. He grinned at me.

'July to September, 1819.'

He brought the volume over to the table and I went through it page by page. Midway in, we found what we were looking for — an entry dated August 6, and headed 'A fine gold box with engraved lid and other decorations. Client: the Comtesse de Compignano.'

'That's not Elisa Baciocchi,' Guastafeste said.

'It's what she was calling herself in 1819. She was no longer a princess, just a mere countess.'

There was confirmation that I was right on the following pages — a series of detailed drawings of Moses on Mount Sinai for the engraver to copy, and then a drawing of a wooden insert in the shape of a violin. The exact dimensions of the insert were given, accompanied by specifications for the colour and thickness of the velvet with which the insert was to be lined.

Guastafeste leaned over the table, studying the drawing.

'I can't see any information about the violin it was intended for,' he said.

'Nor can I.'

I flipped over the page. There was a list of costings for each stage of the box's construction — the underlying metal shell, which wasn't gold, then the gold veneer, the combination lock, the engraving, the pine for the insert, the velvet, even the glue used to secure the velvet, the total coming to 3,200 francs. Everything was recorded in minute detail, the entries written out in a neat copperplate hand, probably with a quill pen. It was clear that Henri le Bley Lavelle had been very particular about record keeping.

'That's a pity,' Guastafeste said disconsolately. 'I was hoping for a maker's name, maybe a description of the violin.'

I peered closer at the ledger.

'What's that there? I can't read it.'

I touched the page with my finger. There was one entry that was uncharacteristically untidy and written in a different hand to the others. It had been inserted between two entries, just below the costings for the velvet lining.

Guastafeste bent lower, focusing on the cramped, spidery handwriting. 'I think it says 'Voyez la princesse de Piombino et Lucca.''

I felt a sudden jolt of excitement.

'Elisa! What's that after her name? A date?'

'October 1807.'

'And the rest?'

'That's hard to make out. It looks like 'Jeremiah' and then another word. 'Posier'? Is that right? Jeremiah Posier. Does that mean anything to you?'

'No.'

'He's not a violin maker?'

'I've certainly never heard of him.'

''See the princess of Piombino and Lucca, October 1807,'' Guastafeste said. 'That was when Paganini was in Lucca, wasn't it?'

'Yes. And when Elisa gave him the other gift she mentioned in her letter.'

'Let's find the ledger for October 1807.'

We went back into the stacks and searched the shelves, pulling out volume after volume until our hands were black with grime and our nostrils choked with dust. But the ledger for October 1807 wasn't there.

'It could be in one of these cardboard boxes, I suppose,' Guastafeste said. 'Or simply lost. We can't expect every record to be here, not after two centuries.'

I gazed at him for a moment.

'You know, we're a pair of idiots,' I said.

'What?'

'Villeneuve looked at the 1819 ledger. He'd

have seen that note about Elisa just as we did.'

I went back to the first stack by the table, and examined the small collection of ledgers on the middle shelf. I should have noticed it earlier: One of the other volumes had finger marks on the spine. I pulled it out and opened it on the table. It was the 1807 ledger we'd been searching for.

I turned over the pages. Almost immediately I found the one we needed. Or rather, I didn't find it. One of the pages had been roughly torn out of the ledger, leaving behind a strip of jagged paper. I could tell from the pale colour of the torn edge that the page had been recently removed.

'Villeneuve?' Guastafeste said.

'Who else could it have been?' I replied.

Guastafeste swore.

'Well, that scuppers that particular line of enquiry.'

'Maybe, maybe not,' I said. 'What's this here?'

I was studying the next page in the ledger. It was a continuation of the record that had begun on the missing page. There were only a few lines of handwriting. One of them read 'Repair to underside of item completed, October 6. Posier hallmarks undamaged.'

There was then a short table of figures, with a total underneath of 150 francs. Below that were the words 'Item despatched to Her Highness, October 8,' followed by the initials HLBL, where Le Bley Lavelle had approved the record.

' 'Her Highness' — that has to be Elisa,' I said. 'This doesn't look like a new commission. Elisa has obviously sent something to Le Bley Lavelle to be repaired. Probably only minor repairs, too — one hundred and fifty francs, that doesn't sound a lot. And the item, whatever it was, was made originally by Jeremiah Posier.'

'I don't understand,' Guastafeste said. 'This is jewellery, not a violin. It can't be what we're looking for.'

'It must have some connection with Paganini's gold box. Why else would there be that cross-reference in the ledger? And why else would François Villeneuve have torn out this page?'

* * *

We didn't linger in the basement. The dust and the damp were beginning to irritate our throats, making us cough. Besides, we'd done all we could there. It was possible that there was more information about the gold box to be found — perhaps in one of the many cardboard boxes — but neither of us felt like looking for it. Guastafeste, in any case, had an alternative plan of action.

'Villeneuve's partner, Alain Robillet,' he said. 'He must know what Villeneuve was up to. Let's go and talk to him.'

We went back upstairs and encountered Olivier Delacourt outside one of the consulting rooms.

'You have finished?' he asked.

'Yes, thank you,' Guastafeste replied.

'You found what you were looking for?'

'Not everything. A page had been torn out of

one of the ledgers — October 1807.'

Delacourt looked shocked.

'Torn out? By François Villeneuve?'

'I presume so.'

'That's disgraceful. Thank you for telling me. I will look into it.'

'And one other thing,' Guastafeste said. 'Have you heard of a goldsmith or jeweller named Jeremiah Posier?'

'Posier? No, I don't think so.'

'He was working round the beginning of the nineteenth century, or earlier.'

'I'm sorry, no, the name is unfamiliar to me.'

'Might Monsieur Jahinny know?'

'Monsieur Jahinny has had to go and see a client. I, too, am engaged at the moment, but please allow me to show you out.'

Delacourt tapped in a code on the keypad beside the door and ushered us into the showroom. A red button on the wall unlocked the front door. Delacourt shook hands, wished us good day, then closed the door behind us and hurried back to his customer.

Guastafeste and I walked the short distance to the Ritz Hotel and took one of the waiting taxis to an address in the Marais, the area between the Centre Pompidou and the Bastille, a neighbourhood that half a century ago had been full of dilapidated mansions and squalid tenement buildings but which had then been redeveloped and gentrified by the middle classes, who had brought with them their penchant for art galleries, chic apartments, and interior-design shops.

The premises from which François Villeneuve and Alain Robillet conducted their affairs were on the less fashionable fringes of the Marais, where some of the original character of the area still remained. The bars and shops here were less trendy, the buildings a touch shabbier. It had the feel of a real working commercial district rather than a spread from a lifestyle magazine. Villeneuve and Robillet's business had a frontage on the street — two large plate-glass windows with a sign above reading FINE ART and ANTIQUES — but there weren't many items on display. One window contained just a chest of drawers and a sideboard, the other a single easel on which a gloomy oil painting of a biblical scene was perched. It was only four o'clock in the afternoon, but the place looked shut up for the night. The lights were off and the steel security grilles had been lowered over the outside of the windows.

Guastafeste tried the front door. It was locked. I put my face to the pane and peered through the glass. I could see a large room inside, displays of furniture and other antiques stretching away into the darkness.

'There doesn't seem to be anyone here,' I said.

'Let's try round the back,' Guastafeste said.

We walked down the access road at the side of the building and into a scruffy rear yard. A big furniture van was parked against a wall. Next to it was a grey Peugeot saloon that was in need of a wash. I glanced up at the building, the windows overlooking the yard. There were no lights on here, either. The back door of the premises was ajar. Guastafeste pushed it open and we stepped through into a storage area that was piled high with old furniture. A flight of metal stairs with open treads led up to the floor above. We went up them.

The landing at the top was dim and narrow, the floor covered with dirty lino. A trickle of feeble daylight seeped out from a door to our left. Guastafeste pushed open the door.

'Hello, Monsieur Robillet?' he called.

There was an office inside — a desk, a chair, a few metal filing cabinets — but no sign of Alain Robillet. Guastafeste walked across the office towards the window. He stopped abruptly and I heard his sharp intake of breath.

'What's the matter?'

'Stay where you are, Gianni,' Guastafeste said calmly. 'And don't touch anything.'

'What?'

'Just do as I say.'

Guastafeste went round the desk and looked down. I edged sideways, then wished I hadn't. On the floor by the window was a man's body. I could see only his head and part of his shoulders, but that was more than enough. On the side of his head, above the ear, was a dark open wound. His face was streaked with congealed blood.

12

I have no clear memory of exactly what happened after that. I can vaguely recall Guastafeste taking me by the arm and guiding me downstairs and into the yard. I felt sick and faint, but the fresh air alleviated the nausea. I sat on a wooden chair that Guastafeste brought out from the storeroom and followed his instructions to breathe in and out slowly and deeply. He had his mobile phone in his hand by that point and was calling the police. I heard his voice, but the words didn't register: They were just a blur of indistinct sounds.

My sense of time must have been impaired, for it seemed only a few seconds later that the first police cars arrived. Suddenly, the yard was swarming with people: uniformed officers, plainclothes detectives, men in white boiler suits carrying cases of forensic equipment. I was moved out of the way and left alone in a corner of the yard while Guastafeste went back inside the building with the policemen. Fifteen minutes later he emerged alone and came over to me.

'How are you feeling, Gianni?'

'I'm all right. It was just a bit of a shock.'

'I can get you some medical attention, if you need it.'

'No, that won't be necessary. I'm fine now. What's happening?'

'The usual scene-of-crime investigations. The

officer in charge wants us to stick around for a while, in case he has any questions, then go over to police headquarters to make statements. We'll probably have to give them our fingerprints, too, to eliminate them from the enquiry.

'We're not suspects?'

'No, certainly not.'

'We found the body.'

'He's been dead for some time.'

'How can you tell?'

'Experience. The look of the body, the blood on the floor. I'll wait for the police doctor's verdict, but I'd say it happened several hours ago.'

'Is it Alain Robillet?'

'I don't know. Probably.'

I shuddered.

'First Villeneuve, now his partner. That's frightening.'

'There's nothing for you to worry about,' Guastafeste said reassuringly.

'He must be a desperate man, the killer. Two murders in a matter of a few days.'

'We don't know that it was the same person.'

'You mean there might be *two* killers?'

'Let's not get into that right now.'

More vehicles were pulling into the yard — a couple of unmarked police cars, another white transit van. The area round the back door of the building had been cordoned off with tape. We watched the officers coming and going, Guastafeste fidgeting impatiently beside my chair. He wasn't accustomed to being a spectator at incidents like this. I knew he wanted to go inside and see what was going on.

The light was starting to fade. The yard, a dingy little enclosure at the best of times, was filling with dusky shadows. It was getting colder. I pulled my jacket tight across my chest and plunged my hands into the pockets. Guastafeste sensed the movement and turned to look at me.

'I'm sorry, Gianni; I should have thought. You must be freezing out here. I'll have a word with someone.'

He strode across to the cordon and spoke briefly to the uniformed officer guarding the entrance to the building. Another officer was called over and given instructions. Half a minute later I was being led to one of the unmarked cars and installed comfortably in the rear seats, the doors closed and the heater on, pumping warm air round my chilled body. Guastafeste joined me shortly afterwards.

'It shouldn't be long now,' he said. 'Someone's going to drive us over to the quai des Orfèvres.'

In fact, it was nearly forty minutes before a plainclothes detective pulled open the driver's door and slid in behind the wheel. He glanced over his shoulder at us but didn't say anything, just started the engine and manoeuvred the car out of the yard, past all the parked vehicles. The journey to the ile de la Cité took only a few minutes. We were escorted inside police head-quarters and gave our statements to a female officer seated at a computer terminal. Neither Guastafeste nor I spoke fluent French, but we had enough between us to provide a reasonably coherent account of what we'd seen. Our fingerprints were taken; then we waited in an anteroom for a further hour before an older, weary-looking plainclothes detective arrived. I recognised him from the crime scene.

'I'm Inspector Forbin,' he said. 'I'm sorry to keep you. These things take time.'

'We understand,' Guastafeste replied. 'Was it Alain Robillet?'

Forbin shrugged.

'We think so. He had credit cards in his wallet that would seem to confirm it, but we can't be absolutely sure until the body has been formally identified. We haven't found anyone to do that yet.'

'Was he married?'

'We don't know. We're trying to trace the next of kin.'

'And the time of death?'

'This morning, between nine A.M. and noon, the doctor reckons.'

'The shop looked closed when we got there,' Guastafeste said. 'Are there no staff?'

'We spoke to a woman across the street. She said the place had been shut up since the weekend.'

'Since François Villeneuve was killed?'

'That's right.' Forbin looked at his watch. 'Where are you staying?'

We gave him the name and address of our hotel.

'And you're going back to Italy when?'

'Tomorrow morning. Is that all right?'

'I'll call you first thing if I need to ask you

anything else. I'll get someone to drive you to your hotel.'

We were both in sombre moods that evening. We had dinner in a small restaurant near our hotel, but neither of us was much inclined to talk. I was still shaken by the afternoon's events, and even Guastafeste, who is no stranger to homicide enquiries, seemed troubled by what he'd witnessed. Any death is disturbing, a violent death particularly so. Guastafeste had seen bodies before. He'd had to deal with the emotional consequences of that. But this was different. On this occasion, he was closer to the distressing events. He wasn't a police officer being called in afterwards — he had actually *found* the body. And what made things worse for him, I suspected, was the fact that in Paris he was an outsider — in effect, a civilian. He couldn't distract himself with the practical demands of an investigation. He had to stand by impotent on the sidelines while others took charge.

I slept badly, troubled by the harrowing images of Alain Robillet on his office floor, and got up early next morning. When I went down to the hotel dining room, Guastafeste was already there, drinking black coffee and chewing pensively on a croissant.

'How did you sleep?' he asked.

'Not well. You?'

'The same.'

'I kept seeing the body,' I said.

Guastafeste nodded sympathetically.

'I told you to keep back.'

211

'I know, but I was curious. I never expected to see . . . well, something as bad as that.'

Guastafeste finished his croissant and drank some coffee. The waiter came to the table and I ordered a *café crème*.

'Do you mind flying back on your own?' Guastafeste said. 'I want to stay on for a few hours. I'm going to see Forbin, talk to him about the case, see if there's anything here that can help us with our investigations in Cremona.'

'No, I don't mind,' I said. 'Our tickets are open, aren't they? We can take any flight?'

'Yes. I'll probably go back this evening.'

'I'm going to go back later, too.'

'Gianni, you don't have to wait for me.'

'No, it's not that. I want to find out more about Jeremiah Posier.'

'How are you going to do that? Go to a library?'

'I thought I'd go to London.'

'To *London?*'

'You remember my old friend Rudy Weigert?'

'The auctioneer? But he's a violin expert. What does he know about jewellery?'

'Very little, probably. But he works for one of the world's biggest auction houses. He'll have a colleague who's a jewellery expert.'

'Well, if you want to . . . How are you going to get there? Fly?'

'I'll take the train. There's a high-speed rail link now. I can be there for lunch.'

★ ★ ★

In retrospect, it was perhaps a mistake. I'd forgotten just what the word *lunch* meant to Rudy Weigert. To me, it was a light meal to be consumed quickly and without fuss — in the kitchen of my house or, quite frequently, at my workbench. To Rudy, it was an excuse for an orgy of gluttony on a scale rarely seen since the end of the Roman Empire.

I exaggerate, of course, but only a little. Rudy was an epicure, and he had the figure to prove it. On a tall man, his stomach would have been an impressive sight. On Rudy, who was only five five, it was a miracle of anatomical engineering. Quite how he carried such a heavy load round was a mystery, perhaps explained by the fact that he generally *didn't* carry it, at least not very far. From his office on the third floor of a modern block off Piccadilly, we took the lift to the foyer, then a taxi to the restaurant he'd booked, which turned out to be less than a hundred metres away — though, given the traffic, it took us close to five minutes to get there. By the time we were seated at our table, we had probably walked no farther than twenty metres in total and burned off, at a guess, half a calorie — if that.

'We should have walked,' I said.

'*Walked?*' Rudy said in a horrified voice, raising one of his caterpillar eyebrows. 'Are you serious?'

'It would have done us good.'

'What, inhaling all those exhaust fumes? No, the only way to stay healthy in London is to avoid exercise altogether, unless it involves the intensive lifting of a knife and fork. Why don't we have a cocktail, to celebrate your arrival?'

Rudy called the waiter over and ordered two martinis.

'Stirred, *not* shaken, you understand?' he emphasised, turning to me when the waiter had gone and saying, 'You've got to watch these wretched barmen, waving cocktail shakers about as if they were maracas. James Bond has a lot to answer for, if you ask me. Alcohol is a very delicate liquid. Any fool knows that shaking it violently destroys the subtlety of the taste. A gentle stir is all that's required.'

Rudy settled himself back in his chair and looked at me.

'How are you, Gianni? You're looking well.'

'I'm feeling well. And you?'

'I can't complain.'

'How's business?'

'Thriving.'

'Sales are holding up?'

'There's a lot of competition, but we're doing fine, particularly at the top end of the market. There are bucketloads of money pouring in from Russia — mostly Mafia loot, but if we turned away customers because they were crooks, we'd be bankrupt by now. And all those new Chinese millionaires are starting to take an interest, too. Property's taking a bit of a hit at the moment, but you can't beat fine art as an investment. An old master, a Strad, they'll always keep their value. I'll take you into the workshops later. We've just had this beautiful Goffriller violin in — two-piece back with a rich red-brown varnish. Dated 1708, but in remarkably good condition. I

214

expect great things of it at the next sale.'

Auctioneers have a reputation for avarice, but the money per se was genuinely unimportant to Rudy. He saw high prices as a vindication of his love for violins, a confirmation of their true worth. If jewellery or antiques or old paintings could fetch a fortune in the saleroom, then it was only right that violins — which were, after all, vastly superior in every possible way to those other types of object — should do the same.

Our drinks arrived, accompanied by little dishes of olives, nuts, and crisps. The waiter handed us both menus, but Rudy didn't even open his.

'I already know what I'm having. The Stilton and walnut tart, followed by a steak. The steaks here are excellent, by the way. A good sixteen ounces or more. That's what in metric? Five hundred grams?'

'Five hundred grams?' I said. 'Half a kilo of meat?'

'Tempting, isn't it?'

'What happened to your diet?'

The last time I'd seen Rudy, he'd claimed to be on a diet, though not one recognisable to a nutritionist.

'Oh, I'm still on it,' Rudy said blithely. 'It's absolute hell. That's why I'm glad you're here. I can have a decent lunch for once without feeling guilty.'

'When was the last time you had a decent lunch?'

'The day before yesterday, I believe. Two days is a long time when you're starving. We'll have a couple of bottles of the Puligny-Montrachet, shall we?'

'Two? Rudy, I can't possibly drink that much wine, especially at lunchtime.'

'Don't worry, I'll help you.'

'When do you have to be back in the office?'

'Oh, sometime this afternoon. You know, the English work the longest hours in Europe, and take the shortest lunch breaks.'

'Well, there's no fear of that with you.'

Rudy laughed.

'We live in an age of fast food and indigestion. In my own way, I'm a one-man resistance movement — though I use the word *movement* with caution.'

He gave a signal to the sommelier and ordered the wine. Then he spiked a black olive with a cocktail stick and chewed it. He smiled at me warmly.

'It's good to see you, Gianni. Really good. I've arranged for us to meet Rupert Rhys-Jones later this afternoon. He's our jewellery expert. Very nice chap. Knows his stuff. Welsh, but we don't hold that against him. So what's this all about? Why are you suddenly interested in jewellery?'

I'd been discreet in my phone call to Rudy from Paris, but now I told him everything that had happened since François Villeneuve had been found dead in his hotel room.

'My goodness!' Rudy exclaimed. 'You *have* been having an exciting few days. And this second man, the partner, you actually *found* his body?'

'I don't want to think about that bit,' I said. 'A

216

body, another murder investigation, I didn't expect anything like that. Antonio brought me along only because he's convinced that a violin is somewhere at the bottom of all this.'

'You sound sceptical. You don't agree with him?'

'I don't know what to make of it. You know the business better than anyone, Rudy. Have you ever seen or heard of a violin small enough to fit in a gold box about this size?' I held out my hands to show him the dimensions.

'Just once,' Rudy said. 'A variety performer I saw many years ago. A very good violinist. He had a tiny violin like that as part of his act — the world's smallest violin. He could play it, too, though it didn't make much of a sound.'

'Paganini was a showman. He wouldn't have had a little violin like that, would he? To amuse his audiences.'

I knew that Paganini often broke up his concerts with interludes in which he would make animal sounds on his violin — a cock crowing, a dog howling, a cat screeching, that kind of thing. On one occasion, in Ferrara, after someone in the audience whistled at the soprano who was sharing the platform, Paganini retaliated by imitating a braying ass — a particularly offensive insult to the locals, who had historically been known as donkeys — and had to be given a police escort from the city to protect him from the mob. I could see that a tiny violin might have appealed to the virtuoso as a publicity gimmick.

'If he'd had anything like that, we'd know about it,' Rudy said. 'There are plenty of eyewitness accounts of his concerts. His playing on a full-size instrument was spectacular enough. He didn't need anything more to captivate the public.'

'That's what I think, too. I've a feeling we're on the wrong track. I'm hoping your colleague might be able to help us get back on course.'

We had our starters; then Rudy had his slice of cow and I a grilled Dover sole before we moved on to dessert and cheese and coffee. It was half-past three when we left the restaurant and returned to Rudy's office. I was so stuffed, I was glad of the taxi this time. Rudy offered me a cognac from his well-stocked drinks cabinet, but I declined.

'You go ahead,' I said. 'But I'd like to be sober when I meet Rupert Rhys-Jones.'

'Oh, Rupert deals a lot with the landed gentry. He's used to drunks,' Rudy replied.

He filled a tumbler with Rémy Martin and brought it with him as we walked along the corridor to Rupert Rhys-Jones's office.

Rhys-Jones was younger than I'd expected — in his mid-to late thirties, a rather delicate-looking man with long, slender fingers and steel-rimmed spectacles over his pale blue watery eyes. He shook hands limply and retreated behind his desk, which, like the rest of his office, was spotlessly tidy.

'How can I help you?' he said.

I told him about the gold box and my visit to Molyneux et Charbon in Paris. Jones nodded, making a steeple of his fingers and resting his chin on it.

'Yes, I'm familiar with Henri le Bley Lavelle,' he said. 'An excellent craftsman. His work comes up for auction quite frequently. The prices are respectable, but nothing special. He's a bit out of fashion at the moment. Modern buyers find him a little — well, *vulgar* isn't too strong a word. His designs are very ornate, almost gaudy. People these days want something simpler.'

'This gold box is quite plain,' I said. 'Though it has a fairly elaborate engraving on the lid. It's what's inside that puzzles me. There's a velvet-lined wooden insert with a cutout in the middle in the shape of a violin.'

'But no violin?' Rhys-Jones said.

'No, but the box was obviously made for one. It was a gift from Elisa Baciocchi, Napoléon's sister, to Paganini, so the violin link makes sense. What doesn't make sense is the size of the box. It's far too small for any violin I have ever seen.'

'And Rudy?'

Rhys-Jones turned his head to look at Rudy, who was slumped back in an armchair, sipping his tumbler of cognac.

'It's a mystery to me, too,' he said.

'Elisa gave Paganini another gift, many years earlier,' I said. 'We don't know what it was, but in Le Bley Lavelle's records there was a mention of a Jeremiah Posier, who seems to have been another jeweller.'

Rupert Rhys-Jones went very still. He stared at me, his eyes unblinking behind the thick lenses of his glasses.

'Jeremiah Posier?' he said slowly.

'Yes.'

219

'You're sure about that?'

'Yes. Why? Who was he?'

Rhys-Jones licked his lips.

'Jeremiah Posier? A violin?' he said. 'Dear God, it can't be. Surely not.' His voice had gone suddenly hoarse.

'Can't be what?' I said.

Rhys-Jones didn't appear to hear me. He gazed at me as if he were in a trance for a few seconds, then rose to his feet and went to the bookshelves on the wall. He took down a massive tome about sixty centimetres tall and a good ten centimetres thick. I'd seen books like it in Rudy's office — I had one or two of them myself. They weren't intended for sale to the general public; they were limited-edition reference books for fine-arts specialists and cost several hundred, sometimes several thousand, euros each.

Rhys-Jones put the tome down on his desk and I saw the title: *Goldsmiths and Jewellers of the Eighteenth Century.* He ran his finger down the list of contents, stopping at a name near the bottom, then turned to a chapter at the end of the book.

'Jeremiah Posier,' he said. 'Court jeweller to Catherine the Great of Russia, and probably the finest goldsmith of his era. He made the great imperial crown for Catherine's coronation in 1762. That's it there.'

He showed me a photograph of the crown.

'It's a Byzantine design — two half spheres, to represent the two continents spanned by Catherine's empire, studded with four thousand nine hundred and thirty-six diamonds, though we generally round that figure up to five thousand. There are pearls along the edges, and a beautiful red gem on the top that's usually referred to as a ruby but is, in fact, a red spinel, a semiprecious stone that you don't find very often in Western European jewellery but which was highly prized in the East. This particular specimen weighs nearly four hundred carats and was brought to Saint Petersburg by Nicholas Spafary, the Russian envoy to China in the late seventeenth century.'

Rhys-Jones lifted his head and gazed at me again. I could sense his excitement.

'The imperial crown is undoubtedly the most spectacular piece of jewellery Posier produced for Catherine, but it wasn't the only item he made her. You have heard of Giovanni Battista Viotti, of course? The great Italian virtuoso violinist. In 1780, he went on a concert tour that took him to Saint Petersburg, where he played for the Empress Catherine. Catherine was not a great lover of music, but she was a great lover of young men. And Viotti was young. In his twenties, handsome and prodigiously gifted. He became the empress's lover and stayed in Russia for a year. When he finally left the country, Catherine — who was famously generous to her paramours — gave him a gift of a jewel-encrusted gold violin that had been specially made by Posier.'

'A gold violin?' I said.

Rupert Rhys-Jones nodded.

'Solid gold and studded with diamonds, rubies, and emeralds.'

He turned over two or three of the thick, glossy pages of the book to reveal a full-colour drawing of the violin. Rudy heaved himself up from his armchair and came to look, too.

'My God, that is exquisite!' he exclaimed.

'Isn't it just?' Rhys-Jones said.

I looked at the drawing. The violin it depicted was about twenty centimetres long and not much thicker than a finger. The vertical sides — the ribs of a normal violin — were studded with diamonds, and round the top edge, where the purfling would usually be, was a continuous row of bloodred rubies. Four more rubies were inlaid into the head of the violin to represent the pegs, and down the centre of the instrument, instead of strings, were four lines of emeralds. Even in the two-dimensional drawing, the jewels seemed to sparkle with light.

'Catherine the Great gave this to Viotti?' I asked.

'That's right,' Rhys-Jones said.

'And what happened to it?'

'No one knows. Viotti took it away from Russia with him; then it disappeared. No one has seen it for the last two hundred years.'

'It's stunning,' Rudy said. 'Where did the drawing come from?'

'From Posier's workshop. He kept a record of it. There are forty diamonds and forty rubies round the edges, each weighing more than a carat, and eighty small Siberian emeralds down the middle. Those four red stones at the head aren't rubies; they're red diamonds, an incredibly rare gem.'

'What would it be worth today?' Rudy asked.

'That craftsmanship, with that provenance,' Rhys-Jones replied. 'I wouldn't dare name a price. The last time a red diamond was auctioned, in America — one weighing less than a carat — it went for nearly a million dollars. Those four red diamonds alone are probably worth five million dollars. And then you've got the other diamonds and the rubies and emeralds, not to mention Posier's cachet. Put it in an auction, I couldn't see it going for less than twenty million dollars, maybe fifteen million pounds, depending on the exchange rate.'

I gazed at the drawing, taking in the delicate golden scroll, the curving lines of brilliant jewels. I knew now what we were looking for. And I knew why François Villeneuve and Alain Robillet had been killed.

13

I spent the night at Rudy's home in the Buckinghamshire countryside, thirty miles northwest of London. Rudy's wife, Ruth, no doubt aware of her husband's lunchtime proclivities, gave us a light dinner of poached salmon and salad; then Rudy and I spent a happy couple of hours playing violin duets, with Ruth accompanying us on the piano.

Both the Weigerts were accomplished musicians. They'd met as students at the Royal Academy. Rudy had realised shortly after graduation that he wasn't cut out for the drudgery of life as a rank-and-file orchestral violinist and had found himself a job with a London violin-dealing firm. Ruth, the more talented of the two, had stuck with music, building a solid career for herself as an accompanist and chamber musician before the arrival of their children — twins, a boy and a girl — had disrupted the settled pattern of their lives.

Ruth's career, by choice, was the one that was sacrificed to the demands of a family. She scaled down her playing commitments for a period, then, finding the trick of juggling children and work too demanding, gave up altogether — not without a sense of relief. She'd suffered badly from concert nerves and had always found performing stressful. With Rudy earning a decent salary, she was content to stay at home with the twins, keeping her hand in by doing some keyboard teaching on the side.

She was still a formidable pianist, putting Rudy and me to shame with her dexterity, her phenomenal gift for sight-reading any piece that was placed before her, no matter how difficult. We played the Bach double-violin concerto, then duets by Vivaldi, Shostakovich, and Moszkowski, Rudy lending me his Gagliano, while he contented himself with one of the lesser instruments from his collection.

It was eleven o'clock when Ruth excused herself to go to bed.

'I'll see you in the morning, Gianni,' she said. She kissed Rudy. 'Don't stay up too long.'

'We're just going to have a little chat. Business, you know.'

'Yes, I know,' Ruth said dryly. 'Just don't have too many glasses of it.'

She left the music room and headed upstairs. Rudy and I went along the hall to his study and Rudy got out a bottle of malt whisky and poured us each a generous measure. The curtains were open, the light from the room spilling out over the patio and the lawn beyond. On the skyline, I could see the undulating silhouette of the Chiltern Hills.

We talked about violins and I recounted my experience with the Cannon and Yevgeny Ivanov.

'You played it?' Rudy said. 'You played Paganini's violin? You crafty old devil, Gianni. What was it like?'

'Incredible. But slightly odd.'

'Odd? In what way?'

'I felt like an impostor, a trespasser. You know, like an uninvited guest at a party. There's an English word for that, isn't there?'

'A gate-crasher.'

'That's right. That's how I felt. Like a gate-crasher. I knew I shouldn't have been doing it, but I couldn't resist.'

'What utter nonsense. When you repair a violin, don't you always try it out afterwards, to make sure the repair is good? So what's the difference?'

'I know, it doesn't make sense. But Paganini is the difference. Just to touch his instrument, never mind play it, sent shivers down my back. I was unworthy of such a distinguished violin. I got this feeling that Paganini was looking over my shoulder all the time I was playing it, screaming, 'Stop! Stop. I can't take any more of this appalling din.''

Rudy laughed.

'He wasn't a god, Gianni. He was a man — and a pretty disreputable man at that.'

'But he played the violin like a god.'

'For his time, yes. But he'd be nothing special today.'

'You think not? I'm not so sure.'

'Things have moved on. The standard of playing is higher than it's ever been. In Paganini's day, only Paganini could play Paganini. Now, every student at Juilliard, or the Royal Academy, or the Moscow Conservatoire can play it. I'll wager that Yevgeny Ivanov plays Paganini better than Paganini did.'

'He was certainly pretty impressive. He's

disappeared, you know.'

Rudy frowned at me.

'Ivanov? What do you mean?'

I told him what had happened, described my encounters with Yevgeny and his mother, his disappearance from the hotel, and his bizarre phone call to me.

'Sounds as if he's cracked up,' Rudy said. 'Had some kind of a nervous breakdown. Either that or there's a woman somewhere.'

'A woman?'

'My guiding principle of human nature — sex. A man does something strange, acts out of character, there's always a woman involved. And vice versa, of course. Or a man, I suppose. He's not gay, is he?'

'I know nothing about his sexuality,' I said.

'It wouldn't surprise me. I know it's crude amateur psychology, but men with overbearing mothers like that, well, they're often gay, aren't they? Poor boy. It's child abuse, really, isn't it, what he's had to go through.'

'That's a bit extreme, don't you think?'

'Well, look at it. He starts the violin at — what? — four, five years old. That's when most of them start. You think it was his idea, no parental pressure? Then his mama stands over him for three or four hours a day, making him practise. You think he wouldn't rather have been out playing football, or watching television? I've seen these kids. They come to the workshops to try out instruments, and they've always got mummy or daddy in tow. They're like those tennis prodigies, the teenagers with some big

227

loudmouth bully of a dad hovering over them every minute of the day. They've had their childhoods taken away from them. I'd say that was abuse, wouldn't you?'

'Some kids like it,' I said. 'You can't generalise.'

'Then they get to their twenties and they've had enough. They rebel, reject the parents who've put them through all that misery. I bet Ivanov's run off with some girlfriend his mama doesn't know about.'

'I didn't get the impression he knows any girls.'

'Well, he should, a young fellow his age. He should have girls coming out of his ears. He could be with a prostitute, I suppose.'

'Antonio thought that, but I can't see it. He has no money, for a start. Ludmilla keeps a very tight grip on the purse strings.'

'He'd have salted something away, ready for the day when he made his bid for freedom.'

'That doesn't really fit with your theory about a breakdown,' I said.

'No, maybe not. I'm making it up as I go along. It's probably all rubbish. You want a top-up?'

We lingered until the small hours, Rudy telling scurrilous tales about his work colleagues and clients; then we went to bed. I slept heavily, anaesthetised by the whisky.

In the morning, we had a late, leisurely breakfast before Rudy drove us into London and dropped me off at St. Pancras station. I caught the Eurostar to Paris, took the shuttle bus

228

straight to Charles de Gaulle, and was back in Cremona by the early evening. I called the *questura*, but Guastafeste wasn't there. He'd stayed on in Paris, one of his colleagues told me. I made myself something to eat — a pork escalope with fried potatoes — and retired to the sitting room with one of the books from my shelves — a biography of Giovanni Battista Viotti.

Viotti is not a name with which most non-musicians are familiar. Even musicians would be hard-pressed to tell you much about his life. His works are rarely heard on the radio, and hardly ever in the concert hall. Yet he wrote twenty-nine violin concertos and is known as the father of modern violin playing.

He was born in northern Italy in 1755, twenty-seven years before Paganini, and, like Paganini, showed a precocious talent for the violin. He went to Turin at the age of eleven and became a pupil of Gaetano Pugnani, another legendary violinist, whose fame today rests almost entirely on a musical hoax perpetrated by Fritz Kreisler, who wrote several pieces for the violin in the early twentieth century, claiming that they were the work of seventeenth — and eighteenth-century composers such as Vivaldi and Tartini. One of the pieces was a 'Praeludium and Allegro' — familiar to every student of the violin — which was attributed to Pugnani. Years later, Kreisler came clean and admitted that all these 'long-lost' compositions were, in fact, his own work.

Pugnani is little more than an obscure

footnote in history now, but in his day he was a musical giant, celebrated for his eight operas, seven symphonies, and innumerable other pieces. He was also much in demand as a soloist, and in 1780 he went on a tour of Switzerland, Germany, Poland, and Russia. He took with him his star pupil, Viotti, who was then an unknown twenty-four-year old with limited concert experience.

In Saint Petersburg, both men performed for Catherine the Great, and — as Rupert Rhys-Jones had said — the empress was so captivated by Viotti that she kept him on in the capital and he became her lover. The affair lasted a year before petering out, allowing Viotti to return to Italy. It must have been an amicable end to the relationship, for Catherine's parting gift of the jewel-encrusted gold violin was fabulously generous, even by her standards.

Exactly what happened to the violin after that was a mystery. The biography I was reading mentioned the gift in passing but made no further reference to it. It was a book about Viotti the musician and its focus was on his career as a violinist and composer. A piece of jewellery, no matter how distinguished its provenance, was of little interest to the author.

But as I read the pages that dealt with Viotti's return from Russia and his brief stay in Italy before he went to Paris for the triumphant debut that was to make him a celebrity overnight, I began to construct a theory about the gold violin — a theory based on the flimsiest of evidence but which, as I refined it, seemed to have an appealing plausibility.

I was still thinking about it when the phone rang. It was Guastafeste. He was back from Paris, catching up with his colleagues at the *questura*.

'I need to talk to you,' I said. 'I'd prefer not to do it on the phone.'

'Give me an hour and I'll be there,' Guastafeste said.

'Have you eaten?'

'No, but . . . '

'When did you last eat?'

'Gianni . . . '

'When?'

'Breakfast.'

'I'll make you something.'

'You don't need — '

'Don't argue, Antonio. I'll see you in an hour.'

I went into the kitchen and made a simple pasta sauce with olive oil, onions, garlic, and tomatoes. By the time Guastafeste arrived, there were ham and black olives and a bottle of red wine on the kitchen table and a pan of boiling water on the hob. I added a few handfuls of conchiglie to the water as Guastafeste walked in, then poured us both a large glass of wine.

'Help yourself to the ham and olives.'

'You shouldn't have, Gianni,' Guastafeste said. 'It's not necessary.'

'You look tired and hungry,' I said. 'I can't do anything about the fatigue, but I can certainly feed you. You're overdoing it; I can tell. You've got to take a break occasionally, you know. Look after yourself better.'

'I'm fine,' Guastafeste insisted, but he wolfed down a slice of ham and some olives in quick succession, then took a long gulp of wine.

I gave the pasta a stir and joined him at the table.

'What news from Paris?' I asked. 'You stayed on longer than you expected.'

'I was waiting for the pathologist's report on Alain Robillet. It was Robillet, by the way. His wife formally identified him. He was killed by a heavy blow to the head.'

'Like Villeneuve.'

'There were differences. Villeneuve was hit with the lamp in his hotel room. Robillet was hit with something much nastier — a hammer or a wrench, the pathologist reckoned. And hit with enough force to leave a hole in his skull.'

I grimaced.

'They didn't find the weapon?'

'It wasn't at the scene,' Guastafeste said. 'They've been searching the surrounding area to see if the killer dumped it somewhere, but they've found nothing so far.'

'Motive?'

'Nothing obvious. It might have been robbery. There was a shop full of antiques downstairs. It was well secured, but Robillet had the keys to the locks. They were in his jacket pocket. It's possible that the killer took the keys, went into the shop and stole something, then returned the keys.'

'Was anything missing?'

Guastafeste shrugged.

'You saw the place. There must have been thousands of items. There's no way you could tell if anything had been taken, not unless you cross-checked everything against an inventory. And Robillet and Villeneuve, according to Inspector Forbin, were not the kind of men who kept inventories. Their business affairs were, let's say, somewhat less than transparent. Half the stuff in their shop was probably stolen in the first place.'

Guastafeste helped himself to another couple of olives.

'Forbin said they mixed with some pretty unsavoury characters. Violent, ruthless characters who wouldn't think twice about smashing in someone's head with a hammer.' 'Forbin knows who these people are?'

'It's a long list.'

I went to the stove and tested the pasta. The conchiglie were just al dente. I drained off the water and put the pasta into a bowl with the tomato sauce. I placed the bowl on the table in front of Guastafeste, then brought grated Parmesan from the fridge.

'You said you wanted to talk to me,' Guastafeste said.

'Yes. I think I know what was in the gold box.'

Guastafeste paused, a spoonful of Parmesan half-sprinkled over his pasta.

'Go on,' he said.

I told him about my meeting with Rupert Rhys-Jones. Then I showed him a colour photocopy of the jewelled violin that Rhys-Jones had had done for me before I left his office.

Guastafeste studied the photocopy in silence for a long time.

Finally, he said, 'How much is it worth?'

'A lot. Twenty million dollars, Rhys-Jones reckoned.'

'And this is what Elisa Baciocchi gave to Paganini?'

'It has to be.'

'Where did she get it?'

'I don't know for certain, but I have an idea. Viotti, as I said, was given it by Catherine the Great, as a memento of their affair.'

'He must have been one hell of a lover.'

'Perhaps. But Catherine wasn't the first woman he loved. There was another woman — in Turin, where Viotti lived before he went to Russia. Her name was Teresa Valdena, the daughter of a wealthy cloth merchant. Teresa was seventeen when Viotti met her, Viotti twenty-one. They fell in love and wanted to get married, but Teresa's father disapproved of the match. Viotti, a penniless music student with few prospects, was not the kind of son-in-law he wanted. Valdena forced his daughter to break off the engagement and forbade her from any further contact with Viotti.

'Viotti went off on his tour of Europe with Pugnani and was away for eighteen months. When he returned to Turin, he found that Teresa's father had sent her away to a convent after she refused to marry the young nobleman he had chosen to be her husband. The convent she went to was at Montecatini, in Tuscany.'

234

'So Viotti never saw her again?' Guastafeste said.

'Just once. He went to visit her in the convent. No one knows what passed between them. Perhaps he entreated her to leave, to come away with him and be his wife. Perhaps she wanted to but couldn't. Perhaps she had already decided to devote herself to a life of religious contemplation. Whatever the truth, the fact is that Viotti went away without her. He returned to Turin, then left Italy for Paris.'

'And the gold violin?'

'He gave it to Teresa.'

'This is guesswork?'

'Yes. But it fits what happened years later — about 1806, 1807, when Elisa was princess of Piombino and Lucca. It's documented in a book I've got about Elisa. Napoléon was running short of cash to keep his war machine going. He ordered Elisa to dissolve all the religious institutions in her principality and confiscate their lands and assets — which would have been quite considerable. Montecatini is near Lucca. Teresa's convent is one of the institutions that would have been closed.'

'So the gold violin — if it was there — would have been confiscated by Elisa's soldiers,' Guastafeste said. 'But not sent to fill her brother's war chest.'

'That's consistent with Elisa's character. She went through all the assets that were seized from the convents and monasteries and kept some of the loot for herself. The gold violin must have been hard to resist. A beautiful piece of jewellery like that. And she was in the middle of a passionate love affair with Paganini. Who better to give the violin to than him?'

Guastafeste scooped up a forkful of pasta and chewed pensively.

'It's only a theory,' I said. 'But it fits the facts. How else did Elisa get the violin?'

Guastafeste nodded.

'It has the ring of truth about it,' he said. 'Catherine the Great gives it as a love token to Viotti, he gives it as a love token to Teresa, and then Elisa gives it as a love token to Paganini. And yet not one of those loves endured. That says something about human nature, doesn't it?'

Was he right? I wondered. Certainly about Catherine and Elisa and Paganini. All moved on to other lovers without much difficulty. But Viotti and Teresa? That was a different matter. No one knows what became of Teresa. Her life was lived away from the public gaze. But Viotti was one of the greatest musicians of his day, his achievements recorded for posterity.

He was a complex man. His first appearance in Paris, playing one of his own concertos — only months after that final meeting with Teresa — caused a sensation. His audience clamoured for more and every concert he gave thereafter was a sellout. But eighteen months after that glorious debut, he walked away from the concert platform and devoted his time to teaching — without remuneration — and composition, his violin concertos being per-formed, but not by him.

A brief spell running one of the Paris opera

houses with the help of Marie Antoinette's coiffeur put him in jeopardy after the French Revolution and he fled to London, where he resumed his career as a soloist. But that revival was cut short when he was accused of revolutionary sympathies and expelled by the English. Three years of exile in Germany followed, during which time he composed but did not perform, and when the expulsion order was revoked and he was permitted to return to London, he rejected any notion of playing in public again and became a wine merchant. Business was clearly not his forte, however, for in 1818 he went bankrupt. He went back to Paris to run the Royal Opera House, but that was not a success, either. When he died, in 1824, he had large debts, which even the sale of his Stradivari violin could not cover.

He was an enigmatic man — kind, generous, and modest, but difficult to fathom. He was renowned in his time as both a composer and performer, but he had the misfortune to be living in an era of great change. With the rise of Romanticism, his concertos, hugely popular before 1800, were soon regarded as old-fashioned, and his classical style of playing was superseded by the flashy virtuosity of which Paganini was the foremost exponent. Viotti's real legacy was not his music, but the pupils he taught — Rode, Baillot, and Kreutzer, who went on to dominate the nineteenth-century French school of violin playing, their influence continuing on into the twentieth century through Massart, Wieniawski, and Kreisler.

Now, as I reflected on Viotti's life, one particular fact stood out: He never married. Was he still carrying a torch for Teresa Valdena? I don't generally subscribe to the concept of a broken heart. An aching heart, yes. We have all suffered from that. But a heart so shattered by lost love that it never fully recovers from the blow? That is much rarer. We are a resilient species. If we were not, how would we survive the vicissitudes that life throws in our paths? The pain, the grief, the misery — they would all overwhelm us and we would just curl up and die. But we cope. We endure. We lose one love, we mourn for a period, and then we move on. In the flash of a star that comprises our life span, it will only be an instant before we, too, are gone.

Did Viotti never recover from the loss of Teresa? Did he carry her memory with him for the rest of his life, a memory so intense that no other woman could erase it? I pictured that final encounter at the convent at Montecatini, Teresa in her nun's habit, Viotti sitting beside her. What did they say to each other? Did they touch hands? Was there a last kiss before they parted? I saw Viotti reasoning with her, perhaps pleading with her to come with him, Teresa shaking her head. Then I saw him giving her the jewelled violin he had brought home with him from Russia. A gift from one woman who had loved him, which he was now giving to another woman who had loved him, but who would never be his. There was something poignant about that.

'So the question now,' Guastafeste said, scraping up the last few conchiglie from his bowl, 'is what did Paganini do with the violin? Did he keep it for the rest of his life? Did he give it away, perhaps to another woman?'

'Coffee?' I said.

'Please.'

I spooned coffee into the steel espresso pot and put it on the hob.

'It would help if we knew where François Villeneuve got the gold box,' I said. 'Elisa had it specially made for the violin, after all, and Paganini must surely have used it. If we knew where the box came from, it might give us a clue as to what became of the violin.'

'There's been progress on that,' Guastafeste said. 'While I was in Paris, my colleagues checked through the stolen-goods register, particularly the fine-arts squad's records from Milan. A gold box exactly matching the one Villeneuve had — combination lock, engraving of Moses on the lid — was stolen from a villa in Stresa ten days ago. The villa belonged to an old lady who'd just died, so it was unoccupied at the time.'

I was opening a cupboard to take out two coffee cups, but I stopped and turned to stare at Guastafeste.

'An old lady? Stresa?' I said. 'Her name wasn't Nicoletta Ferrara, was it?'

Now it was Guastafeste's turn to stare at me. 'How did you know?'

I told him about the Bergonzi violin that Vincenzo Serafin had asked me to authenticate. Guastafeste took a moment to absorb the details; then he said, 'Serafin went to the villa?'

239

'He has a country house up there himself. Nicoletta Ferrara's nephew invited him over to look at the violin.'

'When was this?'

'Recently. The last couple of weeks, I think.'

'So let me get this straight. Serafin visits the villa; then shortly afterwards the house is burgled and a valuable gold box is stolen, a gold box that later turns up in the possession of Serafin's friend François Villeneuve.' Guastafeste paused. 'I think I'm going to have to make another trip to Milan.'

14

The excursion to Paris, and the unplanned detour to London, had taken more time than I'd anticipated, and next morning I was disconcerted to find that I had got behind in my work. An instrument belonging to one of the first violins in the pit orchestra at La Scala was due for collection that very day, yet I'd barely looked at it, never mind begun the fitting of the new sound post and bridge that its owner was expecting.

I cut short my breakfast and skipped my customary mid-morning break for coffee and applied myself intensively to the job. By lunchtime the violin — a rather handsome mid-nineteenth-century Giuseppe Rocca — was finished. I tried it out for a short while; then, satisfied with the sound, prepared to put the instrument back in its case.

A violin case — like a bedroom — reveals a lot about the personality of its owner. Some are pristine, the linings as clean as the day they were made; others are battered and dirty, littered with the detritus of a musician's life — discarded strings, chips of rosin, chocolate-bar wrappers. Renato Lampi's case was one of the latter.

Renato was a big, ungainly man with long, greasy hair and an unkempt beard that always seemed to contain traces of the last meal he'd eaten, sometimes the last week's meals. His clothes were generally crumpled, his shirts frequently stained with splashes of toothpaste or pasta sauce. His violin case was a similar mess. The felt linings, originally a rich dark green colour, were now faded and matted with grime. In places, the material had come unstuck, exposing the bare plywood underneath. The bottom of the shaped recess where the violin nestled was caked with dust and one end had broken away entirely.

I baulked at putting the instrument — now rejuvenated by my work — back into such a squalid environment. It deserved better. I emptied the case, then took my vacuum cleaner and sucked out all the dirt. The broken section was more of a problem. It certainly needed repairing, for at the moment the violin wasn't properly cushioned by the sides of the recess. If the instrument slid round while the case was being carried, it might get damaged.

I lifted out the broken section, thereby revealing a small cavity behind. The damage was clearly not new, because the cavity was full of fluff and dust and other bits of rubbish. There were two stubby pencils that had somehow strayed in, an ebony mute with a chipped leg, and several pieces of paper, including a receipt for a set of new strings that was five years old. I scraped all the rubbish out and vacuumed the cavity; then I fastened the broken section back into place and reglued the felt lining.

It was while I was disposing of the mute and scraps of paper that something suddenly occurred to me. I thought back to our visit to the

Molyneux et Charbon archives in Paris, to one of the drawings we'd seen in the big leather-bound ledgers. I went to the phone and rang the *questura*. Guastafeste wasn't there — he'd gone to Milan — so I left a message asking him to call me when he returned.

It was early afternoon, and I was absorbed in one of the other jobs I'd neglected to do, when Renato arrived to collect his violin. I didn't really have time to socialise, but I did. Living and working alone in rural seclusion can be a dispiriting experience. Sometimes I can go for days without seeing another person, so I always try to be hospitable to my customers. Renato isn't a close friend, but we have known each other for many years, and at our infrequent meetings I always make an effort to catch up on his life.

We went into the kitchen and spent an amiable half hour drinking wine and gossiping about La Scala, whose orchestra, like most professional orchestras, is a hotbed of feuding and adultery. I am familiar with just about all the members of the pit band — I look after the instruments of many of the string players — and Renato was well informed about who was sleeping with whom and who had fallen out with whom. By the time he left, I was feeling quite relieved that I worked on my own. Just hearing about the antics at the opera house was exhausting.

I returned to my workshop, but I had been settled at my bench for less than half an hour when I heard footsteps and looked up, to see Ludmilla Ivanova outside on the terrace. She opened the door and strode in, a determined glint in her eyes that made me sigh inwardly. I knew she hadn't come for a cosy little chat.

'Where've you been?' she demanded.

Her curt manner took me aback a little. I stared at her.

'I'm sorry?'

'I've been ringing you for days.'

'Ringing me?'

'About Yevgeny. The police are doing nothing. They just fob me off with excuses. I thought that friend of yours was going to help, but every time I call the *questura*, they say he's not there. What's going on? Where is Yevgeny? Why has he not been found?'

'He's safe, signora; we know that.'

'We know nothing of the kind. That phone call to you was meaningless. If he's safe, why hasn't he returned? It's Kousnetzoff, I'm telling you. He is behind this.'

'I don't think there's anything to worry about. He said he would be back in a few days.'

'A few days have passed. Where is he? Why is no one doing anything? Why? I'm sick of this horrible little town. I want Yevgeny back; then we can get away from here. I wish we'd never come.'

She went on in this vein for several more minutes, getting more and more worked up about the whole business. My attempts to calm her, to reassure her, were rejected out of hand and I could see that she was not going to leave me alone until I took some kind of action.

'You came by taxi, I assume?' I said when she

finally tired of saying the same things over and over again.

'What's that got to do with it?' Ludmilla said.

I took off my work apron and hung it on a hook on the wall.

'I will drive you back to your hotel now,' I said. 'Then I will make enquiries about Yevgeny and Kousnetzoff.'

''Enquiries'? What do you mean?'

I took her firmly by the arm and escorted her out of the workshop.

'Just leave it to me, signora,' I said.

I had no clear idea of what I was going to do, but I knew I had to do something. Guastafeste and his colleagues were obviously too engrossed with their murder enquiry to spare much time for Ludmilla. She was distressed — understandably so — and I couldn't stand by and do nothing to help her. Her remarks about Cremona had also stung me. I didn't like to hear my hometown maligned, to be somehow blamed for Yevgeny's disappearance. That was unjust. I felt it was my civic duty to restore Ludmilla's faith in Cremona and its citizens by attempting in my own small way to track down her missing son.

I drove us into the city and saw Ludmilla up to her room in the Hotel Emanuele; then I went back down to the foyer and spoke to the receptionist and the assistant manager, both of whom had been on duty on the Monday afternoon when Yevgeny had vanished. I explained that I was acting on behalf of Ludmilla and asked them a few questions about that

245

afternoon. They had already given statements to the police and could add nothing more to them.

Yevgeny had received his phone call from Vladimir Kousnetzoff at about a quarter to four; then forty-five minutes later, at half-past four, he had come downstairs from his room, deposited his key at reception, and left the hotel. There had been no one waiting for him in the hotel foyer, or outside on the street — at least as far as the receptionist could see. That was the sum total of their knowledge. Had Yevgeny received any other phone calls that day? I asked. No. Had anyone come to the hotel asking for him? No. What about a stocky, bald Russian man? Had they seen anyone matching that description in the vicinity of the hotel? No, again.

I thanked them for their time and walked the short distance to the Hotel San Michele, where I spoke to the receptionist on duty, a bubbly, chatty young woman who was only too willing to help me. Yes, she remembered Signor Kousnetzoff. He'd stayed for four nights — arrived on Thursday and checked out early Monday evening. She could tell me that without looking at the register because the police had already asked her the same question. She hadn't spoken much to Kousnetzoff. No one in the hotel had. He'd asked for his messages when he'd been out, but that was about the limit of his conversation. She hadn't liked him, really. His manner was unfriendly, almost rude. She hadn't seen him with anyone else, particularly Yevgeny Ivanov. The police had asked her that, too. She was sorry, but that was about all she knew.

I was wasting my time; I could see that now. The police had carried out all the obvious checks. There was nothing I could do that had not already been done. I took my leave of the receptionist and went back out to the street, crossing over to the other side to return to my car. Almost opposite the hotel entrance was a newspaper kiosk. I skirted round it to avoid the racks of papers and magazines that were half-blocking the pavement, and as I did so, I noticed that one of the racks contained foreign-language newspapers — *Le Monde, El Pais, The Times, The Guardian*, the *International Herald Tribune*. I stopped, something occurring to me suddenly. The kiosk proprietor, from his perch on a stool behind the counter, had a clear view of the Hotel San Michele's entrance — and newspaper sellers, having long periods of inactivity to fill, are not known for their reluctance to take an interest in the affairs of others.

'You don't sell Russian newspapers, do you?' I asked him.

The proprietor sniffed and rubbed his nose with an ink-stained finger.

'No. There's not much call for Russian papers round here. Why?'

'I just wondered,' I said. 'There was a Russian man staying in the San Michele last weekend. Short fellow in his fifties, no hair. You didn't see him, did you? Or a skinny young Russian boy in his early twenties. They might have been together.'

'No, can't say I did.'

'He didn't come over here and buy a paper?'

'Not that I remember. The French fellow did, but no Russians.'

'French fellow?'

'You know, the dead man. He was found in his room with his head bashed in. It was in the news, the TV, the lot.'

'François Villeneuve. You spoke to him?'

'Well, he didn't say much. He just bought a paper. Friday and Saturday, I think. *Le Monde* both times. Funny-looking fellow. Buck teeth and a scrappy little beard.'

'That's all? He just bought a paper?'

'That's what I do, sell papers. Oh, and a map. He bought a map.'

'A map of where?'

'Of Cremona. You know, those town plans showing the streets. Well, most of them. He took a look at the index and couldn't find what he was looking for, so I had to give him directions.'

'To where?'

'The Via Bucco.'

I frowned.

'The Via Bucco?'

'I had to think about it myself, to tell you the truth, and I've lived in Cremona all my life. It was too small to be on the map.'

'Have you told the police this?' I asked.

'Yes, a few days ago. They were questioning everyone round the hotel. Me, the shops and businesses. You know the Via Bucco?'

'Yes, I know it,' I said.

It was near the railway station, a seedy little dead end backing onto the tracks. As far as I could recall, there was only one thing of any interest there. I drove down to refresh my memory, then headed back into the town centre, parked, and walked to the *questura*.

Guastafeste had returned from Milan. He came down to the front desk and suggested we go for a coffee at a bar round the corner. Something in his manner told me that his trip to see Vincenzo Serafin had not been a success.

I waited until we were seated at a table, a double espresso each and a pastry for Guastafeste on the table between us, before I said, 'How was Milan?'

Guastafeste pulled a face.

'Frustrating.'

'Did you bring Serafin in?'

Guastafeste gave a sardonic chuckle. 'If only.'

'What did he say?'

'He was indignant, got himself all worked up into a pompous rage. You know the kind of thing — a law-abiding citizen accused of some outrageous crime by an incompetent police officer.'

'And the gold box?'

'He said he'd never seen any gold box at the villa. The old lady's nephew, Ruggiero Monteveglio, showed him the violin he wanted appraised, but that was all. They stayed in the one room the whole time, never went anywhere else in the villa.'

'Doesn't sound like Serafin to me,' I said. 'He'd have been snooping about all over the place, seeing what the old lady had. How big is the villa? Do you know?'

'I got the burglary report from the Stresa police. It's big. Seven bedrooms, three bathrooms, a view over the lake. Nicoletta Ferrara must have been loaded.'

'What else was stolen?'

'Jewellery, silverware, some paintings, including a race-course scene by Degas — mostly small stuff that was easily transportable. She had some valuable antique furniture, according to the investigating officer I spoke to, but that would have needed a van to remove. Whoever did it knew what they were looking for, and knew how to dispose of it. They were selective. Didn't touch the TV or the DVD player, the stuff the amateurs go for. They picked off a few prize items and got out quickly.'

'There wasn't an alarm?'

'It was disabled — expertly disabled by someone who knew what they were doing. It was a very professional job from start to finish.'

'What do the Stresa police say?'

'Enquiries are ongoing. Which basically means they haven't a clue. This was a slick operation. The house was cased; the burglars went in at night, stole a few specific items to order, and were gone in minutes. There's no forensic evidence worth a damn. No fingerprints, no tyre marks. The houses on either side were both empty — one's a holiday home belonging to a property developer in Milan; the other's occupied by a banker who was away in Switzerland for a week. No one even knows exactly when it happened. The nephew was keeping an eye on the place, but he didn't go there every day.'

'Do the Stresa police know about Serafin?' I asked.

'They interviewed him. The nephew told them he'd been to the house. Serafin gave them the same story he gave me. He was invited there to look at a violin; he's a respected international violin dealer, friends with lots of powerful people, et cetera, et cetera. The evidence is all circumstantial. There's nothing to prove that Serafin had anything to do with the burglary.'

Guastafeste picked up his pastry and bit into it fiercely, his teeth snapping together with an audible impact.

'Nothing except common sense, that is,' he said a touch bitterly. 'But common sense isn't proof. You know, he had the nerve to say that I was hounding him, trying to intimidate him. He said he'd be talking to his lawyer about it. God, I would love to pin something on him.'

Guastafeste let out a long sigh and gave me a rueful smile.

'Sorry, he got under my skin.'

'He does that.'

'You left a message while I was out.'

'Yes. Can I have another look at the gold box? I've had a thought.'

'What kind of thought?'

'It might be nothing. I just want to look at it again, if that's okay. But there's something else, too. Something I've found out since I called you.'

I told him about my conversation with the newspaper seller. Guastafeste listened with

251

mounting concern, his eyes fixed on my face.

'Well, that's the first I've heard of that,' he said when I'd finished.

'He claims he told the police.'

'He probably did. We have a pile of statements this high in the office. We're working our way through them, but there's a long way to go. The Via Bucco?'

'You know what's there, of course?'

'Pietro Lodrino's place, you mean?'

I nodded.

'I checked it out. It's a very short street. Lodrino's warehouse is the only thing there.'

Guastafeste gazed at me pensively, pastry crumbs on his lips.

'You said something a couple of days ago. Why was Villeneuve in Cremona? Why not Milan, where Serafin lives? What was he doing here? I've been stupid. I should have followed it up then.'

He bolted the rest of his pastry, gulped down his coffee, and stood up. 'Thank you, Gianni. I wish to God I had you on my team at the *questura*.'

'You have,' I said.

★ ★ ★

I phoned Ludmilla Ivanova when I got home, to stop her phoning me. I told her that I was still making enquiries about Yevgeny and would continue doing so until I had some news for her. Then I grilled some sausages for my dinner and ate them with a few potatoes and a glass of red wine. After dinner, my daughter, Francesca, phoned from Mantua, as she does at least once a week. We talked for half an hour or more, Francesca telling me about my grandchildren and how they were doing at school and all the things they did in the evenings and at weekends, then asking me questions, probing, checking up on me to make sure I was looking after myself properly — not turning into some unshaven old man who washes once a month and eats food straight out of a can.

When she'd rung off, I gazed up at the photographs on the mantelpiece, my three grandchildren beaming at me, looking different, less familiar in every picture. I saw them a few times a year, heard about them every week, but increasingly — as they got older — I was feeling less and less a part of their lives. I didn't feel part of Francesca's life, either. Or my two sons' lives, Domenico living in Rome now, Alessandro in Brussels, working for a petro-chemical company and coming home once a year, if that. Home? I still thought of my house as their home, but of course it wasn't. It hadn't been for a long time.

My gaze moved along the mantelpiece to the photograph of my wife, a smiling, radiant Caterina sitting by a waterfall in the Dolomites, where we'd gone for a walking holiday. That was how I wanted to remember her — the beautiful, happy woman she had been, rather than the shrivelled husk she became by the end. I wanted to blot out those final months from my memory because that was not Caterina who endured them. Not my Caterina, the woman I'd fallen in love with thirty-five years earlier. It was some pale, unrecognisable shadow of her — a shadow racked with pain and the terrible knowledge of her own death.

My vision began to mist over. Sometimes I feel that my purpose in life has been completed. Why are you gone, Caterina, while I am still here?

I was getting morose. That wasn't good. I needed to snap myself out of it, and there was only one infallible way of doing that. I went into my back room and took out my violin and played a Bach unaccompanied partita, the one in B minor that Yevgeny Ivanov had performed at his recital in the cathedral. I didn't play it very well. There was a time when that would have made me furious with myself, made me rage against my inadequate technique. But my expectations have declined with age. Now I'm just glad even to get through a partita. Bach played badly is better than no Bach at all.

'Don't ring us; we'll ring you,' said a dry voice from the doorway.

I turned and saw Guastafeste leaning on the frame, half-smiling at me.

'Sorry, did I startle you?' he said.

'How long have you been there?'

'Not long. I knocked, but you didn't hear. Don't let me stop you. What is that piece, by the way, Schoenberg's Variations on a Theme by Bach?'

I gave him a narrow look.

'Don't push me,' I growled. 'I know where you live.'

I put my violin back in its case and we went into the kitchen.

'Have you eaten?' I asked.

'You're not cooking me any more meals, Gianni,' Guastafeste said.

'Don't you like them?'

'That's not the point.'

'You haven't, have you?'

'Yes, I have.'

'What, a pastry and a cup of coffee? That's not a meal, Antonio.'

'Do you want to look at this, or not?'

He put the gold box on the table, still in its transparent plastic evidence bag, and slumped down onto a chair. His face was pale and lined, the stress of the murder investigation taking its toll. Since the split with his wife, Guastafeste has become absorbed in his work to an unhealthy degree. He is a handsome, attractive man, but he shows no signs of becoming attached to another woman. And what he really needs is someone — other than me — to look after him.

I poured us both a glass of wine and brought cheese and crackers and grapes to the table, helping myself to a few grapes before pushing the plate towards Guastafeste. He didn't say anything, just cut a thick slice of cheese and ate it hungrily.

'You've been to Lodrino's warehouse, haven't you?' I said.

'Took every available officer and went through his entire warehouse. He'd been careless. One of the items taken from the villa in Stresa was still there — the painting of the race-course by Degas. We brought him into the *questura* and he admitted buying the painting and a few other

255

things, including the gold box, from someone — a Signor Rossi — who came into his shop the week before last. Just wandered in off the street. Lodrino swears blind, of course, that he didn't know the goods were stolen. He said Signor Rossi had incontrovertible proof of ownership, proof that Lodrino has conveniently managed to mislay.'

Guastafeste cut another slice of cheese and put it on a cracker.

'I should have thought of Lodrino earlier. You know his reputation, don't you?'

I nodded, recalling my one and only encounter with the auctioneer and antiques dealer. He'd come to me with a good copy of a Maggini violin, which he'd picked up in a house clearance, and suggested that I might authenticate it as a genuine Maggini and we would split the profits, an offer I had politely declined. He hadn't approached me since.

'A job like the one in Stresa,' Guastafeste said. 'It was well organised, professional. And the stuff that was stolen was valuable, probably easily identifiable. There are only a limited number of people who could dispose of it safely. In this part of Lombardy, that had to be Lodrino.'

'Did you ask him about Serafin?'

'He said he'd never heard of him. But here's the interesting bit. Lodrino said he sold the gold box to two men for five thousand euros in cash.'

'Two men?' I said.

'One was François Villeneuve. Lodrino had done business with him before, in Paris — shady business, no doubt.'

'And the other?'

'Lodrino didn't know him, or his name. But he gave us a description of him. Medium height, stocky, bald. Spoke Italian with a strong foreign accent — Eastern European or Russian.'

'Vladimir Kousnetzoff?' I said.

'No question about it.'

'Kousnetzoff and Villeneuve were partners?'

'Puts a new slant on Villeneuve's murder, doesn't it?'

'You haven't tracked down Kousnetzoff yet?'

'We're doing our best. Sooner or later, he's got to turn up.' Guastafeste picked up a grape, tossed it into the air, and caught it in his mouth.

'So tell me why you want to look at the gold box again?' he said.

'Just something that occurred to me when I was repairing a violin case earlier. You remember when we were in Paris, down in the Molyneux et Charbon archives, we found the original drawings for the box, including the specifications for the lined insert, the wooden frame that held the jewelled violin in place?'

'Yes.'

'It was a hollow insert.'

'You think there might be something underneath it?'

'I don't know. Did your jewellery expert remove the insert?'

Guastafeste shook his head.

'He just examined the outside of the box, particularly the hallmarks. That's all we needed — to know who made it and when.'

I took the gold box out of the plastic evidence

bag. The dials on the combination lock had spun round so that the lock was engaged. I turned them back — *B, E, F, G* — and heard a click. I pulled open the lid. The interior of the box was just the way I remembered it: gleaming gold sides and a recessed insert lined with blue velvet. I tried to pull the insert out, but there was nothing to grip — my fingers kept sliding off the velvet — so I took a table knife from a drawer and slid the thin blade down between the insert and the side of the box. I applied a little pressure, but nothing happened.

'Maybe it's glued in?' Guastafeste suggested.

'I don't think so. It's just a tight fit.'

I brought a second table knife and inserted that at the other end. With Guastafeste holding the box firmly down, I pulled on the two knives, levering them backwards. Slowly, the insert rose up out of the box.

There was nothing underneath it except the dull unpolished gold base and a scattering of dust.

'What did you expect?' Guastafeste said.

I didn't reply. I was disappointed. What had I expected? I wasn't sure. I'd probably expected exactly what I'd found: nothing. But I'd hoped for more. And hope is the most irrational of emotions.

I examined the underside of the insert, still reluctant to accept defeat. I saw only bare pine and the glued ends of the velvet lining.

'I thought . . . ' I began, and stopped. 'I don't know what I thought.'

I put the insert back into the box and pressed

it down to the bottom.

'The violin's gone, Gianni,' Guastafeste said gently. 'It disappeared two centuries ago. No one knows how or where.'

'No one knows, maybe,' I said. 'But someone has an inkling. Someone has a suspicion about what became of it. Why else would Villeneuve and Robillet have been killed? Someone knows more than we do; that's clear. But who are they, and *what* exactly do they know?'

I put my hand on the lid of the gold box to close it. And then I noticed something that had never really registered with me before. The inside of the lid was also lined with blue velvet. I ran my fingertips over it. The material was still soft, the colour hardly faded after all these years. Lack of exposure to light and air — that had to be the reason why it was so well preserved. Had the box been locked since Paganini died? Had the combination been forgotten until Guastafeste and I managed to work it out?

There was something beneath the lining — a piece of board to give it some rigidity. My fingers encountered a tiny protrusion along the front edge — like a sliver of velvet that had come unstuck. I peered closer and saw that it was indeed a sliver of velvet, but it hadn't come unstuck. It was attached to the lining — a very small hand-stitched tag.

I tugged on the tag. The lining came away from the lid along three sides. On the fourth — the back edge — it remained fastened, a strip of velvet acting like a hinge. Between the lining and the underside of the lid was a rectangle of card about the size of a business card. And it *was* a business card. It had Henri le Bley Lavelle's name and address printed on it beneath an elaborate coat of arms incorporating his initials.

The business card wasn't the only thing inside the lining. There was a piece of paper. A piece of paper folded in two, about ten centimetres square. I lifted it out — it felt old and brittle in my fingers — and carefully unfolded it.

There was writing on the paper — faded but legible — writing in two different hands. The first hand — at the top of the page — was bold and clear, the letters large and ornamented with swirls. I read what was written aloud to Guastafeste.

'"San Carlo, March 20, 1819. I undertake within twelve months of this date to pay the sum of six thousand eight hundred francs to Signor Domenico Barbaia.' It's signed Nicolò Paganini.'

'Paganini?' Guastafeste said. 'What is that?'

'It's an IOU,' I said. 'For a gambling debt, I would guess.'

'Who's Domenico Barbaia?'

'He was the impresario who ran the San Carlo opera house, in Naples. And controlled the gaming tables at the opera house. Paganini must have owed him money — a lot of money. Six thousand eight hundred francs would have been a fortune back then.'

Guastafeste frowned.

'If it's an IOU to Barbaia, shouldn't he have had it? What's it doing in a gold box that belonged to Paganini?'

'Because the debt was paid off,' I said. 'Look

at this, lower down the page.'

The second hand was harder to read. It was an untidy scrawl, the letters cramped together, but I could just make out the words.

' "The debt is now considered cleared. Isabella will love this. Domenico Barbaia, May 16, 1819." '

I turned the paper round so Guastafeste could read it for himself.

'Paganini paid what he owed and the IOU was returned to him,' I said. 'That's why he put it in the gold case. What better place to keep it, considering how he'd cleared the debt.'

Guastafeste gave me a puzzled look.

'What do you mean?'

'Isn't it obvious?' I said. 'Paganini didn't give Barbaia six thousand eight hundred francs; he gave him the jewelled violin.'

Guastafeste studied the piece of paper again.

'Are you sure?'

'Six thousand eight hundred francs was a huge sum. And Paganini, in 1819, wasn't the enormously wealthy man he became later. What assets would he have had? His violin — *il Cannone* — that was probably the only thing of any value he owned. And he was hardly going to part with that. His living depended on it. What else did he have that was worth the equivalent of six thousand eight hundred francs, or more? Viotti's gold violin, that's all. There's another clue in the wording. 'Isabella will love this.' '

'Isabella?' Guastafeste said.

'Let's have some coffee,' I replied.

I put the espresso pot on the stove. Then I told

261

him about Domenico Barbaia and Isabella Colbran.

★ ★ ★

Barbaia is one of those characters history has forgotten, but without whom there would be no history to remember. He started his working life as a café waiter in Milan and went on to become the most influential musical showman of his day. He was poorly educated, but shrewd and hard-working and with an eye for the main chance, acquiring the concession to run the gaming tables in the foyer of La Scala and making a fortune on the side with some lucrative contracts to supply the French troops that were stationed in Milan.

At that time, no one went to the opera purely to listen to the music. To many of the patrons, in fact, music was the least of their reasons for going. La Scala was the centre of social life in Milan. For the wealthy with no jobs, it provided relief from the tedium of their days. They would go every night during the season and listen to the same operas over and over again, although *listen* is perhaps not quite the word, for nobody actually listened to much of the music. They went to talk, drink champagne and play cards in their boxes — their miniature salons — and, as the boxes had curtains that could be drawn, make love to their mistresses or paramours or, if they were desperate, their spouses.

Most of the action on the stage was watched with half an eye, or ignored altogether. The

262

socialising really stopped only for the big numbers or the ballet sequence that every opera was obliged to accommodate and which was little more than titillation for the men in the audience — the cue for them to put down their cards, or their mistresses, and admire the dancers' legs. There was even a tradition of the *aria del sorbetto* — the sorbet aria, which was written for one of the supporting singers and gave the audience the chance to leave the auditorium and buy themselves a sorbet. Rossini famously wrote one of these sorbet arias in his opera *Ciro in Babilonia*; it consisted of just a single note repeated — a middle B flat — because he had discovered in rehearsals that the *seconda donna* could sing only that one note in tune.

But undoubtedly the greatest attraction of La Scala were the faro and *rouge-et-noir* tables that were set up in the foyer — the only place in Milan where gambling was permitted. Many people went to the opera and never actually made it to their seats. They got no farther than the foyer, where some would win and some would lose, but the only consistent winner was Domenico Barbaia.

By 1818, when Paganini and Barbaia first met, the impresario had moved from Milan to Naples, where he was running the opera and the gambling at the Teatro San Carlo. He would later go on to be instrumental in the careers of Bellini and Donizetti, but at this stage, if for nothing else, posterity owes him a debt for bringing the young Rossini to Naples and giving him the security that enabled him to develop his genius as a composer.

Barbaia was rough and a little uncouth, but he had a gift for spotting talent and was prepared to take risks to support the musicians he employed at the San Carlo. Rossini's first opera for him was *Elisabetta, Regina d'Inghilterra* — *Elizabeth, Queen of England* — about Elizabeth I's supposed love for the Earl of Leicester, which is rarely heard in the opera house today. Perhaps the most interesting thing about it is the overture, which Rossini — adept at cannibalising his own work — had already used for his earlier opera *Aureliano in Palmira* and liked so much that he would go on to use it a third time as the overture to *The Barber of Seville*.

The title role in *Elisabetta* was written for the San Carlo's *prima donna*, the formidable Isabella Colbran. Colbran was the Maria Callas of her day, Italy's most celebrated, and most highly paid, soprano, who had an astounding vocal range and a dramatic ability that audiences found mesmerising. She was to become Rossini's wife, but at this point — in keeping with the *droit du seigneur* that impresarios exercised over their leading ladies — she was Barbaia's mistress.

Given his astute box-office instincts, it was only natural that Barbaia should attempt to lure Paganini to the San Carlo, and in the spring of 1819, the violinist duly arrived in Naples. Rossini was busy overseeing the revival of his opera *Mosè in Egitto* — *Moses in Egypt* — which had had its premiere the previous year but had not been an unqualified success because of staging problems. In the scene where Moses parted the Red Sea, the audience — much to its amusement — had been able to see the small urchin boy under the set who was operating the mechanism separating the waves. The mechanism — and the urchin boy — proved difficult to change, so Rossini's solution was to write a new aria for the scene to distract the audience. In this he was spectacularly successful. On the first night of the revival, the aria, the moving prayer 'Dal tuo stellato soglio,' made such an impact that the ladies of the audience went into paroxysms and doctors had to be called to treat them. Many years later, when Rossini's body was transferred from Paris to a new tomb in Florence, it was this prayer that was sung on the steps of Santa Croce. And it was this prayer that Paganini used as the theme for his 'Moses Fantasy,' dedicated to Elisa Baciocchi.

Paganini's stay in Naples was clearly not all work and no play. The IOU we'd found in the gold box was unequivocal evidence that he had succumbed to the weakness for gambling that had afflicted him since his youth, when he had had to pawn his violin to pay his debts. There could have been no question of his pawning his violin this time. The Cannon was far too important to his career. He would no more have parted with it than he would have cut off one of his fingers. But the jewelled violin Elisa had given him was a different matter. Precious though it was, it was expendable.

Throughout his life, Paganini was careless in

his relationships with women. He did not have the temperament or the inclination for monogamy, and his lifestyle, in any case, was not conducive to it. He was constantly on the move, travelling from one city to another, playing concerts, then moving on. In modern times, that would be tiring enough — as many an international concert soloist could vouch. In Paganini's day, with journeys made by horse-drawn coach over unmetalled roads, it was exhausting. Few women would have been prepared to put up with such hardships. They would have wanted stability and a settled life, which Paganini was not able to give them. Even when he was in his forties and he fathered a son, Achille, he did not change his ways. A doting, besotted parent, he simply jettisoned Achille's mother — paid her off with a financial settlement she was only too happy to accept — and took the boy with him on his travels.

If he was so indifferent to the feelings of the women in his life, why should Paganini have had any greater attachment to the gifts they gave him? Elisa's present of the jewelled violin was not as generous as it seemed, given that it had been looted from a convent by one of her soldiers, but she must have made it in a spirit of love. Whether Paganini received it with the same sentiment may be open to question, but he hung on to it for many years after their split. If the gaming tables of the San Carlo had not come in his way, maybe he would have hung on to the violin even longer. Was that why he had dedicated the 'Moses Fantasy' to Elisa? I wondered. As a kind of recompense for using her gift to pay off his gambling debt, as a way of alleviating the guilt he must surely have felt? Six thousand eight hundred francs was a considerable sum. Domenico Barbaia would have happily taken the jewelled violin in lieu of the money, and then . . .

'And then what?' Guastafeste said.

'It's there in the IOU,' I replied. ' 'Isabella will love this.' Barbaia gave the violin to Isabella Colbran.'

15

What happened after that? I wondered. What did Isabella do with the jewelled violin? Most jewellery is made to be worn, but she could hardly have pinned a twenty-centimetre-long gold violin to her gown. Did she have it broken up and the jewels reset into more practical forms? I couldn't see it. Only a vandal with no aesthetic taste would have taken apart such a fine work of art, and Isabella Colbran was no vandal. She was an educated, discerning artiste. She would certainly have kept the violin intact, perhaps displayed it on her dressing table, where she could admire it when she was doing her hair and makeup.

Isabella was one of the greatest singers of her day, a beautiful, supremely talented woman, yet her life was fated to end unhappily. When Barbaia gave her the jewelled violin in 1819, her relationship with the impresario was already coming to a close. She had almost certainly started an affair with Rossini, and who could blame her? Rossini was young and good-looking — the baldness and corpulence that was to afflict him later was still just a shadow on the horizon. He was a phenomenally gifted composer with a love for the good things in life and a wit that any woman would find attractive.

Occasionally, I have been known to speculate about which great composer would have made the most convivial companion for a night on the town. Mozart? He was, by all accounts, a warm, gregarious individual, but his childish, scatological sense of humour would, I fear, have quickly become tiresome. Beethoven? Well, his deafness — not to mention his irascibility — wouldn't have made things easy. There might have been some cruel amusement to be had out of scribbling a provocative comment in his 'conversation book' and then retiring to a safe distance to watch the explosion. But that's not something I could ever do to another person, let alone someone as great as Beethoven. Brahms? Too serious and austere. He played the piano in the brothels of Hamburg when he was a young man, but — perhaps understandably — that seems to have put him off sex and drink for life.

No, Rossini would be my number-one choice. A *bon viveur* with a fondness for food, wine, and music — what better companion could you hope for? They say that Rossini wept only three times in his life: once when he heard a singer murdering one of his arias, once after the premiere of *The Barber of Seville* — which was a notorious disaster — and a third time, at a picnic, when the truffled chicken fell in the river. That's the kind of man he was. Leaving aside *The Barber* — the most joyous comic opera in the entire repertoire — how could you not like a man who went out in drag with Paganini during carnival season, the two friends singing and accompanying themselves on guitars? Or who coined the immortal words about Wagner: 'Wagner has lovely moments but awful quarters of an hour.' Or who, when his friend the composer Meyerbeer died and Meyerbeer's nephew showed him a funeral march he'd written in honour of his uncle, remarked, 'Excellent. But wouldn't it have been better if you had died and your uncle had written the march?'

An evening of jovial revelling is one thing. Marriage, however, is quite another — as Isabella discovered, to her sorrow. In 1822, on their way from Naples to Vienna, she and Rossini stopped off to be married at Castenaso, outside Bologna, where Isabella had inherited a large estate from her father. The marriage, far from cementing their love for each other, seems to have been the beginning of the end for their relationship. Isabella was thirty-seven, Rossini thirty. Her stellar career was starting to falter. Her voice was slipping and she could no longer be relied on to sing in tune. Rossini, though, was at the height of his powers, the most famous composer in Italy, with a staggering thirty operas under his belt.

Two years later, after a poorly received performance in the title role of Rossini's *Zelmira* in London, Isabella retired from the stage and retreated to her villa at Castenaso. Her husband, meanwhile, had relocated to Paris, where he was intent on furthering his already-illustrious international career. Physically separated from each other, and probably temperamentally incompatible, the two of them drifted apart.

No one at the time was very sure why Rossini married Isabella. Wags said it could only have been sheer masochism on his part — condemning himself to a lifetime of listening to Isabella's increasingly wayward voice. Others implied that he did it for the money. Isabella was a wealthy woman, her earnings from the stage supplemented by the income from the Castenaso estate, and she gave Rossini a generous dowry when they tied the knot.

Interestingly, no one seemed to consider the possibility that Rossini might have married for love — and maybe he didn't. He was a successful composer, but perhaps he was aware that sooner or later the well would run dry and he would need a nest egg for his retirement. No one could shine as intensely as he had been doing without burning out eventually. Is creativity in a person finite? Would Mozart and Schubert, dead at thirty-five and thirty-one, respectively — or Mendelssohn and Chopin, gone at thirty-eight and thirty-nine — have continued composing so feverishly if they had lived to ninety? Or did they somehow sense their own mortality and so crammed all the outpourings of their genius into a short span of years?

Perhaps Rossini knew that his composing days were numbered — as indeed they were, though it was choice, not death, that terminated his career. Seven years after his marriage, following his last opera, *William Tell*, he stopped composing operas altogether. Just gave up. Never wrote another opera, though he lived for a further thirty-nine years. Why did he stop? No one knows. There have been suggestions that he was lazy, but his record of thirty-six operas in nineteen years must surely refute that. More likely, he'd simply had enough. He had run out of things to say and he was honest enough to admit it. I like him all the more for that. We tend to put the great composers of the past on pedestals, perhaps because we've stopped producing any new ones ourselves, but Rossini had no exalted ideas of his own status. He looked on composition as a job, not an art, and he was always immensely practical about it — hence his habit of moving overtures, and arias, about from one opera to another. If a work was wanted quickly — *The Barber of Seville*, for example, was composed, rehearsed, and staged in just twenty-four days — and no one was going to listen to half of it anyway because they were too busy drinking and chatting, why bother to bust a gut producing something new?

Changing fashion also played its part. Romanticism was bursting forth all over Europe. Mendelssohn, Chopin, and Schumann were the new rising stars of the concert hall, and in the opera houses Meyerbeer and Donizetti were edging out the old guard, of which Rossini — though he was still only thirty-seven — was the standard-bearer. His ill health, too, was a factor. Like Paganini, Rossini had venereal disease. In Rossini's case, it was not syphilis but the less serious, though still incurable, gonorrhea that troubled him.

It was while he was convalescing at Aix-les-Bains after a bout of illness related to this disease that he met Olympe Pélissier, a well-known courtesan who had been the mistress of Balzac and the painter Horace Vernet. They fell for each other, and when Rossini went back to Paris, Olympe came to live with him. Isabella Colbran was out in the cold.

Rossini's desertion devastated Isabella. Shut away in provincial obscurity at Castenaso, bored and depressed, she started gambling to excess and lost a lot of money — although no more than she could afford. It must have been a traumatic time for her. She had been an operatic star for twenty years, fêted by audiences all over Europe. Now she was a middle-aged recluse who had lost her looks, her voice, and her husband. Alone in her villa, with no lover, no children to comfort her, just memories of her glorious career and a husband who had abandoned her, she must have been unutterably miserable. Did she still have the jewelled violin with her? Was it on her dressing table or beside her bed? Or had she buried it away in a drawer, or even got rid of it, because she could no longer bear to have it around — this gift from a former lover that served only to remind her of happier times?

Rossini never came back to her. In 1837, he obtained a legal separation, and eight years later, in 1845, Isabella died at Castenaso, sad, lonely, and neglected. Ten months after that, Rossini married Olympe.

Guastafeste was silent for a long time after I'd finished.

Then he said, 'I've never heard of any of them. Isabella Colbran, Domenico Barbaia, Olympe Pélissier.'

'I know,' I said. 'The peripheral figures in great

273

men's lives are always forgotten.'

'Who inherited Isabella's estate after she died?'

'Surprisingly, I believe it was Rossini.'

'But they were legally separated.'

'Isabella never changed her will. She still loved him, despite what he had done to her. When she died, they say she was murmuring his name.'

'And the violin?'

I shrugged.

'Who knows?'

'Did Rossini inherit that, too?'

'Your guess is as good as mine,' I said.

'If he did, what would he have done with it?'

'Taken it back to Paris with him, I suppose. That's where he lived for the remainder of his life.'

'And where Villeneuve and Robillet lived. Do you think they found something in Paris, something to put them on the trail of the violin?'

'Maybe,' I said.

Guastafeste cut another slice of cheese and ate it with a cracker.

'One thing I'd like to know,' I said. 'Paganini's gold box. How did Nicoletta Ferrara acquire it?'

Guastafeste nodded, chewing on his cracker and cheese.

'I'd like to know that, too,' he said. 'Why don't we go up there tomorrow and see if we can find out?'

* * *

274

The journey took us less than two hours. First the A1 to Milan, then the A8 — one of the many motorways that radiate out from Milan with the sole purpose of getting its citizens out of town as swiftly as possible. Milan is a wonderful place — or so the Milanese are always telling us — it's just that no one actually wants to live there, particularly at weekends. On a Friday evening, the A8 is choked with fleeing families heading north to the lakes and mountains, like refugees from a war zone.

This morning, however, the roads were relatively quiet. There were the usual convoys of lorries, of course, but Guastafeste soon left them far behind in his 150-kilometres-an-hour slipstream. At the Sesto intersection, we turned off the autostrada, crossed over the River Ticino, and took the road along the western shore of Lake Maggiore, the carriageway hugging the edge of the shimmering water, twisting and turning past inlets where yachts and rowing boats were moored in the shallows. In the distance, beyond the northern tip of the lake, I could see the mountains stretching away into Switzerland, the highest peaks glazed with snow.

Stresa was once the favourite summer retreat of the rich and fashionable, of royalty and artists and idle playboys. Dickens and Flaubert passed through the town and Hemingway set part of *A Farewell to Arms* there. It is long past its heyday, but it is still a stylish, attractive resort, the public gardens along the lakeside luxuriant and well maintained, the hotels elegant and smart, their trade no longer sustained by dukes and counts, but by coach parties of Swiss and Austrian tourists.

It was awhile since I had been there. I first went with my parents when I was a child, just after the Second World War, and later I returned with my own children, visiting the zoo in the grounds of the Villa Pallavicino and taking day trips out to the Borromean Islands to see the grottoes and white peacocks of the Isola Bella and the tropical gardens of the Isola Madre. We went swimming in the lake, the kids screaming at the cold water, and hiked up Mottarone, the mountain behind Stresa, from whose summit you can ostensibly see both Switzerland and the Duomo in Milan, though on the day we went, there was a low mist and you were lucky to see beyond the end of your nose.

I remembered it as a bustling, vibrant place, the water-front crowded with visitors and boat skippers touting for trade, the balconies of every hotel garlanded with red geraniums. In summer, it is no doubt still like that, but now, as winter approached, it was quiet, with that sad, closed-up feel of a holiday resort out of season.

The Villa Nettuno was on the outskirts of Stresa, on the hillside overlooking the lake. We turned off the main road through an open pair of steel gates and went up a steep drive to a small parking area at the side of the house. The villa was a stately nineteenth-century gentleman's residence, rendered with a white stucco that had faded to a dirty grey. It had two storeys, the ground-floor windows arched, the ones on the first floor rectangular, with wrought-iron balconies outside them and green wooden shutters. The shutters, like the render, were faded and rather shabby. Some of the wooden slats were missing; others were broken and hanging loose.

Ruggiero Monteveglio was waiting for us by the side door. He was a slender man in his late thirties. He had a squat nose with very open nostrils, which gave him a porcine appearance, and hair shaved close to the scalp to disguise his premature baldness. He was wearing a creased pair of cotton trousers, a frayed jacket, and scuffed suede shoes. In some countries — England, for example — it is fashionable for the very rich to dress down, to disguise their wealth under the trappings of the common man. But this is not the case in Italy. In Italy, that kind of dissimulation would be regarded as ludicrous, possibly even evidence of insanity. If you had it, why on earth would you not flaunt it? Ruggiero Monteveglio didn't look like a man whose aunt owned a villa that, at a conservative guess, was worth two or three million euros.

We introduced ourselves and shook hands; then Monteveglio unlocked the door and turned off the alarm at a keypad on the wall of the hall.

'You've had the alarm fixed?' Guastafeste said.

'Yes, of course. The insurance company insisted on it.'

'You've made a claim for what was stolen?'

'For what I *know* was stolen,' Monteveglio said. 'There may have been other things that were taken that I don't know about. My aunt had a lot of stuff, some of it valuable, some of it junk, and she wasn't good at keeping records. I can't be sure exactly what was taken.'

He opened an internal door and we walked through into a large sitting room at the front of the house. The shutters were closed, but there was enough light filtering in through the slats to show that the room was crammed from wall to wall with furniture.

'I see what you mean,' Guastafeste said.

There were dark wooden antique sideboards and cabinets round the perimeter of the room, and the centre was taken up with armchairs, sofas, and low tables. Every surface was cluttered with objects — framed photographs, vases, ornaments, all manner of bric-a-brac and knickknacks.

Ruggiero Monteveglio picked his way round the furniture and pulled open the windows to throw back the wooden shutters. Light flooded into the room.

'You don't have metal shutters?' Guastafeste asked.

'Unfortunately, no,' Monteveglio replied. 'I kept trying to persuade my aunt to instal them, but she wouldn't hear of it. She said they were ugly and would ruin the look of the house. I suppose she had a point, but . . . ' He shrugged. 'It would have made the place more secure.'

'I've seen the Stresa police report,' Guastafeste said. 'The burglars broke in through the kitchen window, didn't they?'

'That's right. After they'd cut the power to the alarm.'

'And the items stolen, they were in which rooms?'

'This one, the music room, and my aunt's bedroom upstairs. The bedroom is where they found the jewellery. My aunt, as you may gather, was careless about security. She had the alarm — the insurance company wouldn't insure the house without one — but I don't think she ever switched it on. She was the same with her jewellery. She used to leave it lying around on her dressing table or in a box in a drawer. Nothing was locked away.'

I walked over to the windows and looked out. There was a terrace flanked by a stone balustrade running the width of the house. From either end of the terrace, diagonal flights of stone steps descended through the garden, which was a lush jungle of temperate and semitropical vegetation — banana plants, eucalyptus, camellias, azaleas, hydrangeas. Palm trees poked their heads up from the dense undergrowth, some of them short and stubby, some tall and thin, with umbrellas of fronds, like propellers, at the top that looked as if they might take off into the air in a high wind. Out across the water, I could see the ornate terraces of the Isola Bella. One of the steamers that crisscross the lake was heading towards the island, sunlight glinting off its white hull and the rippling waves it was leaving in its wake.

'This is a magnificent setting,' I said. 'Your aunt was very lucky.'

'It's not a bad little hole, is it?' Monteveglio said dryly.

'What's going to happen to the house now? Are you going to sell it?'

'I don't know. I'm not sure I can afford to keep it on.'

'You live in Stresa?'

'In Pallanza. You know it, across the other side of the bay. I have a two-bedroom apartment. You could probably fit the whole thing into this one room and still have space left over.'

'Where was the painting by Degas?' Guastafeste asked.

'Just there.'

Monteveglio pointed. Above the mantelpiece was a conspicuous rectangular section of wall that was a lighter colour than the rest.

'It's been recovered, by the way,' Guastafeste said.

Monteveglio stared at him in surprise.

'The Degas? When?'

'Yesterday. We raided an auction house in Cremona.'

'In Cremona? You have the thieves?'

'Only the fence, and he's saying nothing about the burglars.'

'Just the Degas? None of the other stuff that was stolen?'

'Not so far. The gold box you already know about, of course.'

Guastafeste gazed round the room. There were a lot of pictures on the walls — far too many, in fact. They were squashed so close together that the frames were almost touching. Several of the pictures were clearly the work of the same artist. They had a distinctive style — not really paintings, but more mixed-media compositions, part oil paint, part water-colour, part collage. Some were little more than crude daubs, big splashes of colour, with different objects stuck onto the canvas — pieces of cloth or sacking, strange silhouettes cut from black card, even chunks of what looked like varnished driftwood. A couple seemed to have musical themes — large staves with clefs and random notes painted on them, images of musical instruments that had a surreal, distorted look. In one, a violin as thin and flexible as a sheet of paper was slithering down a flight of steps whose treads and risers were the black and white keys of a piano.

'The burglars didn't take any of these, I notice,' Guastafeste said.

'They had taste,' Monteveglio replied.

'Who's the artist?'

'These were all done by my aunt.'

'She was an artist? A professional?'

'Would you pay for something like that? No, she did them purely for her own amusement. They're all over the house.'

'And not one was stolen?'

'No. Shame, isn't it?'

'I quite like them,' I said, feeling strangely defensive of Nicoletta Ferrara. A lot of work and imagination had gone into these creations and I felt they deserved a little more respect.

'Really?' Monteveglio said incredulously.

'They're very individualistic.'

'Yes, I suppose that's one way of putting it.'

'The gold box,' Guastafeste said. 'Where was that kept?'

'In the music room.'

'May we see?'

The music room was at the far end of the house. It was almost as big as the sitting room and just as cluttered, with glass-fronted music cabinets against the walls and two grand pianos in the middle — a Steinway and a Bosendorfer. There was more of Nicoletta Ferrara's idiosyncratic artwork on the walls, many again with musical subjects. Some were strange collages, fragments of photocopied music arranged to create landscapes or peculiar animals or people's faces.

'Your aunt was obviously musical,' I said.

Monteveglio nodded.

'Yes, it was her great passion. She was an excellent pianist, and a very good violinist, too.'

'The violin you showed Vincenzo Serafin, the Bergonzi, do you know how your aunt acquired it?'

'I believe she inherited it from her father. It had been in the Bianchi family for several generations, I think.'

'That was your aunt's maiden name, Bianchi?'

'Yes.'

'They must have been well-off.'

Monteveglio gave a ghost of a smile.

'They weren't short of a euro or two. They made their money in banking back in the middle of the nineteenth century.'

'And she was your aunt by marriage?'

'She married my mother's older brother, Luca. The money was all hers. My uncle Luca was an investment broker in Milan. Nicoletta came to him for advice on what to do with her inheritance when her father died. Uncle Luca's solution: Marry him. And she did.'

'And your uncle died when?'

'Oh, ten, twelve years ago.'

I looked at a framed photograph on one of the tables. It showed a middle-aged man and woman standing by a fountain that I recognised as the Fountain of the Four Rivers in the Piazza Navona in Rome.

'Is this your aunt and uncle?' I asked.

'Yes, that's them.'

I studied the photograph more closely. Nicoletta Ferrara had a striking face, but she wasn't a beautiful woman. Her features were too uneven, her nose on the large side, her jaw-line slightly masculine. There was a strength, perhaps even stubbornness, in her eyes and the set of her mouth. I'd never met her, but something about her face seemed familiar.

'When Vincenzo Serafin came here, which room did you go in?' Guastafeste asked Monteveglio.

'I showed him the violin in here,' Monteveglio replied.

'But to get here, you would have to pass through the sitting room?'

'Yes, I suppose we did.'

Guastafeste shot me a meaningful glance.

'Apart from the Degas, which of the stolen items were in the sitting room?'

'Well, the silverware was. My aunt kept it in the big glass cabinet in the corner — unlocked, of course.'

'And the gold box?'

'That was on top of that cabinet over there. You're not suggesting that Signor Serafin had anything to do with this, are you?'

'No, no,' Guastafeste said. 'A reputable violin dealer like him. What made you go to him, by the way?'

'He has a house up the road from here, near Baveno. I don't know him personally, but a friend of a friend told me about him. Said he was one of the leading dealers in the country.'

'Do you know where your aunt got the gold box?' I asked.

'I think she inherited that from her parents, too. It was another family heirloom, like the furniture and the violin. I remember it from my childhood. We'd come here for lunch and the box was always there on the cabinet. It fascinated me — the box you couldn't open. You know it had a funny combination lock on it? I used to spend hours trying to crack the code. No one knew what it was, even my aunt. I was sure there was a treasure map inside it. I wanted to break it open and see, but my aunt wouldn't hear of it. She said it was like that English legend of King Arthur and Excalibur. When the right person came along, the box would open. Until then, it had to be allowed to keep its secrets. She claimed it once belonged to a princess, but we didn't believe her, of course. Aunt Nicoletta was like that — fanciful, liked to tell stories, to embroider the truth a bit.'

'Did this princess have a name?'

'Not that I remember.'

'Elisa?'

'No, I don't think so. Why?'

'It was made for Elisa Baciocchi, the princess of Piombino and Lucca. She was Napoléon's sister.'

'Aunt Nicoletta never said anything about that.'

'There's nothing about its origins in the insurance paper-work — a bill of sale or certificate of authenticity? She must have had it valued at some point.'

'It wasn't insured,' Monteveglio said. 'The Degas, the silverware, the jewellery — they were specifically listed on the insurance policy, but not the gold box.'

'It wasn't covered?'

'A lot of things aren't covered. My aunt didn't worry about things like insurance. She didn't really seem to care. If something was stolen or broken, so what? They're only objects, after all. Why worry about them? That was her attitude. You can be indifferent like that when you have as much as she did.'

'Do you inherit all her estate?' Guastafeste asked.

'Most, yes. She left money to various charities, but this house, the stuff in it, it's all mine now. There's too much of it for my liking. I'll probably get rid of the furniture, all the junk she collected over the years.

'Has Serafin made you an offer for the Bergonzi violin?' I said.

'No, he hasn't given me a valuation yet.'

'If I were you, I'd get a second opinion from another dealer.'

'You would? Signor Serafin seemed a very straightforward, honest kind of man.'

'Appearances can be deceptive,' I said.

In the car driving home, Guastafeste was silent until we were a couple of kilometres from the Villa Nettuno. Then he said, 'That was a bit of a waste of time, wasn't it? All we found out was that that lying rogue Serafin cased the joint, then tipped off Villeneuve and his pal Lodrino, who organised the burglary — and we knew that already.'

'Mmm,' I murmured noncommittally.

I wasn't so sure we'd wasted our trip. Something about that photograph of Nicoletta Ferrara was bothering me. Her maiden name, too, had struck a chord. Bianchi. Why did I know the name Bianchi?

I dwelt on it as we headed south along the lakeshore road and onto the autostrada. We were nearing Milan, the traffic starting to thicken, when something happened that took my mind off Nicoletta Ferrara.

Guastafeste received a message over the radio that was clipped to the dashboard of the car. Vladimir Kousnetzoff had been located, the crackly male voice informed us. Guastafeste reached across to punch a button on the handset.

'Where?'

'Bologna. The Hotel Primavera.'

'He's been picked up?'

'Negative. He'd checked out before the

286

Bologna police got there.'

'*Merda!*'

Guastafeste hammered the sides of the steering wheel with the palms of his hands.

'Isn't that just like it?' he said through clenched teeth. 'We finally track him down and he vanishes.'

'Bologna?' I said.

Guastafeste glanced across at me.

'What about it?'

'Isabella Colbran's villa at Castenaso — that's just outside Bologna.'

16

It is two hundred kilometres from Milan to Bologna, but we did the journey in under ninety minutes, the speedometer occasionally touching 180 kph, the rooflight flashing to clear our path through the traffic. I didn't take in much of the scenery — I had my eyes tightly shut most of the way.

Only when I felt the car begin to slow and the g-force that had been pinning me to my seat ease off a little did I dare to open my eyes. I saw a sign reading BOLOGNA — 5KM.

'You have a good sleep?' Guastafeste asked.

'I wasn't asleep.'

'You were breathing very heavily.'

'I think you're confusing sleep with a sustained panic attack,' I said.

We took the ring road north round Bologna, then turned off and followed a smaller rural road to Castenaso. The countryside was flat, bare ploughed fields, which a few months earlier would have contained wheat and maize crops, and scattered farmhouses ringed by lime and cypress trees to provide protection from the sun and wind.

As we went over a level crossing, an illuminated electronic speed sign started flashing red at us, telling us we were going sixty-three kilometres an hour. Guastafeste applied the brakes and we dropped to below the legal limit.

We were on the outskirts of Castenaso, driving past modern apartment blocks, which soon gave way to a few shops. We crossed a bridge over the River Idice, then kept going through a set of traffic lights and almost immediately found ourselves coming out on the other side of the town.

'Was that it?' Guastafeste said. 'Or did we miss something?'

He pulled into the kerb, reversed into a farm track, and drove back the way we'd come.

We hadn't missed anything. That was all there was to Castenaso — a nondescript linear settlement clinging to the main road, with no real centre and no older core that might have been there when Isabella Colbran and Rossini were alive. In their day, it must have been a small, self-sufficient farming community. Now it had become a soulless dormitory town for Bologna, only a few kilometres away.

We parked outside a hardware shop and got out to explore further on foot. A hunched, scruffy-looking fellow was passing by on the pavement. I stopped him and asked if he knew where Isabella Colbran's villa was.

'Who?' he said.

'Isabella Colbran,' I repeated. 'She was a singer. Married to Rossini.'

'Rossini? You mean the builder in Marano?'

'The composer. They had a house near Castenaso.'

'Who did?'

Guastafeste took my arm and led me away, muttering darkly about the limited gene pool

289

and mental faculties of the local populace.

The second person we accosted was no help, either. He was obviously a municipal employee, for he was wearing a luminous yellow vest and was going about his work as if he were suffering from a bad case of somnambulism. He was wandering along the street picking up litter with a long-handled claw and depositing it in a black garbage bag he was carrying. A wirehaired terrier, which might have been his, or a stray with nothing better to do, scampered along beside him, yapping excitedly at the claw. He didn't know who Isabella Colbran was, or Rossini.

'We should've asked the dog,' Guastafeste said sourly as we continued along the street in search of a local who could justify the epithet by actually demonstrating some knowledge of the area.

At the traffic lights, I noticed a small police station and suggested we go inside and ask for help. Guastafeste wasn't keen on the idea. Professional pride, I think. There is a rigid pecking order in the police force, and a city detective like Antonio was reluctant to ask favours from colleagues he no doubt regarded as little more than country bumpkins. We crossed the road instead and approached a group of elderly men who were sitting on benches under the trees by the *comune*. They knew who Rossini was all right, and Isabella, too, but they had some bad news for us about the Villa Colbran.

'It's gone,' one of the men said.

'Gone?' I said.

290

'You didn't know? It was destroyed during the Second World War.'

'All of it?'

'Nearly all. I haven't been there myself, but I believe there are only a few stones left.'

This was a blow. We'd come all this way for nothing.

'Where was it?' I asked.

The man gestured with a hand.

'A few kilometres away. Over the level crossing and right at the roundabout. Look for the Santuario della Beata Vergine del Pilar. The villa was right by it.'

We returned to our car in silence. Guastafeste stared out of the windscreen for a long moment, then said bitterly, 'Another waste of time. Kousnetzoff can't have come here.'

'I'm sorry,' I said. 'I was wrong.'

'It's not your fault, Gianni. It's just frustrating.' He started the engine. 'Back to the autostrada?'

'I suppose so. Why don't we go to the villa on our way? It's not much of a detour.'

Guastafeste shrugged.

'Okay, why not.'

We headed out of Castenaso and into the surrounding farmland, driving along a dead-straight road between fields, drainage ditches on either side of the carriageway, green-houses and lines of poly tunnels gleaming in the sun. The urban sprawl of Bologna had not spread this far yet. It still felt isolated, sparsely populated. On the horizon ahead of us was the tower of a church. As we drew nearer, I could see from the architecture, the dusty red bricks, that it was an ancient building, four, maybe five hundred years old.

'That has to be it,' I said.

Guastafeste pulled into a lay-by just before the church and switched off the engine. We were at a minor crossroads in the middle of nowhere. Apart from a house on the corner across the road, which had obviously been erected fairly recently, the church was the only building in the vicinity. On the traffic island immediately in front of it — in a strange juxtaposition of old and new — was a garish plastic sign advertising a pizzeria.

We climbed out of the car and walked over to the church. It was a simple cubelike brick building with a pitched roof and a tall bell tower on one side, which had a small dome on the top. At the base of the tower was a white marble plaque in memory of Rossini. Guastafeste tried the front door. It was locked. I walked farther along the road. The land behind the church was open fields. I could see no sign of any remains of the Villa Colbran.

'Let's go,' Guastafeste called to me. 'There's nothing for us here.'

I walked back towards him and saw a dark blue Fiat saloon turn off the main road onto the dirt forecourt outside the church. A man in a suit and tie, about my age, got out and looked at us both curiously. I explained why we were there.

'Isabella's villa?' the man said. 'I'm afraid there's not much to see. Just the remains of the entrance and a few fallen stones, and the summerhouse in the woods, but that's virtually derelict.'

He pulled a bunch of keys from his jacket pocket.

'This is the church where they were married, Isabella and Rossini. Would you like to see inside?'

I saw Guastafeste hesitate, about to refuse the offer, and stepped in before he could say anything.

'Thank you. You're very kind,' I said.

'You're lucky I came along,' the man said. 'It's closed up most of the time.'

He unlocked the door and we followed him inside. The interior was gloomy, weak sunlight filtering in through a couple of high windows, one above the door, the other on the right-hand side. It was more a chapel than a church. There were no transepts, just a short rectangular nave, with an altar at the far end. The walls were a dull grey colour and had one or two large cracks in them, which had been crudely filled with cement. There were a few rows of pews and wooden chairs, two confession boxes, displays of flowers that looked plastic, and a collection of those fake votive candles with electric bulbs at their tips that are appearing more frequently in religious buildings — presumably because real candles are deemed uneconomical or a fire risk. The place had that distinctive musty smell that you could bottle and market as Old Church.

'March 16, 1822. That's when they were married,' the man said. 'A small private ceremony with only the priest and two witnesses present. This was Isabella's local church, built by the Spanish College in the sixteenth century — that's its coat of arms next to the altar — in honour of Our Lady of the Pillar in Saragossa. You know the story, I assume? Saint James going to Saragossa, where the Virgin Mary appeared to him and gave him a column of jasper wood and a wooden statue of herself.'

'You're very knowledgeable,' I said.

'I've written a pamphlet about it. This one here.'

He picked up a small booklet from the table next to the entrance and handed it to me.

'Umberto Boscolo, that's me,' he said, tapping the name on the cover of the booklet. 'I've written a lot about the history of the area. It's a hobby of mine. That's two euros — in the box, please. All proceeds go to the church. As you can see, it's in need of all the help it can get.'

'You said it's closed up most of the time,' I said.

Boscolo nodded.

'It's maintained by a few volunteers, like me, all of us retired. There's a service every other Sunday, the occasional wedding, but that's all. The rector covers several other churches in the area, and he holds regular Masses in a number of old people's homes. That's where all the faithful are. They're growing old, dying out. It's very sad.'

I put some money into the slot in the metal strongbox that was fastened to the wall, then leafed through the pamphlet.

'That's the Villa Colbran there,' Boscolo said.

294

He reached out and slid a finger into the centre of the pamphlet, spreading open the page to reveal a photograph of an imposing three-storey white villa at the end of a long drive. In the foreground were two high stone pillars with wrought-iron gates in between, the gates swung back to give a clear view of the house.

'It's an impressive building,' I said.

'That was taken in 1900. Isabella's father, Juan, bought the villa from the Spanish College in 1812. You know the Colbrans were Spanish? Juan had friends at the Spanish court. He had powerful friends here in Italy, too — Eugéne de Beauharnais, the Empress Josephine's son by her first husband, and Joachim Murat, Napoléon's brother-in-law. Isabella and Rossini lived in the villa after Juan Colbran died. It was their country estate.'

Boscolo pointed at another picture in his pamphlet. 'That's Isabella. A handsome woman, don't you think?'

'Yes indeed.'

Isabella was seated for the portrait, dressed in what appeared to be a stage costume — long classical robes and a headdress over her jet black hair. The backdrop was a painted woodland scene, like an operatic set. In her arms, she was cradling a small lyre. She was a tall, full-bodied woman with the kind of fleshy figure that has gone out of fashion in recent times. Her arms and throat were bare, her outfit revealing an expansive cleavage, which the artist had painted in loving detail. She was gazing down and to one side, an enigmatic, slightly melancholy expression on her face.

'The marriage didn't last,' Boscolo said. 'Rossini has always been blamed for that — running off with another woman, Olympe Pélissier — but there are always two sides to marital difficulties, aren't there? Isabella wasn't an easy woman to live with. She was temperamental, moody. She was accustomed to being a famous diva, people cheering and clapping her. She found retirement hard. She didn't adapt well to a quiet country life, to living in Rossini's shadow. He wanted a woman who would look after him, nurse him through his many illnesses. Olympe was better suited to that than Isabella.'

'The villa,' Guastafeste said. 'Where exactly was it?' I could sense he was getting impatient with all this local history.

'I'll show you.'

Boscolo led us back out of the church and a short distance along the side road. He pointed across the fields.

'It was over there. There is a farm track that roughly corresponds to the drive to the villa. And that copse in the distance, that's where the remains of the summerhouse are.'

We thanked him for his help and walked back to the car. Then we drove along the side road and pulled onto the grass verge at the end of the track that Boscolo had pointed out to us. Two hundred years ago, there would have been a grand entrance and driveway just here. Rossini and Isabella would have come and gone through it in a horse-drawn carriage. Now there was just a patch of dried mud and a rutted farm track overgrown by grass and wildflowers.

'Is this really worth it?' Guastafeste said.

'We're here now,' I replied. 'We might as well take a look.'

I slid out of the car and walked up the farm track. A reluctant Guastafeste followed me. Sixty metres on, the track petered out by a tiny mound of old bricks and the stump of a marble pillar, which was all that remained of the Villa Colbran.

I looked round, imagining the building that had once stood there — the white stuccoed walls, the arched doorways, the elegant salons, the manicured gardens and parkland spreading out in every direction. I saw Isabella in the villa, the forlorn, neglected woman withering away within its walls, rattling round in its empty rooms with only a few servants and a gambling habit to comfort her.

I sat down on the marble stump and began to read Umberto Boscolo's pamphlet about Rossini and Isabella. After Isabella's death, in 1845, the villa was rented out and one of the outbuildings was used as a smithy by a local blacksmith who had built the summerhouse in the woods for Isabella. Apparently, the summerhouse was her favourite retreat. She liked to go there to be alone, to think and to sing where no one could hear her. She had lost her voice, and knew it, but still found solace in her music.

In 1848, there was an uprising against the Austrians, who ruled northern Italy. There was fighting in the streets of Bologna, and Isabella's villa was occupied by the Austrian army, which vandalised and looted it, killing both the blacksmith and the estate manager, Lorenzo Costa.

I told Guastafeste this and he gave a shrug of resignation.

'So that's it, then,' he said. 'If the jewelled violin had still been here, if Rossini hadn't taken it back to Paris with him, the Austrians would have stolen it. Either way, it's gone.'

I put the pamphlet away in my pocket and wandered round the pile of bricks. Had Vladimir Kousnetzoff been here before us? If he had, he'd have found the same as we had: nothing.

It was only a short walk to the woods behind the villa. The summerhouse was hidden deep in the trees, a ruin over-grown by vegetation. Its domed roof had partially collapsed and there was a mound of rubble in the centre of the building, weeds sprouting from its surface. The sides of the summerhouse were more intact, and I could see why — they had been constructed by a blacksmith, not a stonemason. There was a low brick base, now chipped and coated with moss, but above that the sides were wrought-iron latticework, all rococo swirls and trefoils and leaf shapes, as if some rampant wild plant were climbing up the building.

I touched one of the metal leaves, then the curling wrought-iron tendrils looping their way up towards what was left of the tiled roof. The metal was in remarkably good condition for its age. It had been painted with bitumen or tar to protect it from the elements. Some sections were rusty and had broken away, leaving gaps, but I could still get an impression of what it must have been like when Isabella Colbran used to come here. There would have been a stone bench inside — I could see the crumbled remains in the shadowy interior, imagine Isabella sitting on it, lost in thought or quietly singing one of the arias that had made her famous.

'Come on, Gianni,' Guastafeste said. 'This isn't serving any useful purpose.'

I nodded. He was right. There was no point in lingering any longer. I followed him out of the woods and back along the track to the car. The road was too narrow for a U-turn, so we drove on, turning left at the next junction, then left again to head back towards the main road. We were on the other side of the old Colbran estate now, a ploughed field and the woods between us and the site of the villa. A car was parked at the side of the road, narrowing the carriageway. Guastafeste slowed to get past and I glanced out through the window.

'Pull in,' I said abruptly.

'What?'

'Pull in.'

Guastafeste brought the car to a stop.

'I saw something over by the woods,' I said. 'Two men, I think, going into the trees.'

'Two men?'

Guastafeste twisted round in his seat and stared hard across the field.

'Are you sure? I can't see anything.'

'They were there,' I said.

'Farmworkers?'

'I don't know.'

We got out and stood by the car for a moment, looking across the field and listening. It was very quiet. I could hear nothing except the gust of the breeze in my ears and the intermittent drone of traffic far away in the distance.

Then a sharp cry suddenly broke the silence — a cry of pain from the woods. I froze.

'What was that?' I said. 'A bird? An animal?'

'That wasn't a bird,' Guastafeste replied. 'It was a man.'

He crossed the road and vaulted over the drainage ditch, then started running across the field. I went after him, struggling to keep up. I was only halfway across the field when I saw Guastafeste disappear into the woods. He was out of sight for a time; then he reappeared on the fringe of the trees. Drawing closer, I could see that he had his mobile phone pressed to his ear.

'Keep back, Gianni,' he said in a low voice.

'What is it?'

'The police are on their way. Just stay where you are. Leave this to me.'

He turned and plunged back into the woods. I moved forward and hesitated. Guastafeste had told me to keep back. He'd said almost the same thing to me in Paris when we'd found Alain Robillet's body. I knew I should heed his instructions, but my curiosity was too strong. I wanted to find out what had happened. Pushing aside the undergrowth, I ventured into the edge of the woods. Then I stopped abruptly, letting out a gasp of shock. In a small clearing a few metres in front of me, a man's body was sprawled on the ground, his arms thrown out to the sides, his eyes and mouth open in a horrific grimace. It was Vladimir Kousnetzoff. There was a bloody red gash on his neck where his throat had been cut.

I stepped back, feeling my legs give way. I averted my eyes, breathing deeply to stop the nausea from overwhelming me. Where was Guastafeste? He'd told me to leave this to him, but I couldn't stand there and do nothing. There was a killer in the woods. I couldn't let Guastafeste tackle him alone. I skirted round the body and kept going through the trees.

It was a dense patch of woodland that had been left untouched for years. There were no paths, few clearings. The trees were crammed close together, the space between them filled in with shrubs and bushes, some so high and thick that they were virtually impenetrable. I forced my way through the vegetation, branches and brambles clawing at my arms and legs. I'd gone maybe thirty or forty metres when I stopped and tilted my head to listen. I could hear a faint rasping sound, like a hacksaw cutting through metal. I squeezed round a thicket of tangled shrubs and saw the wall of the summerhouse five metres ahead of me; saw a man carving feverishly away at the wrought-iron latticework, trying to remove a small section of the ornate decoration. And I knew suddenly what it was. I could picture the section in my mind. I'd seen it but not noticed it.

I edged closer. The man didn't see me, didn't hear me, he was so intent on his work. Then he paused to rest for a second and caught the crunch of my feet on the twig-strewn ground. He turned his head. I stopped dead in surprise, my eyes meeting his. It was Olivier Delacourt, the assistant manager of Molyneux et Charbon, in Paris. Delacourt! I gaped at him, my astonishment turning to fear as I remembered Kousnetzoff's body back in the clearing near the edge of the woods.

Delacourt stared at me, a hunted, desperate look on his face. There was a sheen of sweat on his forehead. He glanced round, checking that I was alone. I could sense the calculation going on in his head. One elderly man, that wasn't a threat. There was time to finish the job at hand, then deal with me.

He went back to his sawing for a moment, hacking away at the last few millimetres of metal with a furious energy until the piece of latticework came away in his fingers. He held the piece, gazing intently at it, panting heavily from the exertion; then he raised his head and fixed me with a piercing glare that froze my blood.

I was breathless; my legs were shaking, my heart pounding. This man was a killer. I took a step back. Where the hell was Guastafeste? Had he somehow got lost in the woods? Had he forgotten about the summerhouse?

Delacourt advanced towards me. I knew I couldn't run away from him. I was too old, and my legs were too weak.

'Antonio!' I screamed. 'Over here, by the summerhouse. Antonio!'

Delacourt raised the hacksaw in his hand, the

blade facing outwards. I reached down and picked up a fallen branch, brandishing it in front of me like a club. Delacourt kept coming, his mouth twisted into a bitter smile, a crazed, feral glint in his eyes.

'The police are on their way,' I yelled. 'You can't get away. Antonio!'

Then I saw Guastafeste. He was creeping out from the bushes behind the summerhouse. But he was too far away to do anything. Delacourt was almost on me. I swung the branch to and fro in front of me to keep him at bay, and to give Guastafeste more time.

'Did you hear me?' I shouted. 'The police are coming. It's all over.'

Delacourt came for me. But as he lunged forward, he caught his foot on a bramble and stumbled. I lashed out with my branch, knocking the hacksaw from his hand. He paused for a second, scanning the undergrowth for the hacksaw. And in that instant, Guastafeste swooped out round the summer-house and launched himself at Delacourt, hurtling into his back and smashing him violently to the ground. The piece of metal from the summerhouse that Delacourt had been clutching went flying into a clump of grass. Guastafeste pinned the winded Delacourt to the earth and in one slick, practised movement cuffed his hands behind him.

'You okay, Gianni?'

I nodded. I felt sick. My head was spinning. I wondered if I was going to faint. I stretched out my hand and steadied myself on a tree trunk. On the ground by my feet, Delacourt was groaning feebly, Guastafeste kneeling on his back.

'You're safe now, Gianni,' Guastafeste said. 'I've got him.'

I stayed where I was for a time, letting my heartbeat and breathing get back to normal. Then I walked slowly across to the summerhouse. My legs were still trembling. My mouth was dry. I could see the gap in the wrought-iron latticework, the rough silvery edges where the metal had been cut through. All these years the summerhouse had been there. How many people had sat in the cool shade of its domed roof, had gazed out through that intricate pattern of twisted iron — and never noticed? Yet why should they have? It blended in so perfectly with the other decorations that it was completely inconspicuous — just an organic part of the whole. If you want to conceal something, put it out in the open, where everyone can see it.

I retrieved the piece of metal from the undergrowth. It was an elongated oval, like a large sweet-chestnut leaf, about thirty centimetres long and ten centimetres wide. The ends were bare, jagged, freshly cut metal, but the other surfaces — the front and back and sides — didn't look like metal at all, they were so thickly coated with tar.

Delacourt twisted his head round and swore at me.

'That's mine. You have no right to it. *I* found it.'

'Tell that to the Bologna police when they arrive,' Guastafeste replied.

He pushed Delacourt's face firmly back into

the earth and looked up, listening. I could hear it, too — the distant sound of sirens getting nearer.

I took out my pocketknife and scraped away some of the black layer. It wasn't easy to remove — it was set hard, like rock. I worked the knife blade deeper and a chunk of the coating broke away. There was an object underneath, an object that wasn't oval but which had been bonded to a piece of oval metal and then disguised with the tar. I chipped away another corner and saw a gleam of yellow, then something else — a bloodred crystal the size of a small pea, and next to it a second crystal, this one clear like a piece of glass. Only I knew it wasn't glass.

I lifted my head and smiled at Guastafeste.

17

Guastafeste stayed on in Bologna, to be present when the local officers interviewed Olivier Delacourt, so I caught the train back to Cremona. It was almost dusk when I arrived home. The sky was overcast, daubed with bulging black clouds that presaged rain. The house was cold and gloomy. I switched on some lights and the central heating and made myself a cup of coffee. I didn't feel much like eating. I'd had a dried-out ham and cheese sandwich at Bologna station — my first food since breakfast — but I didn't want anything else. The afternoon's events had taken away my appetite.

I was listless. There was a hollow feeling of nausea in my stomach. I wondered if I was suffering from delayed shock. I kept seeing Vladimir Kousnetzoff's body lying on the ground, running and rerunning the image through my mind like a loop of film that stubbornly refused to move on to the next sequence. And when, finally, it did move on, it was only to the scene by the summerhouse, to Delacourt advancing towards me with a hacksaw in his hand. I don't know which scene disturbed me more — the corpse with its throat cut, or the killer preparing to do the same to me. I knew I couldn't have fought Delacourt off. If Antonio had come just half a minute later, he would have found me dead. The thought made me shudder, sent an icy tremor through my body that left me chilled to the bone.

I forced myself out of my armchair and went upstairs to find a warm pullover. I was shivering, my arms and legs trembling as if I had a fever. I slipped the pullover on, then put my dressing gown over it and sat on the edge of the bed for a few minutes until the shaking stopped. I was considering whether to go straight to bed, or go back downstairs to make myself a bowl of hot soup, when the telephone rang. I picked up the receiver on the bedside table, thinking it would be Guastafeste. It was Yevgeny Ivanov.

'Gianni?' he said. 'I need to talk to you.' He spoke in English, his voice almost a whisper, hoarse at the edges.

'Talk?' I said.

'Can you come to me?'

'Where are you?'

'A house near Lodi.'

'Lodi?'

'You know where that is?'

'Of course. You want me to come now?'

'Yes.'

'What is this, Yevgeny?'

I couldn't disguise my irritation. It was nearly dark, and I had had a traumatic day.

'I want to sort things out. Please, Gianni. You're the only person who can help me.'

The appeal was so heartfelt that I softened a little.

'Whereabouts near Lodi?' I asked.

'Close to the river. Outside a village called Galgagnano.'

I thought about it. Lodi wasn't far, a small medieval town midway between Cremona and Milan.

'Gianni?' Yevgeny said tentatively. 'I am sorry to trouble you. I would be very grateful if you would come. I have no one else to turn to.'

'How do I find you?' I said.

He gave me directions; then I hung up. I didn't really want to go. I was tired, emotionally drained. The last thing I felt like was an earnest, and probably difficult, conversation with a troubled young man. But I couldn't bring myself to let him down. I liked Yevgeny. His faith in me was flattering. He'd said he needed my help. It would have been callous to reject his plea. Besides, if I stayed here, I would only dwell disturbingly on Kousnetzoff and Delacourt, and I'd had enough of both of them.

It was spitting with rain outside. I picked up my waterproof jacket and went to my car. By the time I reached the main road, the heavens had opened and I was driving in a torrential downpour, the sky so dark that it felt like the middle of the night. It took me twenty minutes to get to Lodi, then a further fifteen to find the house. It was down a rough farm track, a small one-storey stone cottage on a hillock above the River Adda. I could just make out the course of the river in the broad floodplain below me as I dashed from my car to the door of the cottage.

The door was already open. Yevgeny was standing in the hallway. Next to him was a slim, pretty young woman in her early twenties. I gave

308

a start as I recognised her. She was the student who'd been accompanying Vittorio Castellani at the post-concert reception in Cremona's town hall two Saturdays ago.

Yevgeny took my hand and squeezed it hard, then clung on to it as he spoke.

'Thank you for coming. It is very good of you. Is it raining?'

'Yevgeny, what are you doing here?' I said, extricating my hand.

He glanced at the girl beside him.

'This is Mirella,' he said. 'She was at the reception.'

'I know.'

I looked at her. She averted her eyes guiltily. So Rudy Weigert had been right. Sex — the key to all human behaviour.

'She is music student at the university in Milan,' Yevgeny said.

'This is your house?' I asked her.

'No, it belongs to a friend.'

'And you've been here all this time?'

The question was addressed to Yevgeny. He looked down sheepishly.

'I have not behaved well,' he said. 'My mother will never forgive me.'

'Mothers are very good at forgiving,' I said. 'Now, why don't you tell me exactly what's been going on.'

We went into the living room off the hall. It was a small room with a kitchen area at one end and an open hearth, in which the remains of a fire were glowing dully. I'd already worked out from the three doors off the hall that this was a one-bedroom cottage: living room, bedroom, bathroom.

Yevgeny and Mirella sat down next to each other on the sofa, leaving me to take the armchair by the fire. I could feel the welcome heat on my legs. Yevgeny grasped Mirella's hand in his own and she slid closer to him, their shoulders touching. They looked terribly young, and terribly awkward.

'This is not easy,' Yevgeny began. 'I feel so bad about it. All the trouble I have caused, the worry. Did you speak to my mother — after my telephone call?'

'Yes, I spoke to her.'

'And?'

'She was concerned, of course. She was hurt that you had rung me and not her.'

'Yes. I know that must have made her unhappy.'

'But I reassured her that you were all right and would be coming back soon. What are you doing out here, Yevgeny? Your mother has been worried sick. She has had to cancel at least one of your concerts. You're damaging your career.'

'I am not sure I want a career anymore,' Yevgeny said quietly.

'What do you mean?'

He gave a facial shrug.

'I am not sure I want to go on with the life I have been living. I do not think it is right for me.'

'Are you not happy?'

'No, I am not.' He glanced at Mirella. 'I mean with my music, my playing. In other areas, well, yes, I am happy now. Very happy.'

He smiled at Mirella and they gazed softly at each other for a moment, as if I weren't there. I'd forgotten just how intoxicating and all-consuming young love can be — and how irritating to others.

'Let's start at the beginning,' I said, suppressing the urge to bang their silly heads together. 'At the reception after your concert. That's presumably where all this began.'

Yevgeny nodded.

'We meet there,' he said. 'After you leave. We start talking; we get on well. We swap mobile numbers. Then on the Monday afternoon, Mirella call me, ask if I want to go for a drive. Mama is not there; she has gone shopping.'

'She thought you'd gone off with Vladimir Kousnetzoff,' I said.

Yevgeny's eyes opened wide with surprise.

'Kousnetzoff? Why would I go with him?'

'He phoned your hotel room that afternoon, didn't he?'

'Yes, he did.'

'Why?'

'Because he want to manage my career. He has approach me before, but he is wasting his time. I always tell him no. Mama thought I go to meet him? She knows I would never do that. What do I want with agent? I have her.'

'That's not how she sees it. She was convinced you'd walked out on her. Or even that Kousnetzoff had kidnapped you.'

'*Kidnapped* me? But that is ridiculous.'

'Worried mothers don't always think rationally. Why didn't you leave her a note saying where you'd gone?'

'I do not think I will be gone a long time. We go for drive; then we go to bar; then we have a meal in a restaurant. Those are ordinary things to most people our age, but I have never done them. I have never been out for a meal with a girl. Mama has never allowed it.'

'You could have phoned her later.'

'Later? I meant to, I really did, but . . . ' He paused. 'I drink too much wine. We go back to Mirella's flat, in Milan, and, well, things happen.'

He looked away, colouring slightly.

'Yes, I understand,' I said quickly. This was not an area into which I wished to stray.

'It's all my fault,' Mirella interjected.

'No, no . . . ' Yevgeny protested.

'It is. I could've driven you back the next day, but I didn't. We came out here instead.'

'But that is what I want,' Yevgeny said.

He looked directly at me, his expression tense, grave.

'You do not know what it is like for me, the life I have been leading since I was a child. I needed to get away for a while. I needed space to think. I know I should have called Mama, but after I stay away that one night — the first night I have ever been apart from her in twenty-three years — I could not face it. I could not face her anger, her disappointment in me. I have always been a disappointment to her.'

'I don't think you have,' I said.

'Oh, I have. Nothing I do is ever good enough.

312

Right from early age, my only clear memories of Mama are her saying, 'You can do better than that, Yevgeny.''

'I'm sure she's only ever wanted you to fulfil your potential. She's always had your best interests at heart.'

'I know that.' He straightened up, his posture defiant now. 'But why should I not go off for few days? Why should I not be with Mirella? Why I have to tell my mother where I am all the time? I am not a child. She must see that.'

He swallowed hard.

'Gianni, you must help me tell my mother this. Tell her that things must change. I do not know how. You must give me advice. You have age, experience.'

He was gazing at me imploringly. I could see the confusion and anguish in his eyes. He'd been foolish and thoughtless, but I couldn't bring myself to be too hard on him.

'I've never been under the delusion that age and experience qualify you to give advice to anyone,' I said.

'But I need it,' Yevgeny said. 'It is partly because of you that I have done this.'

'*Me?*' I said incredulously. 'What have I — '

'No, do not take it wrong way,' he interrupted hurriedly. 'I am not blaming you. It was Sunday that did it, that finally make me decide that something in my life has to change.'

'Sunday?'

'When we play quartets at your house. I enjoy it so much, just playing music for pleasure — no pressure, no expectations. I have been playing

313

the violin for nearly twenty years. I start when I am four. I can read music before I can read the alphabet. It has been my whole life. Everything else has been unimportant. The violin was all that mattered. Scales, practice, exams, performances. That is all I know for twenty years and I get tired of it. I want something more. And on Sunday, you show me that music can be fun. Nothing else. Just fun. And fun is what I have never had — in music or anything else.'

He looked at me anxiously, seeking my approval, and I caught a glimpse of the little boy in him. The four-year-old in short trousers trying desperately to please his mother, and still trying now he was a grown man. I noticed Mirella squeezing his hand tightly, pressing closer to him in an instinctive gesture of support. I couldn't really blame her for any of this. She wasn't the cause; she was just the catalyst for a reaction that was always going to occur, sooner or later.

'You want to give up your career?' I said.

'Not give up. I just want to do it different. Make some changes, get off treadmill.' He glanced at Mirella again. 'Get more of a life outside music.'

'Then talk to your mother about it.'

'That is the problem. I cannot talk to her. I have tried, but she will not listen. She always knows best. To be honest, I'm scared of her, scared of how she might react.'

I stood up from my armchair.

'Get your things. I'm taking you back to Cremona.'

He didn't argue. He knew what had to be

done. I was there simply to set the wheels in motion.

They went into the bedroom to gather up their belongings, and I found a poker by the hearth and knocked out the remains of the wood fire. The handle of the poker was dusted with soot, which came off on my hands, so I went along the hall to the bathroom to wash it off.

I was drying my hands on a towel when I noticed the handwritten notice stuck to the wall, giving instructions about how to operate the cottage's hot-water system. The handwriting was familiar. I stared at the notice, studying the shape of the letters, looking for the individual characteristics that make each person's handwriting distinctive. I realised suddenly where I'd seen it before — in the margins of the book about Elisa Bonaparte that I'd borrowed from Vittorio Castellani's office.

I went back out into the hall. Yevgeny and Mirella were emerging from the bedroom in their coats, Mirella clutching a small holdall.

'It was good of Professor Castellani to let you use his cottage,' I said.

Mirella looked at me blankly.

'Professor Castellani?'

'This is his house, isn't it?'

'No, it's Marco's.'

'Marco?'

'He was at the reception, too. Marco Martinelli. He's an associate lecturer in the music department. This is his family's cottage. Loads of people use it; Marco doesn't mind.'

She eyed me apprehensively.

'You're not wanting me to come with you, are you? To see Yevgeny's mother.'

'No, I don't think that would be advisable just yet,' I said. 'Perhaps later.'

I've never seen anyone look so relieved.

'Okay,' she said.

'I'll leave you to say good-bye to each other,' I said tactfully. 'I'll be waiting in the car, Yevgeny.'

So it was Marco's book that I took from Castellani's office, I thought as I ran through the rain to my car. Why would Marco have had a book about Elisa Baciocchi? And for the second time that day, a surname was bothering me. First Bianchi, now Martinelli. Why did the name Martinelli sound familiar?

★ ★ ★

I phoned Ludmilla from the foyer of the Hotel Emanuele, then left Yevgeny in an armchair and went upstairs alone. Ludmilla was waiting for me, standing in the open doorway of her room, her eyes scanning the empty corridor behind me.

'Yevgeny . . . ' she said.

'We need to talk first,' I said.

'He is well? Tell me he's all right.'

'He's all right,' I said.

'Where's he been? Why hasn't he come up with you?'

I closed the door and made her sit down. She perched on the edge of her chair, her hands clutched tightly together, her lips pinched. Her whole body was tense.

'I want to see him,' she said. 'Why isn't he

316

here? What's going on?'

I pulled out another chair and sat facing her.

'All in good time, signora,' I said.

'You've got bad news, haven't you?' she said. 'What is it? He's signed with Kousnetzoff, is that it? Tell me. Is he leaving me? I must know.'

'He is not leaving you,' I said.

'Then why isn't he here?'

'He asked me to speak to you first.'

'Speak to me? Speak to me about what?'

'About the future.'

'The future? What do you mean?'

I told her where Yevgeny had been, and with whom. And I told her what he'd said to me at the cottage and then later in the car as we drove back to Cremona. She stared at me for a long moment, absorbing everything I'd said; then her eyes flashed angrily.

'What nonsense is this? He's going to throw away all these years of struggle for a girl? Has he lost his mind?'

'He's throwing nothing away,' I said calmly.

'Of course he is. Who is she, this Mirella? A student, you said. An opportunist, no doubt. Some pretty little thing with an eye for a meal ticket, latching onto Yevgeny because he's on his way to the top. Dear God, men! What is the stupid boy playing at? I want to meet this Mirella. Is she downstairs, too?'

Ludmilla stood up and headed for the door. I cut her off before she could reach the handle.

'This is none of my business,' I said. 'But Yevgeny has asked me to talk to you, and I have not finished yet. Please sit down.'

'Who are you to tell me what to do? He's my son. I will sort this mess out with him.'

'Signora, please sit down.'

I held her eyes. She stared back at me belligerently. I was blocking her exit, and she knew I wasn't going to step aside without a fight. She glared at me for a few seconds longer, then swirled round and strode back across the room.

'So finish what you have to say,' she snapped. 'Then I'll deal with Yevgeny and this . . . this gold-digging girl.'

'I cannot talk to you while you are in this state,' I said.

' "This state"?'

'You are angry.'

'I have a right to be angry, don't you think? He has disappeared for a week. No note, no phone call. I have been to the police; they have been searching for him. And now he comes back and expects everything to be all fine and rosy.'

'I understand why you're angry,' I said. 'He has behaved very badly, caused a lot of trouble and pain. He knows that. But getting angry with him isn't going to help.'

'Isn't it? He needs to have some sense knocked into him. He needs to see just how foolish he's been, how this girl is using him. He should get rid of her now and concentrate on his career again. He has concerts coming up. Since the Premio, the offers have been pouring in. He cannot afford to waste the opportunities he is being offered. It's what he's always dreamt of. What we've both dreamt of.'

'Maybe Yevgeny has other dreams, too,' I said.

'Nothing is as important as his career.'

'To him, or to you?'

'What are you saying?'

'I'm saying that he can have a successful career and other things, too. A social life, friends. Don't paint him into a corner. Don't make him choose between you and Mirella.'

'*Mirella?* A girl he has known for just a few days? I am his mother. We have been together for twenty-three years. You think that counts for nothing?'

'It counts for so much that you shouldn't put it at risk,' I said. 'He's not a child. Twenty-three-year-old men need more than their mothers. Listen to me, Ludmilla. All he wants to do is to make a few changes, to do things a little differently. He's not abandoning his career, or you. Don't overreact. He has a girlfriend, that's all. That's normal for a boy his age. Mirella might last a month, or she might last a lifetime. There's no point in guessing which now. Just let things take their course. Give Yevgeny the freedom to make his own choices, and his own mistakes. Because if you don't, he will break away from you now and never come back.'

There was an uncomfortable silence. I resisted the temptation to fill it. I'd said what I had to say, what Yevgeny had asked me to say. It was up to Ludmilla now to take the initiative. To take it, or to reject it.

'Why didn't Yevgeny talk to me about this?' Ludmilla said eventually. 'Why did he send you?'

'You want the honest answer? Because he's scared of you.'

She flinched.

'Scared of me? Don't be ridiculous.'

'He said he'd tried to discuss it with you, but you would never listen.'

Ludmilla looked away pensively. Her forehead creased. I tried to interpret her feelings from the pattern of wrinkles and saw hurt and puzzlement and disbelief.

'He actually said that? That he was scared of me?' she asked, turning back to me.

'Yes. I'm sorry.'

We fell silent again.

'Will you ask him to come up?' Ludmilla said softly.

'You're ready?'

'Yes, I'm ready.'

I went to the phone and spoke to the receptionist in the foyer. Then I opened the door and waited for Yevgeny. He came slowly along the corridor, his gaze fixed on my face, searching for some kind of signal — a signal I couldn't give him, for I didn't know what Ludmilla was going to do. Just before the threshold, he paused, unsure whether to enter the room. Then he steeled himself and came on. He regarded his mother warily, bracing himself for a confrontation.

Ludmilla said something in Russian. I didn't understand the words, but she didn't sound angry. Yevgeny replied in the same language. They looked at each other uncertainly. I knew it was time for me to go. I gave Yevgeny a quick

320

smile of encouragement and headed for the door.

I was at the far end of the corridor, about to go down the stairs, when I suddenly remembered why I knew the name Bianchi.

18

Antonia Bianchi — there it was on page seventy-four of one of my biographies of Paganini. And alongside it was a portrait of Antonia that bore an uncanny resemblance to the photograph of Nicoletta Ferrara, née Bianchi, I'd seen at Stresa. They had the same mouth and nose, the same look of stubbornness in the eyes — so many similarities, in fact, that even without the clue of their surnames, I would have suspected that they were related.

Antonia Bianchi was a singer who became Paganini's companion for a few years in the 1820s, and the mother of his only child, Achille. She was twenty when she met the violinist. Paganini was forty-one. They were together for four turbulent years but never married. Paganini, of course, was not an easy man to live with, but Antonia seems to have been almost unhinged in her fits of temper and jealousy, attacking her partner in public and attempting more than once to smash his precious Guarneri del Gesù to bits. The son she produced was the only thing that kept Paganini and her together for those few years.

Without Achille, on whom he doted, Paganini would have walked out on Antonia long before he actually did. When the acrimonious split finally came, Paganini gave Antonia two thousand scudi to relinquish any claim over

Achille, and from then on father and son were inseparable.

Two thousand scudi? I wondered about that sum as I read through the relevant pages of the book. It wasn't a large amount, particularly when compared with the phenomenal fees Paganini was charging for his concerts. Antonia doesn't appear to have had any great maternal urges and may well have been glad to get rid of her son. But given her violent, vindictive nature, it was perhaps a little surprising that she should have let Paganini off so lightly. Or had she?

The money was clearly not the only thing she took with her. Paganini must also have given her the gold box that Henri le Bley Lavelle had made for Elisa Baciocchi. How else did it come to be in Nicoletta Ferrara's house? By the time of the split, it was several years since Paganini had paid his gambling debt to Barbaia with the jewelled violin. The gold box would have been no use to him, so parting with it would probably have been no great sacrifice. The Bergonzi violin, too? Had that also been Paganini's, and had he included it in the financial settlement with Antonia? Paganini had a reputation for being a miser, but he could be extremely generous when he chose. He gave innumerable benefit concerts for charity and a large gift to the struggling Hector Berlioz. In his will, he left an annuity to Antonia, showing he had not forgotten her, though many years had passed since their parting. They had not been happy together, but she was the mother of his son and he made sure that she was properly provided for.

Did he give her anything else? Or did Antonia take anything else with her when they separated? I pondered on those questions as I got ready for bed; then they slipped from my mind as sleep overtook me. I had a bad night, waking regularly every couple of hours, tormented by nightmares about Vladimir Kousnetzoff and Olivier Delacourt. It was a relief when morning came and I could retreat to my workshop and lose myself in my work.

Nearing lunchtime, I heard footsteps on the terrace and looked up from my bench, to see Guastafeste outside. We went into the house and I made us both a cheese sandwich and a green salad.

Guastafeste waited until I'd poured two glasses of red wine and was seated at the table before he said, 'Are you all right, Gianni?'

'Why shouldn't I be all right?'

'Yesterday — that can't have been easy for you. There was Paris, too. Finding Alain Robillet's body, then Vladimir Kousnetzoff's. We have people we can call on, you know. Trained counsellors who are used to treating trauma. Do you want to talk to one of them?'

'I don't need a counsellor, Antonio. I have you to talk to, though to be frank, I don't really want to talk. Not about the bodies anyway. I'm more interested in what happened after I left Castenaso.'

'Delacourt confessed,' Guastafeste said. 'He admitted killing Kousnetzoff and Robillet. A falling-out among thieves, it would seem. He thought they'd double-crossed him, tried to cut

324

him out of his share of the jewelled violin.'

'They were all in this together?'

Guastafeste nodded, taking a bite of his sandwich, then wiping his mouth on the back of his hand.

'Delacourt had a long-standing business relationship with Villeneuve and Robillet — buying and selling stolen jewellery. It was Delacourt who first got the scent of the jewelled violin. He came upon the entries in Henri le Bley Lavelle's records by chance and mentioned it to Villeneuve and Robillet. They had a contact in Saint Petersburg — Vladimir Kousnetzoff — who was also interested in the violin. Kousnetzoff wasn't just a musical agent. He had another business on the side — smuggling stolen fine art and antiques out of Russia and using Robillet and Villeneuve to find wealthy buyers in the West. Kousnetzoff knew all about Jeremiah Posier and the jewelled violin he'd made for Catherine the Great. He'd recently acquired some of Posier's private papers, including a letter dated 1848 from the estate manager at Castenaso, enquiring about the provenance of the violin.'

'The estate manager?'

'Lorenzo Costa.'

'The one who was killed by Austrian soldiers when they were billeted at the villa after Isabella Colbran's death.'

'Yes,' Guastafeste said. 'And who decided to hide the violin from the soldiers by getting the local blacksmith to weld it into the ironwork of the summerhouse. The blacksmith who was also killed by the Austrians.'

'Taking the secret with him to the grave,' I said. 'How did Delacourt know where to look?'

'He didn't. He and Kousnetzoff knew the violin had been at Castenaso. They went there a few weeks ago but, like us, found only ruins. Then the gold box surfaced and that distracted them temporarily, gave them another lead to follow. It was only a couple of days ago that they remembered the summerhouse and went back to Castenaso for a second look, taking with them a hacksaw.'

'We should have guessed in Paris,' I said. 'We asked Delacourt if he'd heard of Posier and he lied, said no. Any jeweller worth his salt would have known who Posier was.'

I took a sip of my wine.

'What happens to the violin now?'

'It will have to go to a jewellery expert, someone who can clean off all the tar and restore the violin to its original condition.'

'And then?'

'Who knows? It will probably end up in a museum — on display in a glass case.'

Guastafeste ran his hands through his thick black hair.

'You have to wonder at human greed, don't you?' he said. 'What people will do for a piece of metal adorned with a few mineral crystals. To kill two people for that — it doesn't make any kind of sense.'

'Two? Aren't you forgetting François Villeneuve?'

'There's a complication,' Guastafeste said.

'Delacourt denies killing Villeneuve. He says he wasn't even in Cremona when it happened.'

'Do you believe him?'

'I'd like to say no. That would make everything so much simpler. Delacourt killed them all, Villeneuve, Robillet, and Kousnetzoff. Case closed. But I think he's telling the truth. He's admitted two murders. Why not admit the third — if he did it?'

'But then who . . . ' I began.

'Kousnetzoff's a possibility. Unfortunately, we can't ask him.'

'Why would Kousnetzoff kill Villeneuve?'

'To get his hands on the gold box, perhaps. Lodrino sold it to both of them, after all.'

'But the box was in the hotel safe, and only Villeneuve had access to it. Killing him wouldn't have got Kousnetzoff the box.'

Guastafeste shrugged.

'I don't know, Gianni. Maybe we'll never know for sure.'

'What did Delacourt have to say about it? Did you ask him?'

'Yes, we asked him. He said he didn't know. It wasn't him — he was adamant about that. More than that, he couldn't — or wouldn't — say.'

'So Villeneuve's case is still open?'

'I'm afraid so. We're going to have to go back to the beginning, look again at all the evidence. Examine Villeneuve's movements from the time he first arrived in Cremona; where he went, who he met. Check the forensics, see if we can pick up a lead.'

'Lodrino?'

'He has a watertight alibi for the time Villeneuve was killed.'

'Serafin?'

'His alibi stood up — unfortunately. It's not just his mistress, either. Several other people can vouch for his being in Milan all that Sunday morning. No, I have a feeling the killer is someone we haven't thought of yet. Someone who's been out of the frame so far. Someone who knew Villeneuve, or met him during his stay and was also interested in the gold box. Interested enough to kill for it . . . Gianni?'

He was gazing at me curiously.

'Are you okay?'

'What?' I said.

'You seemed to shut off just then. Your eyes went blank.'

'Martinelli,' I said.

'Who?'

'Martinelli. I've just remembered. Felice Baciocchi's cousin's daughter married Ignazio Martinelli.'

'What are you talking about?'

'Villeneuve's room at the Hotel San Michele,' I said. 'Did you find any fingerprints you couldn't identify?'

'Of course. It was a hotel room. Dozens of people must have passed through it. Why?'

'I want to give you something for your forensics people to examine.'

'Forensics? Gianni, what is this?'

'If I'm right, there's someone I think you need to see.'

I didn't wait downstairs in the foyer this time, but went straight upstairs to the first floor, Guastafeste by my side. The corridor smelt of fresh paint. The workmen who'd been plastering earlier in the week had moved on to decorating. Their ladders and dust sheets encroached on the corridor, forcing us to tread carefully as we passed.

Marco Martinelli was in the office next door to Vittorio Castellani's. It was a tiny room. One desk and chair would have been enough for the limited space available, but two more desks and chairs had been brought in and somehow crammed together to enable three people to work there — though the conditions were so claustrophobic, I couldn't imagine anyone managing to get much done. The walls were lined with shelves that were overflowing with files and books, and on the floor were more books and files in cardboard boxes.

Fortunately for us, Marco was alone. He was pressed against one wall of the room, typing at a computer keyboard. His eyes were bloodshot and tired. He glanced up and stopped typing as Guastafeste and I squeezed through the door and found a tiny patch of floor on which to stand.

'Vittorio isn't here,' he said. 'He won't be in until tomorrow now.'

'It's you we wanted to see,' I said.

'Me?'

I manoeuvred myself onto one of the other chairs and lifted my feet over a box.

'It's cosy in here, isn't it?'

'It's hell,' Marco said.

'But only temporary, I trust.'

'That depends on how you define *temporary*.'

'That's your office down the corridor, isn't it? The one where the ceiling fell in.'

'Yes.'

'And those boxes of books in Professor Castellani's office are yours, too?'

'Yes. Why do you ask?'

'I'm afraid I borrowed one of them.'

I glanced at Guastafeste, who held out the transparent plastic evidence bag he was carrying for Marco to see. Inside the bag was *Napoléon's Sisters: Caroline, Pauline, and Elisa.*

'This is yours, isn't it?' Guastafeste asked.

'What's going on? Who are you?' Marco replied.

'Just answer the question, please.'

'Yes, it's mine. What of it?'

Guastafeste flipped out his police ID card.

'Antonio Guastafeste, Cremona *questura*. I'm investigating the murder of François Villeneuve in the Hotel San Michele in Cremona nine days ago.'

Marco gave a sharp involuntary cry and put a hand to his mouth. The colour drained out of his cheeks. He looked down at the desk, breathing audibly, his chest rising and falling rapidly. Then he looked back at Guastafeste, his face tight and ashen.

'What's that got to do with me?' he said. 'I've never heard of François Villeneuve, or the Hotel San Michele.'

'Villeneuve was hit over the head with a table lamp,' Guastafeste said. 'There were fingerprints on the lamp that match the fingerprints on this book. *Your* book. How do you explain that?'

Marco didn't answer. I could see him thinking, going through his options. He looked at the door. In a less cluttered office, I believe, he might have considered making a break for it, but he was pinned against the wall by his desk, and besides, Guastafeste and I were between him and the exit. So he tried to brazen it out instead.

'Let me see that again,' he said, peering at the evidence bag. 'No, I was wrong. It's not my book. I've never seen it before.'

'The book doesn't really matter,' Guastafeste said calmly. 'It's your fingerprints that count. And I'll bet my pension that the prints on the table lamp are yours. When we get to the *questura*, we'll take your prints and get a proper match.'

'You're arresting me?' Marco said.

Guastafeste nodded. Then he cautioned Marco and made him aware of his rights.

'You're arresting me?' Marco said again. 'For murder?' He was breathless, staring in disbelief at Guastafeste.

'That's correct.'

Guastafeste took a pair of handcuffs from his jacket pocket. Marco leaned back in his chair, pressing himself against the wall, his hands raised defensively.

'Now wait a minute. Murder? It wasn't murder. I swear it wasn't.'

'No?'

'You've got it all wrong.'

'You admit that you hit him?' Guastafeste said.

'Look, it wasn't what you think. I went there to talk to him, that's all. Just to talk. I didn't want an argument; I didn't want a fight. It was only later I found out. When I heard the news, saw it on the television.'

'You went to Villeneuve's hotel room?'

'But not to kill him. I didn't kill him. It just happened.'

'Why did you go there?'

'To talk to him. That's all I wanted to do: talk.'

'About what?'

'About the Moses box.'

'The gold box with the engraving of Moses on the lid?'

'Yes.'

'How did you know Villeneuve had it?'

'I overheard him at the reception. In Cremona, after Yevgeny Ivanov's recital. He was with another guest — a tubby little man with a black beard. They were discussing it.'

'And what was your interest in the box?'

'It wasn't so much the box; it was the music I wanted.'

'The music?'

'Paganini's music.'

'The Serenata *Appassionata?*' I asked.

'Yes.'

Marco pulled out a drawer of his desk and removed a brown manila envelope. From the envelope he produced a thin sheaf of yellowed manuscript paper. I saw the handwritten title at the top of the first page — 'Serenata

332

Appassionata' — and the dedication, 'To Princess Elisa Baciocchi.' It was Paganini's handwriting. Below that was the tempo marking, '*Adagio ma non troppo*,' and then the music itself — the treble and bass clefs of a piano part in D major, common time, the notes scrawled untidily across the staves.

'This is the piano accompaniment?' I said. 'And the violin part?'

'That's what I've been looking for,' Marco replied. 'It's obsessed me for years.'

'Where did you get this?'

'It belongs to my family, passed down through the generations.'

'From Elisa to Felice Baciocchi, and then by marriage to the Martinellis.'

'That's right. But the violin part has always been missing. My grandfather used to talk about it to me when I was a child — Paganini's long-lost masterpiece. No one else in my family was interested. They thought he was just a senile old man making up stories. He talked about the Moses box, too — that's what he called it, 'the Moses box' — a gold box with Moses and the Ten Commandments on the lid. He said it had belonged to Paganini, too, but it had disappeared years ago. That's why I pricked up my ears when I heard Villeneuve talking about it. If he had the Moses box, perhaps he might have information that would lead me to the violin part of the Serenata *Appassionata*.'

'You didn't know about the jewelled violin?' Guastafeste asked.

'What jewelled violin? I wanted only the

music. I thought if I could find it, it would boost my career. A new, undiscovered work by Paganini, which would get me a tenured post. And it would put one over on Castellani. The great Vittorio Castellani, that smug, patronising bastard, treating me like a typist, a servant. I'd show him.'

'And did Villeneuve know anything about the music?' I asked.

'I didn't find out.'

'What happened in his hotel room?' Guastafeste said.

Marco hesitated.

'I didn't intend to kill him; you have to believe that. You have to. I went to talk to him. He wouldn't tell me anything. He tried to throw me out. I refused to go. He started shouting at me. I lost my temper. I know I shouldn't have. I picked up the table lamp . . . I didn't think I hit him that hard, but he went down. He was on the floor. I thought I'd just knocked him out. I panicked, opened the door, and ran. It was only later that I found out he was dead.'

Marco glared defiantly at Guastafeste, then at me.

'He was stupid, stubborn. He should have told me. All I wanted to know about was the music. That music is mine. I've spent years looking for it. It's *mine*, you understand?'

Marco slumped forward over the desk and covered his face with his hands, his whole body shaking. Guastafeste pulled him to his feet and handcuffed him. Marco offered no resistance. There was no fight left in him.

We went downstairs to the foyer and Guastafeste called the *questura* and asked them to send a police van to pick up Marco. Once they'd arrived, we drove back to Cremona in Guastafeste's unmarked car. He was subdued, uncharacteristically quiet. He'd got his man, got his confession, but there was little satisfaction to be had from it. Things are rarely that simple.

I, too, was quiet. There was one other loose end to tie up, one more mystery to solve. I was working out how I was going to do it.

19

Ruggiero Monteveglio was waiting for me outside the Villa Nettuno. We shook hands and I apologised for disturbing him again. I hoped this wasn't going to take up too much of his time.

We went inside the house and through to the music room. The shutters were closed, so Monteveglio switched on the lights. I studied the artwork on the walls, stopping in front of the collage of photocopied music that had caught my attention on my previous visit. It was an interesting example of Nicoletta Ferrara's work. She had photocopied various pieces of classical music, then cut the photocopies up into small sections, most just a few bars long, and arranged them in patterns across a sheet of thick board. I recognised several of the pieces immediately: There were the opening four bars of Beethoven's *Kreutzer* Sonata, part of Tartini's *Devil's Trill* Sonata, snippets of the Brahms violin concerto, and several sections from Bach's unaccompanied sonatas and partitas. It was like a musical jigsaw, or something devised as a party game — identify the composers and the works.

All the extracts seemed to be violin music, and they were all photocopies of printed music — with one exception. In the lower corner of the board was a segment of handwritten music, the opening few bars of a piece I didn't know. It was a single stave in the treble clef, a key signature of

336

D major, common time, with the tempo marking '*Adagio ma non troppo.*'

'Where did your aunt do her art?' I asked.

'She had a studio,' Monteveglio replied.

'In the house?'

'In the boathouse down by the lake.'

'There's a boathouse?'

'On the other side of the main road. You go through a tunnel to get to it.'

'May I see it?'

'If you wish.'

We went out onto the terrace and down the steps through the garden. It was an overcast day, cooler than the previous time I'd been there. A stiff breeze was blowing in from the lake, ruffling my hair and plucking at the sleeves of my jacket.

The paths were all overgrown by vegetation, the damp air filled with the scents of pine and sage and wild garlic. In a niche in the wall, a spring bubbled out from a crack in the rock, filling a stone basin before overflowing and running away down a rill that was half-smothered in ivy and weeds. I caught a glimpse of a classical statue in a shady hollow next to a huge cypress tree, the figure of a man with a trident in his hand.

'Neptune?' I said.

'There are statues all over the place,' Monteveglio replied. 'Most of them you can't see for the undergrowth. Aunt Nicoletta had only the one gardener. She could have afforded a whole team, but she seemed to prefer the place wild and untamed. I think it appealed to her wilful nature.'

Perhaps I, too, had a wilful nature, for I found something intensely alluring about this wilderness. It had an atmosphere, a mystery that well-kept gardens lack. Every corner, every turn in the path brought the promise of a surprise, of a hidden treat.

We rounded a large clump of azaleas and I saw a dark opening in the ground ahead of us — the tunnel beneath the road. We plunged inside it. It was cool and moist. The smell of damp earth increased, oozing out from the moss-coated walls.

'This is the only house in the area with its own tunnel,' Monteveglio said. 'Everyone else has to walk across the road to get to the lake.'

We stepped out onto a small beach. The shingle crunched beneath our shoes. The water was clear and choppy, the waves lapping the shore. To our right was an old wooden boathouse with a red-tiled roof. The lower section of the building was partly below water level and had two big doors on the lake-side to allow a boat to enter and leave. The upper section had windows on all four sides, plus skylights in the roof.

We climbed a flight of worn wooden stairs and Monteveglio unlocked the door. I could see at once why Nicoletta Ferrara had used the room inside as a studio. It was filled with light, and from the windows was a view of Lake Maggiore and the Alps that would have inspired anyone to want to paint.

The studio had apparently remained untouched since Nicoletta's death. An easel was set up in the centre, an uncompleted canvas on it, and

there were more canvases — finished and unfin-
ished — leaning up against the walls. A workbench
down one side was covered with oil paints and
acrylics and pots of glue, and next to the bench
was a small photocopier.

'Do you mind if I poke round a bit?' I asked.

Monteveglio shrugged indifferently.

'Feel free.'

There were several chests of drawers of
varying sizes underneath the workbench. One
had wide, shallow drawers and contained large
sheets of card and paper. Another was full of
half-used tubes of paint and dirty brushes. In the
third chest, I found what I was looking for — the
music Nicoletta had used for the collages in the
villa. There were books of violin sonatas by
Beethoven, Mozart, Bach, and others; concertos
by Brahms, Tchaikovsky, Bruch; a miscellany of
smaller pieces by composers such as Sarasate,
Vieuxtemps, and Wieniawski. I pulled each
drawer out in turn until I saw the name
Paganini. There was a thick stack of his
compositions — the twenty-four caprices, the
Moto Perpetuo, the 'Moses Fantasy,' the
concertos . . . and there at the bottom a few
loose sheets of handwritten music.

I waited for a moment, feeling my heart
beating faster; then I lifted the sheets out of the
drawer and placed them carefully on the surface
of the workbench. My fingers were trembling. I
gazed down at the notes for a long time, singing
the music in my head, hearing it as a violin
might play it — hearing it as Paganini might
have played it.

It all made sense now. There would not have been just the one copy of the Serenata *Appasionata*. Paganini gave the original music to Elisa Baciocchi, its dedicatee, but he would also have kept a copy for himself. On her death, Elisa's music passed to her husband, Felice, and from there to the Martinelli family, though somewhere along the line the violin part had gone missing, leaving only the piano accompaniment behind. Paganini's copy remained in his possession, but somehow it must have ended up with Antonia Bianchi after their separation. And from Antonia, it had been handed down through the generations to Nicoletta Ferrara.

I touched the pieces of paper with my fingertips and felt the same unsettling tingle I'd felt that afternoon when *il Cannone* had been brought to my workshop. I have always believed in spirits. I don't mean pale apparitions in clanking chains. I mean elements of the past lingering on into the present. I have a powerful sense that places still contain something of the people who once lived in them, that objects retain the imprint of their original owners. These things can't be seen or heard or smelt. Those senses are too sophisticated and developed. At our most basic level, we are not creatures who see or hear or smell. We are creatures who feel. I could feel a part of Paganini in these dog-eared sheets of paper, just as I'd felt it in his violin.

'Are you all right?' Monteveglio asked me in a concerned voice.

I turned my head.

'Yes, I'm all right.'

340

'Only you look as if you've seen a ghost.'

'Do I? A ghost?' I said. 'Yes, I suppose I have.'

★ ★ ★

Guastafeste was the first guest to arrive. Well, the first after Margherita, who had driven out early from Milan to help me prepare lunch. Everything was under control. The chicken was in the oven, the vegetables peeled and chopped, the pasta sauce simmering gently on the hob, so with nothing else needing doing in the kitchen, the three of us went through into the sitting room with a glass of wine each.

It was almost six weeks now since Olivier Delacourt and Marco Martinelli had been arrested. I had not forgotten the traumatic events at Castenaso — I don't suppose I ever will — but they had receded in my memory and no longer gave me nightmares. The homicide cases had not been closed. Guastafeste and his colleagues were still preparing the evidence for the court hearings and trials that were to come, but the pressure was off him. He was looking fresh and rested, the shadows gone from round his eyes.

'Is that a new jacket you're wearing?' I asked him.

'Yes, I thought I'd treat myself. What do you think?'

'Very nice.'

'The colour suits you,' Margherita said.

'Thank you. I don't indulge myself very often, but . . . well, it's been a busy few weeks. I think

I've earned a little reward.'

'How's it all going?' I asked.

'The magistrate is going easy on Marco. I think the charges are going to be reduced to manslaughter. There are extenuating circumstances. It seems clear that he didn't intend to kill Villeneuve. Villeneuve had an unusually thin skull. Marco's young; he's never been in trouble before. I think he'll get off with a pretty light sentence.'

'And Delacourt?'

'He's a different matter. Two brutal murders, one committed in France, one in Italy. The legal red tape is going to be a nightmare, but I'd say he's going down for a long stretch. That reminds me. I've something to show you.'

Guastafeste took a photograph from his jacket pocket and passed it across to me.

'The jewellery restorer has finished cleaning up the gold violin. That's what it looks like now.'

I studied the photograph. I could hardly believe what I saw, the transformation was so astounding. The shapeless, black, tar-covered object that had been cut from the summerhouse at Castenaso was now a glittering, magnificent piece of jewellery — as bright and glorious as the day it had first left Jeremiah Posier's workshop in Saint Petersburg. The gold was polished to a fine sheen, the diamonds, rubies, and emeralds scintillating like tiny white, red, and green stars.

'Not bad, is it?' Guastafeste said. 'Every stone was intact, too.'

'It's stunning,' I said.

I showed the photograph to Margherita. She

342

let out a low gasp of appreciation.

'That is beautiful. I've never seen anything like it.'

'What's going to happen to it?' I asked.

'That's a decision for the Ministry of Culture,' Guastafeste replied. He grinned sardonically. 'So we could be in for a long wait.'

'It should be on display somewhere,' Margherita said. 'People ought to be able to see it.'

'That would be good,' Guastafeste said. 'But I wouldn't hold your breath. A lot of people are going to be interested in it. I can smell the stench of lawyers already. Viotti's heirs probably have a claim over it; the Church, too. It was stolen from one of their convents, after all. Maybe Isabella Colbran's descendants, as well. You want my educated guess? It will be locked away in a storeroom in Rome for ten years while everybody argues over it; then it will mysteriously disappear, along with all the official paperwork, and surface a few months later — unbeknown to the world, of course — in the private collection of some billionaire in America. Or China, if you want to get really depressed.'

'You're probably right,' I said.

I looked at the photograph again, thinking of all the people who had possessed the violin over the years — from Catherine the Great through Viotti, Paganini, Domenico Barbaia, and Isabella Colbran — and Olivier Delacourt, who had killed to possess it. It was a fabulous piece of jewellery, but no object, no matter how special, was worth a human life.

I handed the photograph back to Guastafeste

343

and stood up. I'd seen a taxi pulling into the drive at the front of the house, Yevgeny and Ludmilla Ivanova inside it. I went out to greet them. Yevgeny had his violin case in one hand and a bottle of wine in the other. He was looking less gaunt than before. His face and body were filling out. Above all, he looked happy. He gave me a big affectionate hug and smiled.

'Gianni! It's good to see you.'

'How was New York?' I asked.

'Fantastic.'

'They loved him,' Ludmilla said.

I turned to look at her, a little wary of what kind of reception I might receive. But she spread out her arms and embraced me warmly.

'Thank you for coming,' I said.

'It's our pleasure,' Ludmilla replied.

'Come inside. Lunch won't be long.'

Father Arrighi was the next to arrive, timing his appearance once again, with unnerving accuracy, to the exact moment when Guastafeste was distributing his potent custom-made aperitifs. Then, twenty minutes later, came the moment I had been dreading. A small white Fiat turned into the drive and Mirella got out.

This wasn't her first encounter with Ludmilla — that had been some weeks earlier, an undoubtedly nervewracking event at which, I am glad to say, I had not been present — but it was probably only the second or third time they'd met, and I was apprehensive about the outcome.

I had briefed Margherita and Guastafeste beforehand and they carried out their

344

appointed tasks with commendable efficiency. While Margherita engaged Ludmilla in intense conversation, Guastafeste drifted across to the sitting room door and loitered there, blocking the exit, but only after I had slipped out with Yevgeny and taken him into the kitchen to meet Mirella. I gave the two of them five minutes alone together, then escorted them to the sitting room, where Yevgeny introduced Mirella to the others. Though clearly nervous, Mirella handled herself well, and Ludmilla behaved impeccably. She kissed Mirella on both cheeks and even managed a facial contortion that could charitably have been interpreted as a smile.

After that, everyone seemed to relax. Yevgeny and Mirella retreated to a corner, where they conversed in low, intimate whispers, while Ludmilla held court in the centre of the room, describing to the rest of us Yevgeny's triumphant New York debut.

Lunch passed without incident, in no small measure due to Margherita, who had the enviable knack of stimulating conversations to which everyone could contribute, then nursing them expertly, as if she were tending a wood fire, allowing flames to flare occasionally, sparks to fly, and embers to glow without ever fully dying down.

'I'm so glad you're here,' I said when we'd left the others and gone into the kitchen to make coffee.

'You think it's going well?' Margherita said.

'Really well. Mostly thanks to you.'

345

'Hardly. I'm not doing anything at all.'

'You're holding everything together.'

'Yevgeny and Mirella seem very happy.'

'It's nice to see, isn't it?'

'Even Ludmilla must have noticed how different he is. When you think about the last time they were here . . . He's come out of his shell, matured. He's comfortable with himself, and with others.'

I smiled at her.

'Women do that to us.'

She arranged the coffee cups on a tray and poured milk into a jug.

'I'm not looking forward to the next bit, though.'

I could hear the anxiety in her voice.

'You'll be absolutely fine,' I said.

'I'm not good enough, Gianni. I wish now I hadn't said yes. You should have got a professional in. It's going to be really embarrassing.'

I put my arm round her shoulders and squeezed.

'That's utter rubbish, and you know it.'

'It will be. Yevgeny's one of the best violinists in the world, and what am I? A complete amateur.'

'We're among friends,' I said. 'It's not a performance; it's just a bit of fun. And don't run yourself down like that. You're a very good pianist.'

She wasn't to be reassured — I could tell from her face while we drank our coffee. She looked nervous, and she didn't say much. But when the moment finally came and she sat down at the keyboard in the music room, the tension seemed to evaporate from her. She'd been practising her part for weeks. She knew she could do it. She nodded at Yevgeny, watching his bow arm; then the first sonorous chords of the Serenata *Appassionata* rang out across the room.

Rarely have I felt so privileged, so enormously lucky. Here we were in my house, just seven of us, listening to a piece that had not been heard for two hundred years. And what a piece it was. Paganini's music is not renowned for its depth. His compositions were mostly written to showcase his virtuosity, to astound audiences with breathtaking pyrotechnics. But the Serenata *Appassionata* was different. Instead of a violin solo with perfunctory piano accompaniment, this was a genuine duet for the two instruments — music created not to show off, but to show feeling. This was a piece written from the heart. Paganini was a young man when he composed it, a young man in love, and that fact was manifest in every note, every harmony. The artificial harmonics, the left-hand pizzicato and all the other tricks for which he was famous were absent. There was just a simple melodic line of exquisite beauty, perfectly complemented by the rippling counterpoint of the piano, then a development section full of lover's fervour that more than justified the *Appassionata* of the title, before the melody returned, lingering long in the air, in the silence after the two instruments had stopped playing.

What had Elisa written in her letter to

Paganini? 'I can still hear that haunting melody in my head. I think of it as your ghost, a spirit that is constantly with me . . . '

I knew now what she had meant. That melody, that love song, would be with me, too, for a very long time.

Twenty seconds, thirty passed. No one spoke. No one wanted to be the first to break the moment. Then Guastafeste began to clap.

'*Bravo!*' he called. '*Bravissimo!*'

Ludmilla, Mirella, Father Arrighi, and I joined in the applause.

Yevgeny beamed and bowed to us. Margherita smiled shyly, holding my gaze for a time. Then I went to her and hugged her.

'That was wonderful. Truly wonderful.'

'You're sure?' she said.

'You don't believe me? Let's ask Yevgeny.'

'You were magnificent, signora,' Yevgeny said. 'And what a piece of music. It must be published. And recorded, too. What do you think, Mama?'

'I think it can be arranged,' Ludmilla said.

'Let's make it soon. The whole world must hear it.'

I pulled open the French windows and we spilled out onto the terrace. Guastafeste fetched a bottle of wine and filled our glasses and we drank a toast to the Serenata *Appassionata*. Then Yevgeny and Mirella drifted away down the garden. Margherita slipped her arm through mine and we strolled across the lawn.

'I'll treasure that forever,' Margherita said.

'So will I.'

'Does it have to be published and recorded? It seems a shame to share our secret with anyone else. Can you imagine what it must have been like to be Elisa Baciocchi? Having music like that written for you, hearing it for the first time, knowing it was a love token from a man like Paganini, a man you adored.'

'We can't all compose,' I said. 'But there are many other ways of showing love.'

At the bottom of the garden, Yevgeny and Mirella were holding hands. They disappeared behind a trellis and I caught a glimpse of them kissing.

'What time were you planning on going back to Milan?' I asked.

'I hadn't thought about it.'

'You don't have to, you know.' I paused. 'You could always stay the night here.'

She turned and looked at me, smiling.

'I'd like that,' she said.

We do hope that you have enjoyed reading this large print book.

Did you know that all of our titles are available for purchase?

We publish a wide range of high quality large print books including:
Romances, Mysteries, Classics
General Fiction
Non Fiction and Westerns

Special interest titles available in large print are:
The Little Oxford Dictionary
Music Book
Song Book
Hymn Book
Service Book

Also available from us courtesy of Oxford University Press:
Young Readers' Dictionary
(large print edition)
Young Readers' Thesaurus
(large print edition)

For further information or a free brochure, please contact us at:
Ulverscroft Large Print Books Ltd.,
The Green, Bradgate Road, Anstey,
Leicester, LE7 7FU, England.
Tel: (00 44) 0116 236 4325
Fax: (00 44) 0116 234 0205

Other titles published by
The House of Ulverscroft:

FLASH POINT

Paul Adam

In McLeod Ganj, home of the Tibetan government in exile, the Dalai Lama is secretly dying. When fearless camerawoman Maggie Walsh receives the tip-off, she smuggles herself into the compound and films the pictures that will make her fortune. But her escape is thwarted by Tsering, an idealistic young monk. When Maggie is released, the Dalai Lama's death has been announced, so she heads for Tibet. Tsering, too, is heading there. The reincarnation of the Dalai Lama has already been born, and visions in the oracle lake will reveal the chosen child. As their paths overlap, Tsering and Maggie are drawn together. For, once the Chinese Army discover who they are looking for, there is no way they'll be allowed to leave Tibet alive . . .

ENEMY WITHIN

Paul Adam

Tom Whitehead had never heard of Operation Gold Dust. Why would he? No reason for a respected academic, loving husband and father of two to be aware of an international investigation into internet paedophilia. Until he finds himself at the centre of it . . . Raided by the police at dawn, and in the full glare of the paparazzi, Tom is hauled away for questioning. About the pornography found on his computer at work. About the fact it was paid for with his credit card. About the overwhelming, conclusive evidence against him . . . He discovers that he has been under investigation for some time. The police acquired his details from the National Criminal Intelligence Service — via the FBI. But why? And how?

THE LOST

Claire McGowan

When two teenage girls go missing along the Irish border, forensic psychologist Paula Maguire has to return to the home town she left years before. Swirling with rumours and secrets, the town is gripped with the fear of a serial killer. But the truth could be even darker. Surrounded by people and places she tried to forget, Paula digs into the cases as the truth twists further away. What's the link with two other disappearances from 1985? And why does everything lead back to the town's dark past — including the reasons her own mother went missing years before? As the shocking truth is revealed, Paula learns that sometimes it's better not to find what you've lost.

EYE CONTACT

Fergus McNeill

From the outside, Robert Naysmith is a successful businessman, handsome and charming. But for years he's been playing a deadly game. He doesn't choose his victims. Each is selected at random — the first person to make eye contact after he begins 'the game' will not have long to live. Their fate is sealed. When the body of a young woman is found on Severn Beach, Detective Inspector Harland is assigned the case. It's only when he links it to an unsolved murder in Oxford that the police begin to guess at the awful scale of the crimes. But how do you find a killer who strikes without motive?